SWORD AND SCION

THE COURT OF EXTRAVAGANT SECRETS
BOOK 4

JACKSON E. GRAHAM

YOUNG**OAK**PUBLISHING

Young Oak Publishing LLC
Hayden, Idaho

Young Oak Publishing LLC
P.O. Box 682
Hayden, ID 83835

Cover design by Uncompleted Canvas LLC
Logo design by KJ Designs
Author photograph by Rachel Stewart Photography

Quotations from (NIV) New International Version of the Holy Bible used by permission of Bible Gateway.
New International Version **(NIV)**
Holy Bible, New International Version®, NIV® Copyright ©1973, 1978, 1984, 2011 by Biblica, Inc. ® Used by permission.
All rights reserved worldwide.
Text set in Times New Roman

http://jacksonegraham.wixsite.com/jackson-e-graham

Library of Congress Control Number: 2020904234

ISBN: 978-09996059-74 (sc)

PRINTED IN THE UNITED STATES OF AMERICA

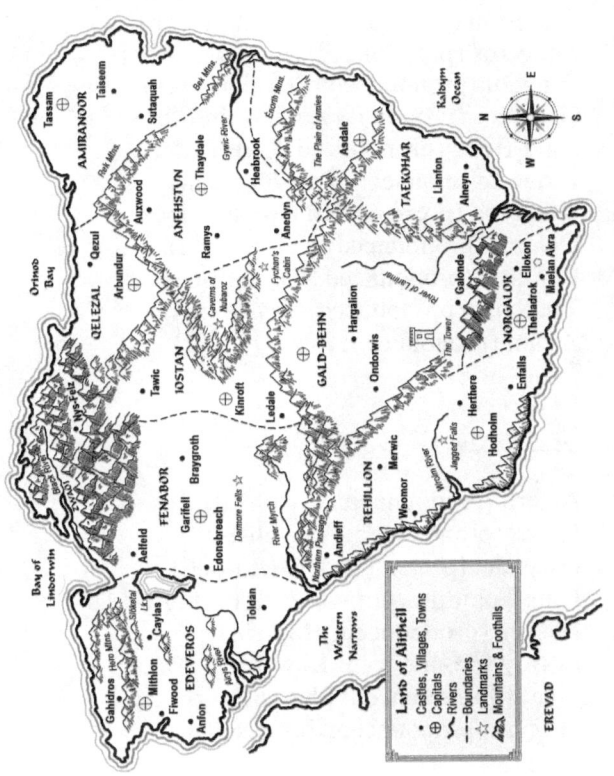

PRONOUNCIATION GUIDE

Places

Amiranoor (pronounced: Ah-**meer**-ah-norr)
Anehstun (pronounced: **Ah**-ne-stoon)
Edeveros (pronounced: Eh-**dev**-ah-ros)
Fenabor (pronounced: **Feh**-nah-bore)
Gahidros (pronounced: Gah-**high**-drōs)
Gald-Behn (pronounced: **Gahld-Ben**)
Iostan (pronounced: **Eye**-oh-stann)
Norgalok (pronounced: **Nor**-gah-lock)
Qelezal (pronounced: **Kell**-eh-zall)
Rehillon (pronounced: **Rey**-hill-on)
Taekohar (pronounced: **Tay**-ko-harr)
Zwaoi (pronounced: **Z-why**)

Characters

Ayleril (pronounced: **Ay**-luh-ril)
Eyoés (pronounced: **Aay**-oh-ess)
Gwyndel (pronounced: **Gwin**-dell)
King Fohidras (pronounced: Fo-**high**-dras)
Haeryn (pronounced: **Hay**-rin)
Lòfroy (pronounced: **Low**-froy)
Sharaf (pronounced: Sha-**roff**)
Taesyra (pronounced: Tay-**seer**-ah)

Months for the World of Alithell

Iaudyn
Nósor
Dichán
Biarron
Iaulan
Merchen
Yílor
Thurdál
Aevoran
Rotanos
Rynéth
Bivyn

**Don't miss these other titles by
Jackson E. Graham:**

Sword and Scion 01: Into the Dark Mountains

Sword and Scion 02: The Allegiance of Avarice

Sword and Scion 03: The Reign of Delusion

To my brother Logan.
I have to work really hard
to keep my plot twists a secret from you.

Ivory towers bent in struggle
Like the broken backs of sufferers.
In this war of succession there are no victors,
For all have bled the cost.
Purple and ermine are now broken
Awaiting shame's weighty token.
Their tears mocked, their name blackened,
All for naught but a game ill-played.
For I foretell, another will come unbidden
To claim the prize so contested for.
A banner of white and red.

Scop's Lament, Gauteron Nikordos of Caylas, 2009 SE,
Recounting the Shaming of House Wynrence during the
Edeveran Wars of Succession

"As far as the east is from the west, so far has he
removed our transgressions from us."
(Psalm 103:12, NIV)

"Do not join those who drink too much wine or gorge
themselves on meat, for drunkards and gluttons
become poor, and drowsiness clothes them in
rags." (Proverbs 23:20-21, NIV)

PROLOGUE

2208 SE, Castle Garifell, Fenabor

After years of failure, Lòfroy never expected to behold fortune again—now, he found himself staring it in the face. As he strode through the halls of Castle Garifell, he grappled with his thoughts behind the privacy of his iron helm. Disregarding the servant leading him, he eyed the sleek, stylized portrait of a woman's pensive face hanging on the deep brown walls, illuminated by the sun streaming through the windows opposite. His heart pounded beneath his breastplate as he contemplated the hand fate had dealt him.

The promise of a kingdom to call my own. But how can one man bring about the impossible?

His gauntlets clinked as he clenched his fists and hurried his pace. Once a man was forced to earn his bread by sweat rather than intelligence, he could not afford to entertain such wild fantasies.

Or so he had once thought.

As his escort slowed before a closed door, Lòfroy set his musings aside. His strange circumstances continued to stir his curiosity. The servant withdrew a jingling ring of keys and inserted one of them above the door handle. At the click of the lock, Lòfroy advanced, barely giving the servant time to withdraw.

Collecting himself, the mercenary pushed the door inward and stepped inside with a boldness despite his uncertainty.

The room was bare, except for a chandelier hanging above his head, its arms rounding like the smooth curves of a ship's prow. As he closed the door behind him, Lòfroy found his gaze drawn to the figure across from him. A silent figure stared out the open window, his back turned to hide his face. His squared shoulders and commanding poise spoke for him. To his own surprise, Lòfroy found himself intimidated by the utter control the man exuded. Lingering at a distance, he swallowed."Are you the Sage?" he asked.

"I am," the man replied. The rich voice boomed in Lòfroy's ears, despite his helm.

Averting his gaze, Lòfroy gathered his thoughts, feeling trapped inside his armor as he felt the dominating presence settle upon him like a dark fog. At first, he had doubted the fantastical tales the mystics told about their Sage. Now, he realized his skepticism for the falsehood it was. He was in superior company —and the time he had spent under the tutelage of the Sage's mystics had proved only a trivial preparation.

"You took a new name?" the Sage inquired.

Catching his breath, the mercenary nodded. "I shall be Lòfroy, your greatness," he replied, masking his unease behind his own smooth voice.

As he leaned against the windowsill, the Sage tapped his forefinger on the wood with hollow knocks. "You wonder how I can fulfill my promise. I sense your uncertainty, Lòfroy," he said. "The Baronship of

Edeveros will belong to you if you are patient enough to receive in at its due time."

Lòfroy shook his head and wandered forward, his eagerness to accept the man's words clashing against his rationale. "How can this be?" he asked

"You have learned my Ten Precepts. What is the first?" the Sage asked.

Hastily stepping back, Lòfroy bowed under the question. "The impossible is always within our grasp," he answered, and as he repeated the phrase under his breath, he began to believe it.

The Sage nodded. "You must remember this, Lòfroy. The impossible is achieved in small increments, not large ones," he said, clasping his hands behind his back. "The borders of Zwaoi are fading. Swarms of Hobgoblins continue to raid the north of Iostan, and Tawic has been abandoned. The Dwarves of Nubaroz may fight to protect the North, but they can only stem the tide for a short time."

Breathless, Lòfroy envisioned the power lingering just within his grasp. "The Hobgoblins are brutes. What would my kingdom have to do with their blind rampage?" he asked, disgusted by the thought of the ugly savages soiling the spoils of his fortune.

The Sage paused, as if absorbed in thought. "The Kingdom of Alithell could never last forever. Destruction is the destiny of every empire—such is the natural state of things," he said. "The time will come when all of Alithell will bow to a new king. And when that day arrives, you, Lòfroy, will find yourself rewarded with power. On one condition."

"And what would that be, your greatness?" Lòfroy asked, shifting his stance. As he spoke, a lingering uneasiness settled deep within him, till he felt the sharp sting of sweat trickle into his eye. The air he breathed suddenly turned foul, and his heart thudded like a limp, rotting muscle within his chest. Still, he persisted and disregarded his acute discomfort. He was glad he didn't have to look upon the man's face.

The Sage was silent. Gripping the edge of the windowsill, he straightened. "That you swear allegiance to me now. That you will obey me without question," he said.

At the forcefulness in the man's words, Lòfroy wavered. The promise of riches and power lured him with its song, and in its light, he viewed the command with favor. "Very well," he replied.

The Sage nodded. "Then go to Edeveros and hide the majority of your force outside the capital, Mithlon. You are to keep the Baron, Galeras Estworth, under surveillance for me. Suggest your services to him as a mercenary and make sure he does not do anything rash. Be ready to act when I give you the command. Your task is as simple as that," he said.

Lòfroy hesitated. "That is all?" he asked.

Glancing partially over his shoulder, the Sage smirked. "If you wish to busy yourself, then I can remedy your boredom," he remarked. "There is a man in Edeveros who brought suffering upon your childhood. You know who I speak of."

A sudden coldness chilled Lòfroy, and a lead weight sank into his stomach. For the first time in years, he felt fear settle in his bones—an old companion. "You are certain?" he asked, his voice rising barely above a whisper.

The Sage laughed to himself. "I have prophesied it. Violence is the tool of the strong, Lòfroy," he said. "Now is the time to use it."

Gritting his teeth, Lòfroy bowed in homage. "I am grateful for the opportunity, my liege," he said, "and I will exact the payment that is long overdue."

1

30th of Aevoran, 2209 SE

"The hounds have given chase, Lord Stonneter,"
the Huntsman announced, the patter of rain moistening
the shoulders of his thick cloak. "The boar will be ours
before the evening is out." With a wrinkled and
weatherbeaten face, he anticipated the Lord of Anfon's
answer. As he awaited the inevitable, he steeled
himself to endure it.

With a laugh of triumph, Lord Belos Stonneter
adjusted his riding gloves, chin lifted high with a wry
smile. He barely acknowledged his Huntsman's
presence. "Any chance of Groundclaws joining in on
the fun? It would be a pity for such a fine chase to be
ruined, Fedrik," he said. He shot an irritated glance at
the Huntsman, and his lip curled in disgust as he eyed
the man. While he had come to expect Fedrik to wear
such humble attire, the sight of the muddy, wet
garments made him squirm.

Feeling the nobleman's condescending stare,
Fedrik crumbled underneath his scrutiny and lowered
his gaze. He pinched the skin of his hand in irritation.
"Far be it, Lord Stonneter. Perhaps the dragons have
found a herd of stags to satisfy their appetites. There
have been no reports raised by the nearby villagers of

dead livestock," he said. His burdened years were shrouded behind his joyless face.

Satisfied his subordinate had understood the implied reprimand, Belos glanced sidelong at the woman riding beside him. Her long, copper-red hair bounced in curls around her head. An old L-shaped scar was carved on her cheekbone. Lord Stonneter felt a quiver of apprehension as her sharp gaze pricked him like the tip of a blade. Furrowing his brow in an unconscious attempt to resist, he met her half-emerald, half-blue eyes—and quickly looked away. He had heard too many rumors about this woman to challenge her.

From her saddle, Gwyndel sighed to herself and shot a withering look toward Lord Belos. His contemptuous treatment of his kind and knowledgeable Huntsman burdened her. The Lord of Anfon, though modest in his leadership, was keen on putting forth his own low opinion of his Huntsman. Her features softened as she observed Fedrik. Seized with an urge to comfort her sullen companion, Gwyndel moved her horse alongside Fedrik.

The baying of hounds echoed through the forest. Fedrik sat up in the saddle and spurred his steed to a gallop, the fog enveloping him as he rode into the trees. Lord Stonneter grinned and galloped in pursuit, his light blonde hair tossed by the wind. Gwyndel bolted after him.

The mist chilled her face, dampening her skin. Rain glistened off the leaves of the oaks and willows, and the rich green grass swayed in the breeze. At the musky smell of damp wood, Gwyndel remembered the countless spring mornings she had spent alongside Fychan, scouting for game in the early morning hours. Shadows lingered among the evergreens and maples like hidden wights. Such was the territory of Edeveros —opulent in beauty and history.

Gwyndel squinted against the wind. The forest soothed her ire at Belos' arrogance.

Sometimes it is the prey that hides in the forest, not the predator. Vakros once thought otherwise.

Gwyndel smiled as she thought of her husband. Having spent much of his life in the harsh, wintry land of Norgalok, Vakros had been taken aback by Taekohar's lush trees, deep green mountains, and grassy plains. At first, he had been wary of the encroaching forests, fearing hidden predators. Yet after nearly five years of living in Taekohar, he had come to not only tolerate them, but to enjoy the solace found among the trees. Gwyndel burst out from the tree line, tugging on the reins to bring her steed to an unsteady halt. With a snort, the horse shifted its weight on the uneven ground below. Realizing she was alone, Gwyndel shook her head in frustration. Although she did not care for the self-absorbed lord's company, she strove to be a polite guest.

The grey clouds dimly reflected on a trickling creek weaving in a winding path through the underbrush. Gwyndel paused, her eyes roving the trees and the shadows, and probing the thin wisps of mist that hung in the boughs above.

The sudden, guttural squeal of a wild boar sent her heart pounding in fright. Gwyndel urged her horse to a gallop toward the sound. She dove back into the shadowed forest, and the ugly calls of the boar were joined by the blowing of a horn. Through the wind batting her ears, Gwyndel could hear the triumphant exclamations of Lord Belos amid the chaos. Baying hounds hurled threats at their quarry.

Gwyndel and her horse scrambled to a stop in a clearing, coming once again into the fold of the hunters. Cornered by the mounted woodsmen, a fat boar thrashed about with squeals of feral rage, struggling to fend off the hounds nipping at its flanks. The thrill of the hunt filled Lord Stonneter's eyes as he yanked his spear from its saddle sheath. Fedrik leapt from his seat and signaled to the three woodsmen with him. Weapons drawn and gleaming, the three woodsmen slowly lined the edges of the glade, eyes pinned on the boar. Lord Belos followed the boar's thrashing movements in preparation to strike.

Escaping the hounds, the boar dashed toward the treeline, and the woodsmen pounced too late. With defiant squeals, the boar vanished into the rustling underbrush. Gwyndel slumped in the saddle and shook her head at their misfortune.

With a bitter curse, Lord Belos Stonneter lowered his spear and patted his horse on the neck, struggling to calm his steed. He snorted in disgust and regarded Fedrik with a harsh squint. "Well done *Huntsman*," he snapped, wiping away the wet hair plastered to his face by rain. "I thought you would have the sense to find

quality woodsmen to assist you. Not sluggards." His
fingers tightened around the reins, and he turned away
in his outrage. Ears reddening, Fedrik kept silent and
bit his tongue. Slumped under the weight of the
nobleman's biting criticism, he crouched beside one of
the hounds, tending a small wound in the creature's
leg. He worked with care, regarding the hound with
sympathy. Upon her saddle, Gwyndel recoiled at such
unfair treatment.

Why does Fedrik take undeserved scorn to heart?

Intending to reproach Lord Belos, she sidled her
horse beside him, and her eyes flashed blue with the
wisdom of the Keeper of the Sword Imperishable.
Gwyndel tensed at a sudden rustling from the brush
and spun toward the sound, shouting, "To your left!"

The boar exploded from the foliage with a piercing
squeal. Startled, Fedrik cried out as one of the
woodsmen accidentally collided into him, knocking
him on his back. The hounds encircled the boar and
leapt at it with snarling jaws. Knocking one hound
aside, the boar charged Fedrik, tusks lowered. Gwyndel
drew her dagger and hurled it with a flick of her wrist.

The boar squealed in pain as the blade sunk into its
shoulder. In a single movement, Lord Belos wheeled
his horse around and heaved his spear. The boar was
knocked off its feet by the blow, and fell shuddering at
Fedrik's feet.

Dismounting, Gwyndel dashed to Fedrik's side and
knelt beside him. The man stared at the lifeless boar,
sobered by his near brush with death. Laying a
comforting hand on Fedrik's shoulder, Gwyndel shot a

cutting glare toward Belos. "Could we not end our hunt with this thrilling kill?" she asked.

Leading his horse, Belos Stonneter strode beside the dead boar and yanked his spear free with a grunt. He reluctantly met Gwyndel's pointed gaze. "Of course, Gwyndel," he conceded. "As a guest in my house, I am glad to honor your request."

Watching the interaction, the three woodsmen turned their cold stares to where Fedrik lay stricken.

Their own hunt was just beginning.

2

18th of Aevoran, 2209 SE

Haeryn Irongaze fell to the ground just in time. The dragon's tail swept over him with a whoosh of air. Rolling onto his back, he scrambled to his feet and hastily raised his shield for protection. The white, green, and yellow colors upon it were smudged with dirt. His sweat-soaked hair lay plastered to his forehead. A mighty roar drowned out the shouted commands of the attacking force. Haeryn's eyes widened, and he sought refuge within the lines of the soldiers and Foresters. Despite their difference in rank, they fought together as one. The men ducked in turn to avoid the dragon's thrashing tail. Haeryn leapt back as it missed him again.

The beast's winged forelimbs were planted in defiance, and its thick, bulky head roved back and forth to confront the large force surrounding it. Its amber eyes flared with the wrath of a cornered beast. The dragon had chosen to menace a small hamlet, and such a threat commanded attention—and brought peril.

Enraged, the dragon swiped the ranks with its clawed wings. Several of the soldiers went flying. In retaliation, a flurry of arrows littered the air as the Foresters let fly. The dragon fell back with cries of pain, seeking refuge in the cave it had been ousted from. A hasty command rose from the Forester ranks. Men previously hidden above the cave burst from cover. With grunts of effort, they toppled several boulders down the slope in a landslide. Its escape blocked off, the dragon snapped at them with its jaws, trodding over trees as it fought back. Haeryn leapt aside as a tree fell, the impact shuddering through the ground.

A tall knight whisked Haeryn to safety, lowering his great-sword. The man lifted his visor, revealing a keen face that belied his age and wisdom. "Where's your helmet?" he asked, his voice terse.

Haeryn met his Master Knight's pointed look. "I was overheated, Sir Thrynnis," he answered.

Sir Thrynnis rolled his eyes and shook Haeryn by the shoulder. "That may be a valid reason—but only in certain circumstances! Such carelessness could cost a warrior his life!" he exclaimed. Even under the fervent reprimand, Haeryn's smile shone in his eyes. In the years of training they had spent in each other's company, Sir Thrynnis had become a second father to him.

The dragon's screams of fury arrested their attention. Baring its teeth, the creature raised up on its hind legs with maw wide, and the soldiers fell to the ground to protect themselves from its flaming wrath.

A guttural, choking sound emanated from the dragon's throat. Falling back on four legs, the creature shook its head and tried to release a column of fire. Again, the flame within the dragon's chest burned out.

Sir Thrynnis shouldered his great-sword. "Be vigilant. The poisoned arrows have negated the creature's fire-breathing for a time. But do not let down your guard," he said. Shutting his visor, Sir Thrynnis clapped him on the shoulder and disappeared among the ranks struggling against the beast, shouting orders to the soldiers under his command. Inspired by his Master Knight's staunch resolve and authority, Haeryn squared his shoulders.

As Haeryn moved to rejoin the battle, a figure in chainmail and a purple tabard collided into him with a growl of contempt. Haeryn fell on his back with a grunt, and cried out as the boy kicked him in the side with his sabaton.

The boy laughed, his mockery cutting through the din of battle to taunt Haeryn. "Get up, snow-boy," he jeered, yanking Haeryn to his feet. "Watching you flail in battle is nearly as satisfying as watching you squirm at my blows."

Livid, Haeryn shoved the boy away with his shield, advancing on him as he stumbled back. Glaring at his tormentor with an unblinking stare, Haeryn raised the tip of his sword to the boy's throat. "You think you can taunt without punishment and terrorize the squires into silence. But *I*, will not tolerate it," he said. "Tread carefully, Tarrew." Before the boy could reply, Haeryn spun on his heels and leapt into the battle.

Robbed of its fire-breathing, the dragon snapped a wayward soldier in its jaws and crouched to spring like a loaded ballista.

Haeryn's chest tightened.

If it pounces, there will be no survivors.

Realizing the inadequacy of his sword against a tough hide, he sheathed it. He glimpsed the wide, tapered spearpoint of a partizan lying not far away. Facing the dragon, Haeryn snatched up the polearm and tightened his grip upon the shaft, its blade sparkling.

Remember the weak spots.

At the sudden blast of a bugle, a volley of arrows arced upward, and the beast roared in pain as several struck home. Taking advantage of the dragon's distraction, Haeryn sprinted headlong toward it and hurled the partizan.

The dragon screeched in agony. Clawing at the weapon embedded in its eye, the dragon spun away to flee from the men. The ranks of soldiers and Foresters seized their opportunity. They rushed forward, weapons raised.

Haeryn joined the charge with a smile of victory.

Victory belongs to the strong, and the strong alone.

3

20th of Aevoran, 2209 SE

Eyoés closed his eyes, savoring a deep breath of
the early autumn air. The crisp, clean scent of greenery
mixed with the bold, savory aroma of freshly baked
pies. The wind whispered as it stirred through the trees.
Like the comforting presence of an old friend, the late
morning sun warmed Eyoés' back in goodwill. He
opened his eyes, taking in the beauty around him with
a smile of contentment.

Castle Asdale had grown much since its
restoration. The grassy thoroughfares that had once
woven among the houses were now replaced with
cobblestone. Numerous shops and cottages lined the
streets. Shelves of wares were placed outside the shops
to lure customers inside, and the sounds of tradesmen
working at their crafts mingled with the pleasant
atmosphere. Banners of vibrant color hung from every
house, rippling in the breeze. Asdale boasted
Taekohar's characteristic knotwork motifs, featured on
lintels and pennants across the city with captivating
charm. Trees cast their branches over the streets to
provide shade. The beauty seemed as alive as the
people who walked by.

Eyoés watched a group of children dashing through
the streets, laughing and screaming in delighted fright

as they chased each other. Leaning back in his seat, he chuckled to himself. He was fortunate that the Guide had led his people into happiness and prosperity.

Eyoés spurred his horse on, and the mounted servants behind him matched his pace. Ayleril rode beside Eyoés and flashed a warm, but hasty, smile. "Let us hurry, Eyoés," he entreated. "You promised the people you would attend today's Hanesion drama, and the people look forward to your appearance."

Eyoés glanced at Ayleril. "Of course, my friend. I am a man of my word," he said. He urged his horse to a trot. The people ceased what they were doing and bowed in honor as he passed through the streets. Children waved and laughed in greeting. Eyoés' heart swelled in response to the adoration of his subjects.

They rounded a bend in the road, and the narrow street opened into a public square. A cascading fountain graced the center of the plaza. Not far away, a pageant wagon awaited the crowds. Skirt curtains hid the wheels and framework from view. A stage balanced precariously atop the wagon. Stylized reliefs carved into the wooden stage drew the eye to those standing upon it. Actors crowded together with their backs turned to the growing crowd, whispering among themselves in preparation for the imminent performance. Opposite of the pageant wagon, a covered dais had been assembled for the guest of honor. Eyoés shifted uncomfortably at the prospect of being on display before the audience.

Musicians gathered at the base of the pageant wagon. As they placed their chairs in a semicircle formation, they gathered their instruments together and hastily tuned them. The rolling, echoing beauty of the telyn and lyra harps joined the lute in harmony as the musicians played from memory. One of the minstrels sang in the language of old Taekohar, filling the air with words of foregone poets. Eyoés sighed, savoring the tale the notes told.

Dismounting, he gave a welcoming smile and waved in friendship to the growing crowd. The people parted before Eyoés with bows of respect. Climbing the stairs of the covered dais, he brushed aside his green cape and sat upon one of the chairs. Ayleril remained close at his side, discreetly motioning for the servants to attend to the horses.

The actors atop the pageant wagon ended their private meeting, and set about preparing the stage for the performance. The crowd quieted down and turned their attention to the pageant wagon with expectation.

A scuffle near them drew Eyoés' eye, and his peacefulness faded. Two men spoke heatedly. Though their words were indistinct, Eyoés could feel their discord in stark contrast to the peace of Asdale. Disturbed, Eyoés turned away, saddened. Despite appearances, the tranquility of Asdale had a tenuous hold. More often than Eyoés wished to admit, the sheriffs often brought to him news of petty quarrels and discontentment. The strife grieved him.

Ease has cultivated entitlement and robbed Asdale of its peace. The people can feel it too—it is in their eyes and their false smiles. They seek relief, though they search for it in the wrong places.

A desire to retreat back into the comfort of the keep seized Eyoés. His thoughts were interrupted as Ayleril laid a hand on his forearm, watching the unfolding crisis with him. With a sympathetic look, Ayleril gave a quiet sigh. "There is little you can do for them, Eyoés," he whispered. "A baron may be able to enforce laws, but he cannot enforce a change of heart. The Hanesion is about to begin." As a servant placed a goblet of fine mead into his hand, Eyoés stared at the minstrels playing in front of the pageant wagon.

As the musicians drew the last note of their song, all fell quiet. Hastening down from the platform, the actors hid themselves behind the stage—save one. Turning to the audience, the man gave a dramatic bow. Dressed in an elaborate tunic of black and silver, he struck a grand pose. "Most gracious crowds, we are grateful for your presence at today's Hanesion drama," he said with a grin. Looking toward the Baron, he extended a hand in his direction. "And we are most honored by the appearance of our benevolent Baron Eyoés Kingson, member of the Five Heroes of Alithell and the scion of Élorn the Protector of Taekohar!" he exclaimed. Cheers and clapping rose from the crowd as they turned to Eyoés with exclamations of gratitude and loyalty.

With a gracious smile, Eyoés waved good-naturedly at his people. Remembering his humble upbringing, he was grateful for the fondness the people showed him.

I only wish to inspire the people to follow the King's leading. Not to further my own prestige.

The actor upon the stage raised his voice. "Without further delay, we bring to you the riveting—and at times humorous—tale of Eyoés Kingson and Throst Ravenstrong!" he declared, withdrawing from the stage as soon as the words were spoken.

Eyoés choked on his mead. Clearing his throat, he pressed a fist to his mouth and froze in his seat. His mind reeled at the unexpected subject matter. In the years following his return from Rehillon, Eyoés had allowed only small hints of the incident to become public knowledge. Consequently, much of the people's scant understanding was tainted by rumors and speculation. Yet it shocked Eyoés that an amateur playwright would venture to create a complete drama from innumerable half-truths. He suspected the playwright had chosen the popular tale to advance his own reputation. Calming himself, he settled in his chair to endure the inevitable.

Several wide-eyed actors fumbled with a prop table as they precariously carried it up the steps of the stage. They dropped it in position and scurried down the stairs out of sight. At a command from the head actor, the minstrels took up a wistful, dark song with their instruments, grooming the emotions of the audience for the best possible reception. As the music entranced the ears of the crowd, several actors in fine costumes hastened to take their seats around the table.

The melody paused to signal the performers, then continued with renewed emotion. Atop the stage, the actors began to argue among themselves, pounding their fists upon the table and raising their voices into a cacophony. Eyoés shook his head at this mock Council of Lords.

He cringed as he spotted another actor lingering on the outskirts of the council, his gaze wandering like some ignorant child. The flame emblem embroidered upon the man's shoulder made his identity clear. Ears reddening, Eyoés tugged at his collar in embarrassment over the man's amateur impression of himself.

It is clear from his demeanor that he cares little about this performance—or about my self-esteem.

One of the actors raised his voice. "We cannot let the Rehils be divided! Lord Ravenstrong has turned the people against you, my Baron! Something must be done—a hero must rise up in our midst," he cried, looking intently at the one seated at the head of the table.

The false Vikar Amberster regarded the man with patience and poise—an excellent actor in comparison to the rest of the lot. Vikar raised his hand, and the councilmen were hushed. "Peace! Consider your words, my friend. I see something must be done, but who will rise up to challenge the cunning and might of Throst Ravenstrong?" he declared.

Another actor entered the stage, and Eyoés recognized him as the one who had introduced the play. The man came to stand haughtily before the council, shoulders held back and hands at his hips. "I thank you for your compliment, Vikar my liege," he said, earning a laugh from the crowd.

Eyoés' face turned grim. A chill made him shudder as he recalled the day he'd first seen Throst.

No one can convey his poise, intelligence, and deceit. A single glance was enough to convince a man of his lies. Even after seven years, his memory unsettles me. A true portrayal of his character may have proved harder to witness than this poor performance.

Roughly pushing his chair away, Vikar stood to face Throst. He gripped the edge of the table with vehemency. "It was no compliment. We all know of your treachery. You have divided the people and possess a false authority that I can never hope to challenge," he retorted, his words full of passion.

Throst laughed in disdain and waved Vikar's words aside. He turned toward the crowd. "Any attempt to oust me will end in your own destruction, Vikar, and your people will consider *you* the villain. None can best me," he challenged, puffing out his chest.

Then, emerging from the edge of the stage, the actor portraying Eyoés leaned toward Throst with an indignant cry. "Then *I* challenge you, man to man. I am Eyoés Kingson, the bane of Skreon the Murderer and the Baron of Asdale—the city that rose from its ashes to become the jewel of Alithell," he declared, sweeping his hand out toward the crowd. "I will best you. And all of Rehillon shall be set free of your lies and corruption!" Eyoés cringed in his seat at the horrid script.

The false Throst wheeled around to face his challenger, his face reddened with contrived anger. "Then we shall duel beside the Wrolm River! I shall crush you upon its shores!" he shouted. The minstrels played a final discordant note, and the actors hastily reworked the stage for the next scene.

Sipping his mead, Eyoés turned his attention away from the Hanesion play.

Perhaps it is better this way—simple and ridiculous. The true machinations of Throst unsettle the mind and haunt his victims. It was not some trifling contest of nobles.

As he turned to speak to Ayleril, Eyoés hesitated. A servant whispered in his advisor's ear. Ayleril raised an eyebrow. With a nod and a wave of his hand, Ayleril dismissed the servant and caught Eyoés' eye. Glancing at the stage, he rose from his seat and leaned close to Eyoés' ear. "You have received a messenger from the Castle Sanctum," he whispered.

Dismissing the poor performance, Eyoés looked up to the sky and gave a sigh of relief.

4

Ayleril nodded to admit a lone figure to the dais. An unimposing, olive-skinned man ascended the steps. Simple sandals shod his feet, and a crisp sapphire blue habit rippled down to his ankles. His hair was cut short in the fashion of holy men. The man's wide grin revealed a pearly white smile as his kind eyes fixed on Eyoés. Standing in respect, Eyoés bowed.

The man lowered his head in humble acknowledgement. He lifted his right hand, putting his forefinger and thumb together in the customary sign of reverential greeting. "I am Sharaf, ascetic of the Castle Sanctum," he said with a rolling tongue. "Baron Eyoés Kingson, I am most humbled to meet you."

Established during Alithell's great days of old, Amiranoor's Castle Sanctum had attained a legendary reputation among the territories as a beautiful monastery. The ascetics' compassion for others and their devotion to the King—though at times distinct and unfamiliar—was highly respected. Eyoés remembered with fondness their steadfastness in producing books and promoting the use of libraries throughout Alithell. Calm settled upon him.

He endured the unfolding drama with disinterest. Searching the audience, he saw they were captivated by the pitiful performance.

They seek relief through entertainment rather than addressing their troubles. Such trivial things will never bring the contentment that only the Guide provides. It will take a potent reminder to wake them from their dithering.

In hopes of securing relief for Taekohar's malady, Eyoés had dispatched a letter to the Abbot of the Castle Sanctum. He hoped his status, and his friendship with his fellow Hero, Sabaah, would convince the Abbot to grant his request. As Eyoés stood before Sharaf, he anticipated the future with confidence.

With a gracious smile, Eyoés motioned for Sharaf to sit in one of the spare chairs beside him. The ascetic inclined his head and placed a hand on his chest. Moving past the chair, he instead seated himself cross-legged on the floor beside the baron's chair. "As a member of the Castle Sanctum, I am content without provided comforts," he answered, looking up to Ayleril and Eyoés. "Please do not regard it as an insult." The extreme inflection in his words emphasized his insistence.

Taking a seat, Eyoés glanced curiously at Ayleril and waved the matter aside. "Of course not," he insisted, fascinated by the man's peculiar habits. He brought his focus back to more important matters. "What does Abbot Behnassos say to my request?" he inquired, leaning forward in his seat with hope.

Sharaf let his eyes roam across the vista of Asdale's beauty and prosperous growth. "He agreed to found an abbey in Asdale as you requested," he answered. "But preparations must be made, and it will take time. Perhaps years."

Eyoés' face fell, and he pressed his fist to his mouth in thought. His eagerness clashed with an understanding of the need for patience as he sought for a solution. As his eyes wandered, the scene playing out onstage caught his attention.

The false Eyoés and Throst stood face to face, swords in hand. They alone commanded the stage, and the minstrels took up the lonesome, dark song once again. The strain of the harp, lyra, and lute escalated. Enthralled by the tale unfolding before them, the crowd sat in captive silence.

The duel began, and the crowd watched, breathless. Sword beat upon sword in a wild, uncoordinated flurry of blows that completely disregarded the true art of swordsmanship. Throst cowered, unprepared for the strength and supposed skill of his opponent. With one last blow, he lay on his back, with the false Eyoés towering over him, sword poised at his enemy's chest.

Throst raised his hands in supplication. "Have mercy! What must I do to pay the ransom of your sword and deliver myself?" he pleaded.

The actor portraying Eyoés withdrew his sword, his fierce gaze holding his fallen enemy fast. "Accomplish twelve labors for me and I will consider you acquitted," he answered, raising his voice to a grand declaration.

Pinching his brow in disgust, Eyoés averted his eyes from the performance. The reminder of his people's belief in conditional pardon sorrowed him.

The people think all forgiveness should be earned with sweat and tears. And now, because of this drama, they think I agree with such falsehood!

He forced himself to focus on the first steps he could take to achieve his goal instead of entertaining his distress. Eyoés glimpsed a birch tree beside the covered dais where he sat and raised an eyebrow. "What materials are necessary, Sharaf?" he asked.

Sharaf pursued his lips. "Stone, usually," he answered. "Wood is not often an available option for the more distant villages and towns of Amiranoor."

Eyoés stroked his short beard. "Perhaps an abbey of wood shall suit our needs. There are several craftsmen who are skilled in woodworking. They will be more than eager to construct a small abbey of timber if the pay is sufficient. I regret to say that I am unsure if they would approach the task with much piety," he said.

Sharaf nodded in thought. "That is a reasonable option. And in the meantime, the Abbot sent me to represent the Guide and his loyal devotees to your people through service," he remarked.

Heartened by Sharaf's humility, Eyoés reached over and clasped the man's forearm in friendship. "You have my thanks and gratitude, Sharaf. I will work to assemble the men and materials for the abbey's construction," he said.

A servant hastened up the steps of the dais and bowed before Eyoés, panting from his rush. "My Baron, a diplomat from Edeveros has arrived in Asdale. She requests your presence with a most urgent summons," he urged. Brow furrowed, Eyoés shared an intrigued glance at Ayleril. The chances of a diplomat's journeying across Alithell for an audience with him over a simple matter were slim.

He stood, casting one last distasteful glance at the Hanesion drama. "Come Ayleril. I am eager to attend to business rather than to witness such an ill-written spectacle," he said.

5

20th of Aevoran, 2209 SE

The friendly voices of the soldiers and knights around Haeryn rose in greeting as the sentries atop the wall waved a welcome. Banners upon the palisade of Asdale's farradoth fluttered briskly. Ahead, a tall gate opened to admit them. Haeryn let his eyes roam over the pointed tips of the palisade and their formidable height.

After the reconstruction of Castle Asdale and its firm establishment as the renewed capital of Taekohar, Eyoés had focused a concentrated effort into strengthening the territory's army. He issued a decree directing the major castles of Taekohar to section off specific areas of their castle grounds for the effective training of a large garrison. These farradoths contained barracks for the knights, as well as a field for their daily drills. In his years of training, Haeryn had come to know Asdale's farradoth as well as his home village in Norgalok.

Haeryn's mind wandered back to the battle against the dragon only a few days prior. With a gleam of youthful pride in his eyes, he sat a little straighter in the saddle. Though he alone was not responsible for the dragon's defeat, his moment of courage filled him with a sense of accomplishment.

Sir Thrynnis rode alongside him with his visor lifted. The knotwork filigree upon his fitted pauldrons brought a hint of tradition to his broad, resolute shoulders. His vambraces struggled to encompass his brawny forearms, and his gauntleted fists were like hammers ready to carry out the law's decrees without partiality. As his horse trotted forward, his chainmail clinked. Haeryn inspected the coat of arms emblazoned on his Master Knight's surcoat. Shaped in the manner of a blue shield, the crest was divided by a diagonal line. White delf squares rested upon a charge of checkered potent. Haeryn smiled as he recalled the meaning of the symbols.

Loyalty that instills him with both respect and selflessness. Peace for all under his authority. Justice, that holds unfairness in contempt.

Within the enclosed walls of the battle school, log cabins were lined up and sectioned by rank on either side of the farradoth. Trees offered sparse shade and natural beauty to the otherwise barren expanse of the drilling field.

The gates closed firmly behind them, and Sir Thrynnis raised his hand to signal the company to halt. As one of the most respected and well-known knights of Taekohar, he dismounted, thereby giving the others permission to do so as well. Haeryn dismounted along with the other soldiers, patting his speckled brown and white horse with a whispered word of gratitude.

The knights and soldiers removed their gear from their saddles as stableboys rushed out to usher the horses inside. With their steeds attended to, the company took up their supplies and started for their respective barracks.

Haeryn picked up his gear with a grunt of effort and headed for the largest of the nearby cabins. As the squire of the renowned Sir Thrynnis, he shared a roof with his Master Knight. Every morning before training, they shared breakfast, discussing the day to come and strengthening the camaraderie between them. Striding down the weaving dirt path, Haeryn hastened to the door and fell against it, pushing it inward.

The rich scent of pine welcomed him. Daub chinked the gaps between the logs in stripes of white against the rich brown walls. A stone fireplace against the leftmost wall was dusted clean of the charred remains of past fires, and fresh-cut logs were assembled in a neat pile within. Sparse furnishings served the cabin's practical needs.

Readjusting his grip on his supplies, Haeryn turned to a small doorway. He hastened into the room, throwing his bag of supplies upon his bed. His own room, though barely the size of a servant's quarters, was to him as warm and pleasant as the most luxurious castle. Leaning against the bedpost, he unslung his shield from his back and laid it atop the bag of supplies. He shrugged his shoulders to ease his sore muscles and examined his shield. A sense of strength and purpose stirred him from his weariness at the sight of his own personal coat of arms. Marred by combat, the stark and vibrant design upon the shield was scarred by gouges. Haeryn picked it up. A simple touch-up would suffice, although the scarring would still be noticeable.

He reached under his bed, groping about blindly. His hands fell on a small, rectangular box, its surface soft with dust. Haeryn pulled the box out and rose to his feet. He undid the latch and lifted the lid. Examining the brush and canisters of paint within, he closed the box and tucked it under his arm. Taking up his shield with his other hand, Haeryn strode out of the cabin.

He squinted against the sunlight. A small cluster of trees drew him, promising a place of respite from the rigors of travel. He set his shield and box of paint on the grass and sat at the base of a tree. Haeryn tipped his head back, gazing up into the deep green boughs. Despite the rigorous drills and chores, he often found himself enjoying the familiarity of the farradoth—but he did not forget his purpose. Protecting the weak.

His expression grew melancholy as his thoughts returned to the snowy wastelands of Norgalok. Closing his eyes, Haeryn imagined the frigid touch of the snow upon his skin, and the howling of the wind in his ears. Memories of his home village made his stomach lurch. His eyes opened, eager to shut out the memory. Glancing around him, he reached into the leather bag on his belt. His hand closed upon a small, round wooden object, and he drew it out, opening his fist. A small pendant lay in the middle of his palm, bearing the snowflake emblem of the Kinsfolk upon it, engraved and painted in red. His brows furrowed, and he stared, blind to all else.

I must remember the pit I've risen from. The gods proved themselves false. I do not need guidance to determine my path. Justice and leadership are my future.

Closing his fist around the pendant, Haeryn returned it to his pouch and lifted his eyes to the shield that lay before him. He opened the box of paints and prepared for his work in peace. Dipping the brush into one of the bottles of paint, he began his repair. The smooth consistency of the paint caused the brush to glide across the rough wood, filling in the gaps and restoring the familiar colors and emblems to their former glory. Although the lines and shapes of his coat of arms were imperfect, Haeryn did not mind. Whatever unique mistakes he made were his own. Despite its imperfections and scars, he was still proud to have earned his coat of arms by saving Sir Thrynnis' wife from a bandit.

The upper top of the shield was exposed silver, ornamented with the symbol of a staring eye. A field of green covered two-thirds of the shield's surface, separated from the silver by an alternating trefly-club border. A symbol of hands clasped was placed upon the green field. Finishing the last stroke, Haeryn wiped the brush clean with a spare cloth as he regarded his shield.

Vert, four fois or, a chief trefly-counter-trefly argent. Symbolizing chivalry, loyalty, and protection. Chivalry—the heritage of the knight. Loyalty—to both Taekohar and to my adopted family. Protection—the deliverance of those trapped in injustice.

With a smile of contentment, Haeryn returned the paints and brush to their box and sealed it. Standing, he bent down to pick up his shield. A shout of pain sounded from the drilling field, shocking Haeryn from his quietude. He straightened, tense for action as his eyes roved the field. Pressing up against the pine tree with his heart pounding, he awaited the blast of horns from the farradoth's palisade, warning of danger. No blast came.

Haeryn stepped away from the pine, searching the farradoth's drilling field. His pulse quickened in familiar outrage as he caught sight of three figures not far away. One of the figures raised his hands in supplication, and Haeryn heard the boy's pleas of tormented grief. The other two figures laughed at this show of weakness. The leader of the two shoved the supplicant to the ground. Haeryn's expression darkened, and he clenched his jaw to contain his wrath at the sight of Tarrew. He was disgusted that Gaery had joined him.

Stepping over his shield, Haeryn sprinted across the expanse and rammed his shoulder into Tarrew, knocking the wind from him and sending him sprawling. Haeryn came to a brisk stop and instinctively fell into an offensive stance. Gaery, startled by his sudden appearance, threw a wild hook. Haeryn ducked aside and swept Gaery's feet from under him.

Wheezing, Tarrew rose. "You mongrel," he gasped, his face reddening.

Seething, Haeryn seized Tarrew by the collar of his shirt. He glared at Gaery. "Get up," he snapped. Gaery leapt to his feet, standing rigid at Haeryn's commanding presence.

Turning back to Tarrew, Haeryn drew him close. "Look at me," he said, voice raw as the winters of Norgalok. Reluctantly, Tarrew returned his potent stare. Haeryn let the silence speak for him. He nodded at their victim. Grateful, the boy scrambled to his feet and fled. Haeryn shoved Tarrew away, causing him to stumble back. "You are squires, as am I. Act like it," he demanded, his iron gaze holding both of the oppressors in rapt attention.

Gaery cowered with a nod of obedience. Tarrew, however, could not allow such a challenge to go unpunished. With a smirk of contempt, he drew himself up to his full height. "Your prowess on the drilling field does not intimidate me, Haeryn," he said, his smirk widening into a smile. "Besides, I wouldn't want to upset the baron's little boy, now would I?" He chuckled as he let the insult take its toll.

Haeryn drove his fist into Tarrew's stomach, and the arrogant squire doubled over, wincing in pain. Seizing a fistful of Tarrew's hair, Haeryn sheared it off with his dagger. Tarrew cried out as he felt the ugly, barren patch on his head.

Before Tarrew could wreak his revenge, Haeryn kicked him away. He threw the fistful of hair to the ground and sheathed his dagger. "I'll warn you again —"

A strong hand gripped him by the shoulder and yanked him back. Heat flushed to Haeryn's face as he wheeled to face his attacker—and suddenly stood at attention.

Sir Thrynnis now turned his wrath upon Tarrew. He drew back his hand and slapped him, pointing toward the barracks. "LEAVE!" he commanded. Tarrew scurried away, nursing his wound. Face blanched in fright, Gaery fled from where he had been watching.

Haeryn swallowed as Sir Thrynnis turned to him. The knight came toward his squire and sighed, glancing back to where the two ruffians fled. "I can't say they didn't deserve it," he began, turning back to Haeryn. "But this is the fifth time in your service that you have overstepped your bounds and taken justice into your own hands. You disregard the mandates of the Farradoth. The squires are responsible for putting forth a good example for the page boys. Such behavior is not befitting a squire *or* a knight. Understood?" Though stern, the Master Knight's rebuke was easier for the youth to bear. The man's kindness and wisdom inspired Haeryn once again, despite the reprimand.

"Yes sir," Haeryn answered. Then, falling at ease, he turned away. "But surely you will not stand by! Justice must be satisfied."

Sir Thrynnis' gaze softened, and he laid a comforting hand on Haeryn's shoulder. "I'll give the squires a stern talking to after the evening meal. Perhaps they'll see the error of their ways." he answered, his disappointment at the predicament evident in his voice. He turned Haeryn around to face the gates of the Farradoth. "You will be a knight in time. Remember it," he said, lowering his voice for privacy. "Your father sent an urgent summons for you."

6

The vivid daylight was overtaken by the subtle glow of lantern-light as Haeryn descended the spiraling staircase into Castle Asdale's lower recesses. Ayleril led the way, his robes furling behind him like a grand flag. They both were content to embrace the silence. Though Ayleril's calm temper had sometimes been at odds with Haeryn's sense of justice in the past, the man had become a trusted friend.

Running his right hand along the smooth stone wall, Haeryn traced the clean, neat junctures. Though cold, the stone's barren surface was pleasant to the touch in its uniformness. From the smallest corner to the grandest hall, he noted the cleanliness of Asdale's keep. Haeryn let his eyes roam across the familiar banners placed at intervals along the stairway, portraying legends of old or abstract knotwork designs. It pleased him that his father took such great care to assure his home's longevity, down to the smallest details.

Haeryn eyed one of the banners. Its circular design drew the eye further in with its ever tightening knots. Such art was foreign to him—a vast difference from the harsh and stylized art of Norgalok. Taekohar had begun to adopt its own distinct cultural identity through dress, music, and art—and Haeryn eagerly strove to adopt the lifestyle of his new home.

As the stairway opened into a broad chamber, Haeryn turned his thoughts to his father's urgent summons. He squinted as he tried to recall anything that could have required his attendance. Haeryn tossed the hair out of his face, his mind full of conjecture and uncertainty as to his summons.

Ayleril nearly left me behind in his rush. What could Father want?

Arcing over his head, a vaulted ceiling alone inspired respect—but the chamber was stripped of the normal trimmings of nobility in accordance with the wishes of its occupant. Ayleril bowed to the boy with a wink and departed.

Pacing about the chamber, Eyoés lifted his head at the sound of Haeryn's footsteps. With a brief smile, he embraced his son. "Thank the King you're back in time! Our guest must depart as soon as possible," he said. He motioned for Haeryn to sit on his humble throne. Haeryn sat, glimpsing a figure lingering in the shadows.

A short, stocky woman moved from beside a pillar, her deep saffron dress weightless as it quivered. Her dirty riding clothes had been exchanged for the fashionable court attire she had brought along. Lavish white traceries were embroidered upon it. Spotless ruffles bloomed out of her sleeves, almost hiding her hands from view. A caul and circlet crowned her head, adorned with small, sparkling stones. Haeryn recognized the origins of her manner of dress instantly. Edeveros—the birthplace of heroes.

Recollections of his father's tutoring in history returned to him. As the first territory established in the Kingdom of Alithell, Edeveros had a rich heritage. Champions had emerged from their green highlands and forests, proving their mettle in the War of Adrógar. Their unparalleled etiquette and raiment mirrored their legendary prowess. Haeryn came to his feet and bowed before the woman with the utmost honor.

Watching his son's response, Eyoés beamed. Haeryn had grown much in the past five years. His smile weakened as he turned to the woman. "Please recount again the purpose for your visit," he said. Eyoés glimpsed Haeryn's inquisitive expression.

The woman's light eyes fixed on Haeryn, examining him from head to foot in silent scrutiny. She gave an amiable smile. "You are Haeryn the Irongaze, squire of Sir Thrynnis of Asdale, and son of Eyoés?" she inquired. Glancing awkwardly at his father, Haeryn nodded.

Despite his position of authority, Eyoés struggled to dismiss the sinking feeling in his stomach. He fixed his eyes on his son. Tears welled in his eyes, and he swallowed the lump in his throat.

If what she claims is true, Haeryn—my son—may leave and never return.

Desperate to hold fast to Haeryn, he dismissed the thought. Eyoés knew that, despite the woman's news, Haeryn would not so easily be torn from him. Drawing herself up, the woman faced Haeryn and commenced

her message. "Nearly two years ago, Lady Roseen
Estworth of Gahidros asked that the archives be
searched to discover the fate of House Wynrence—the
first noble line of Edeveros. After much inquiry and
searching, it was discovered that, centuries after being
stripped of their power during the Edeveran Wars of
Succession, the last Wynrences established a small
coastal settlement in Rehillon. For a time, that was all
we could reckon of their fate," she explained, clasping
her hands in front of her and gliding about the room
with genteel grace. "That was until Caywen and Vikar
Amberster heard of our search. As friends of Roseen,
they delved into their own records to aid us. And it was
in the Great Library of Hodholm that they found the
answer we had been searching for."

She turned to Haeryn, stepping toward him and
lifting his chin so their eyes met. "A settlement was
mentioned in a passing reference in a local census,
when an elderly couple reported an attack by Norgalok
raiders in 2195. They were the only survivors, and
claimed their baby nephew Vasil was stolen,
presumably for slave labor when he came of age. The
Registry of 2192 records the birth of a son named
Vasil, born to Arthyan and Ellenor Wynrence, who
were residents of that settlement. Due to Norgalok's
secession from the Kingdom of Alithell, it is
impossible to look any further into the matter. The
birthdate on the Registry and the year of the raid offer
compelling evidence, as well as your current age. An
additional confirmation is the mention of your former
slavery in your father's letter to Gwair when you came

to Taekohar in 2204. From what I see, your skin is not nearly as light as those of the Norgalokans, which indicates you are not a native southerner," she said. "Haeryn, we have reason to believe you are the last of the Wynrence line."

Haeryn doubted his hearing. His chest tingled as with a handmaid's needles, and his stomach clenched. A thousand rebuttals rose to mind all at once, the sheer volume of them striking him mute. He hunched in his seat, his blank stare twisted in confusion. His mouth opened, though he struggled to voice his turmoil. "What?" he muttered.

The woman lowered her eyes, the potency of his disbelief compelling her to explain. "I do not deliver this news flippantly. My journey was difficult. With King Fohidras' new system of roads still underway, the only path I could take was through the wilderness on an arrangement of peasant trails," she said.

Haeryn looked up at her with brokenness in his eyes. Faint memories of his childhood flashed through his mind—the biting snow, the day of the sacrifice, the fear that had haunted his life as far back as he could remember. "I thought my parent's names were Freok and Thakka..." he said, his voice falling away. Covering his mouth, he leaned against the armrest of his father's seat. He felt conflicted.

Taekohar is my home. Now I am told it is not? Who am I truly?

The Edeveran heroes once confined to old books were now his flesh and blood. His family. His legacy.

He wondered if this would be his chance to further justice.

Eyoés moved beside his son and laid a hand on Haeryn's shoulder. His expression was pained, and his hands shook. He patted his son on the shoulder, struggling to make sense of this revelation. "How certain are you?" he asked the woman.

The emissary grabbed a nearby chair and sat, clasping her hands in her lap in the manner of a gentlewoman. She met Eyoés' gaze fixedly. "Eyoés, if he is fifteen years of age at this moment, the dates match up exactly," she answered, turning to Haeryn. "But in the Registry there was also mention that there was a star-shaped mark on Vasil's left ankle—"

Haeryn yanked off his boot and rolled down the edge of his sock. Eyoés stifled a gasp at the star-shaped birthmark. "The Norgalokans said I was cursed because of this," Haeryn said.

Eyoés willed himself to silence rather than sway his son with his own opinion.

Perhaps that is why Haeryn's parents in Norgalok gave him up for the sacrifice.

The woman leaned forward and laid a hand on his knee. "It is now beyond doubt. Your people need you, Haeryn. Hard times have befallen Edeveros. Even though the Wynrence claim to the Baronship has long expired, you stand as a symbol of Edeveros' former glory. Should the last Wynrence return to his ancestral homeland, hope will spark anew and stir the people to remember their honorable roots, desiring something better for their homeland. Establish your lineage in Edeveros for their sake—not your own."

Haeryn sat in silence, pummeled by the new identity thrust upon him. A desire to embrace it swelled in his heart—but as he saw the love in his father's eye, he doubted.

Eyoés saved me from death. He welcomed me into his home and life in Taekohar. Am I responsible for the commonfolk of another territory? How can I abandon Taekohar?

Exhausted by the questions, Haeryn stood, running his hand through his hair. "I need to think," he declared, snatching his boot from the floor and jamming his foot in it. He strode to the stairs, his mind no longer focused on the other two within the room.

Eyoés did not move to detain him. Eyes softening at the sight of his son's distress, he watched Haeryn stomp up the stairs and out of sight.

What does the Guide desire of Haeryn? And what role am I to play?

7

Haeryn returned to the farradoth, deaf to the calls of welcome from the sentries upon the palisade. As the gate shut behind him, he stopped, pondering the surrounding buildings and drilling field. The breeze rustled through the trees and whispered through the grass, attempting to comfort him in a tongue he did not understand. Haeryn looked up into the clear blue sky, anxious to settle upon a course of action.

He strolled onward, his thoughts turned inward as he walked through the training field. The shouts of drilling soldiers sounded dull and distant to him, hearkening back to ancient days of warriors and legends. He stopped under the branches of an oak and leaned against it, closing his eyes.

I know who I wish to become. I shall never abandon Taekohar. But the people of Edeveros need me. The opportunity for leadership has come. What should I do?

With every thought, Haeryn's restless heart ached. As his mind toiled, the memory of Eyoés' comforting smile and his loving embrace offered solace.

At least I am not alone in this.

A familiar, mocking laugh startled him. Haeryn saw Tarrew scorning him from a safe distance with a glint of nervousness in his eye. "I heard you were summoned by your father," he said, voice low. "How does it feel to be the son of a coxcomb, reaping the benefits of someone else's hard work?" Haeryn tensed, and Tarrew fled, fearing the next flash of fury.

Sinking back against the oak, Haeryn sighed. His breath caught in his chest as Tarrew's insult echoed in his mind. He bit his tongue, indignant at the suggestion that his father was a pompous noble.

He shook his head, overwhelmed by the uncertainties. Haeryn pushed away from the oak and strode toward his home. The dirt path blurred in his vision as he crossed the distance. Pushing against the door to the cabin, he entered, blind to all but his own troubled mind. He closed the door, staring into the fireplace as he leaned against the mantle.

"You met with your father and the emissary," Sir Thrynnis said, sitting at the table with a tankard before him. He met the unsettled gaze of his squire. "You are not the only one ill at ease," he remarked.

Haeryn's shoulders sagged. With a sigh, he sat across from his Master Knight and angled away from him, cracking his knuckles. "A part of me rejoices at this revelation. But I feel torn. I admire the old heroes, but Edeveros is distant and unknown. To accept the Wynrence name is to reject my adoption into Taekohar. At least, that is what it seems like to me," he said.

His brow furrowed. "Regardless, I know this—I wish to be a knight of Asdale, not a pampered nobleman. I want to *help* others—to suffer at their side and protect them from evil with my own two hands."

Sir Thrynnis smiled and laughed to himself. "If only there were more men like you," he said. "That is why I made you my squire. You have the spirit of a knight, Haeryn. That will always be with you." Swallowing a sip of mead, he placed a hand on Haeryn's shoulder. "Yes, nobles have a reputation of ruling others from a distance. In some cases, it breeds a weak connection to the people. But not always. Look at your father. He loves Taekohar's people!" he declared, inclining his head and returning Haeryn's keen look. "Being a Wynrence does not mean treating your people with indifference—or even adopting the full responsibility of nobility. Home is not the land of your forefathers. It is the land of your loved ones."

The tension within Haeryn's heart eased, and as he mulled over Thrynnis' words, they warmed him like a wool mantle. He relaxed in his seat, letting the assurance enfold him. Haeryn clasped his hands. "If I take this name as my own, what will come? Am I to leave Asdale for Edeveros?" he inquired.

Drinking the last draught of his mead, Sir Thrynnis shrugged. "That is your decision to make," he said, pushing the chair away and standing up. "You've always wished to help those who cannot help themselves. And skill alone does not make a great leader. The key to your growth might very well await you in Edeveros." He patted Haeryn on the shoulder and departed, his words still hanging in the air.

Haeryn sat on the edge of his bed, staring at the closed door to his room. His folded tabard was cradled in his hands, the coat of arms upon it urging him to cling to Taekohar. He did not look at it. Instead, his eyes were riveted upon his door, envisioning the journey that lay beyond it. The words of his Master Knight churned in his head, growing stronger with consideration.

The key to your growth might very well await you in Edeveros.

Still, Haeryn hesitated. The Kinsfolk pendant in his belt pouch returned to his thoughts. At the memory, Haeryn heard the words of Sir Thrynnis strive against his doubts.

Home is not the land of your forefathers. It is the land of your loved ones.

Haeryn looked down at the tabard in his hands. At the sight of the familiar coat of arms, his eyes prickled with tears. His journey from waif to squire flashed before him. He knew Taekohar would always be his home. Nothing would take its place.

Images of poor commoners arose in his mind, their eyes revealing their eagerness for the return of the Wynrences. Haeryn clenched his jaw and tightened his grip on his tabard. "Taekohar is my home—but Edeveros is my quest," he declared.

8

3ʳᵈ of Rotanos, 2209 SE

A drizzle of rain showered down from the bleak grey sky, dampening Gibusil's wings with a glistening sheen. Fine mist hung over the green moors, tumbling down into the gorges. To the north, mountains and rocky outcrops pierced through the mist's covering like castle towers. Small copses of trees were scattered across the landscape, dwelling in the shadows of the hills and valleys.

Eyoés patted Gibusil's neck, sending a spray of rainwater flying off the griffin's golden coat. Gibusil chirped in delight at the rain's cool touch, glancing over his shoulder at Eyoés. A leather eyepatch covered the griffin's right eye, strapped securely around its head. A pang of sadness pricked Eyoés. In the years following their return from Norgalok, Gibusil had grown accustomed to his impairment. Yet despite the griffin's adaptability and skill, Eyoés knew it would prove a dangerous weakness.

Gibusil swooped low, piercing the shroud of mist, soaring not far above the land. The landscape shifted, and a gorge furrowed between two descending hills below them. A woodland of conifers and birch surrounded them, the songs of the birds and the whispers of the wind beseeching the travelers to bring them news. As Gibusil increased his speed, the forest blurred.

Eyoés' face fell as he looked out over the home of Haeryn's ancestors. Glancing over his shoulder to where the youth sat, Eyoés noted the youth's staunch manner, and the determined set to his brow. Eyoés felt a flicker of uncertainty as he recalled his son's declaration to him of his decision. Haeryn declared Taekohar was his true home.

But what if the call of Edeveros becomes stronger?

The gorge opened into an expanse of flat moorland, hemmed in by rising hills and outcrops of rock. Not far in the distance, a township rose in the open landscape, surrounded by several farms. Hamlets dotted the landscape at various intervals, each claiming several farms as its own. Like threads, roads weaved the townships and hamlets together. Wagons, horses, and other travelers passed along the streets. Rising out of the ground like a red fountain was a forest of crimson. Eyoés felt transfixed by the deep red leaves and the silvery branches he glimpsed underneath.

Besieged by the red forest, Castle Mithlon towered over the landscape, set upon a flattened section of exposed stone. Clusters of towers clung to its bleached white walls. From the highest tower, a grand flag billowed. A simple red stripe cut diagonally across a white field, marked with three white X's along the band. Haeryn squinted, recognizing the coat of arms that flew proudly above the grand capital of Edeveros.

Argent on a bend gules three saltires coupled argent.

Haeryn leaned forward for a better view. "The crest of the Estworths," he said, stirred by the gallant tales of Arógym and other heroic Estworths. Rigorous training in heraldry had become a standard training regimen for the squires of Asdale's farradoth. Though identification of a coat of arms was nigh impossible in the chaos of battle, a general understanding was necessary in regard to knightly relations with other territories.

Haeryn's smile of admiration faded, and his eyes narrowed. The emblem of a fox's head was emblazoned on the flag's upper right corner—a foreign element.

They both fell silent, looking warily at the banner. Eyoés shuddered at the poignant memory of Rodmer Estworth lying upon the shores of the Jagged Falls in Rehillon, slain in his final act of villainy.

Gibusil dove toward the road leading to the castle, and the two riders clung to the griffin's back with white knuckles. Cries of shock erupted from the travelers upon the road. The people ducked as the griffin shot over their heads and glided above the crimson forest. Eyoés cringed in his seat, his ears growing red at the people's shock.

Gibusil soared feet above the forest canopy, and a cloud of red leaves stirred in his wake, torn from their branches. The shower of raindrops pricked Haeryn's face as they sped through the rain to Castle Mithlon.

Eyoés pulled on Gibusil's reins, and the end of the forest came into view. The griffin slowed his approach, and the crimson trees fell away to a section of open land before the gates of Mithlon. Under Eyoés' guidance, Gibusil steadied his pace and glided down before the walls of Castle Mithlon. Haeryn heard the shouts of the sentries as they saw the griffin's approach. His heart raced as he saw crossbows being readied upon the ramparts. Gibusil eased to the ground, his huge spread of wings casting a looming shadow.

When the griffin had landed, Eyoés slid from the saddle. Haeryn followed. They raised their hands in a gesture of peace, stepping toward the guards. "I am Eyoés Kingson, Baron of Taekohar and member of the Five Heroes. This is my son, Haeryn the Irongaze. We must speak with Neifon Vassaros," Eyoés declared.

Eyoés and Haeryn ascended the wide steps to Mithlon's doors, escorted by a company of ostentatious sentries. Rain pattered on the sleek armor of the soldiers, its rhythm adding to the cadence of their march. Haeryn noted the grand horsehair plumes draping down the back rim of their helmets. Their kite shields were painted with the likenesses of flowers and budding branches, reminding Haeryn of his own battered shield.

Not much combat to be had in Mithlon, apparently.

A sharp snarl startled Eyoés, and he spun with heart racing. Gibusil crouched defensively, watching with his single eye as the stable servants surrounded him. One of the attendants approached the griffin from its blind side. Gibusil spun toward the man, his crown of feathers flaring as he shrieked a final warning. With a cry, the servant fell upon his back, shielding himself with his hands as his face blanched.

Eyoés burst through the escort of soldiers and dashed to where the man had fallen. He stepped in front of Gibusil with hands outstretched. Though he strove to keep his expression placid, the tightness in his eyes betrayed his unease. "Heel, Gibusil," he coaxed, his voice calm as he strove to pacify his agitated griffin. Ever since his wounding in Ellokon, Gibusil had fought to regain his confidence. Fear had taken its toll on him.

With a final snarl toward the stablehands, Gibusil lowered his head with a rumbling chirp of obedience. Stroking the griffin's beak, Eyoés closed his eyes with a sigh of relief. Looking into Gibusil's eye, he gestured toward the servants gathering around their fallen friend. "No harm will come to you—I promise," he said, promising a return of the loyalty the griffin had shown him over the years. Tears pricked his eyes at the sight of his steadfast companion's distress.

Gibusil, satisfied by his master's confidence, allowed the servants to lead him to the nearby stables. As his companion disappeared behind the large doors, Eyoés turned back to the escort and hurried up the steps. Seeing Haeryn's pity for the creature, Eyoés wrapped an arm around his shoulder. "Gibusil will regain his fearlessness in time, son," he said. "Perhaps one day you will have a griffin of your own."

The doors of Mithlon's keep commanded their respect, instilling a humility meant to prepare them for homage. Stylized branches and leaves trimmed the deep blue doors, and gold filament was inset upon them. The ancient land of heroes appeared to have aged little since the War of Adrógar. Eyoés felt the hair stand on his neck.

I envisioned my father Élorn here, fighting alongside the likes of Arógym and the other warriors of renown.

For a brief moment, Eyoés felt he'd entered one of the tales of his childhood—like some messenger approaching the gates of Mithlon to deliver great news of triumph. Glancing to Haeryn beside him, he smiled at his son's admiration.

The leader of their escort seized a silver knocker and beat upon it. Immediately, the massive doors swung inward, seeming to glide on their hinges. The guards escorted Eyoés and Haeryn inside as the doors shut firmly behind them to guard their rear.

The total stillness of the famed castle froze it in time. Their footsteps echoed throughout the expanse of halls, with nothing to answer. Only the faint flickering of the flames within candled sconces acknowledged their entry. As Eyoés discerned the traceries of bronze inlaid within the smooth marble floor, he lightened his steps to avoid scuffing his boot across them.

A wide swath of marble and granite stairs spilled into the entryway. On either side, railings carved in the likeness of interweaving branches hemmed them in. Guarding the stairs with solemn looks, two statues stared at Haeryn and Eyoés. One, clothed in lavish robes, held a book and scepter in one hand. The other boasted sleek plate armor, grasping a shield emblazoned with an ancient crest. Eyoés laid his hand upon the railing, appreciating the carved marble's sleek and rolling shape. As they crested the top of the stairs, marble hallways lined with columns spread in innumerable directions. They turned right into a tall, narrow hallway and hurried their pace. Sconces forged in the shape of flowers emitted a strong, yet exquisite aroma of amber, vanilla, cinnamon, and cedar.

Despite the grand impression, Eyoés found the renowned halls disappointing—the lavish filigree and extravagant architecture, though stunning to the eye, struck him as superficial.

Mithlon's beauty pales in comparison to the grandeur and awe of Gald-Behn.

The escort came to a halt, withdrawing behind them into a semi-circle formation. Eyoés raised an eyebrow as the soldiers stood at attention. He turned to where Haeryn scrutinized the hallway. As he followed his son's gaze, a grin spread across Eyoés' face.

A slim man strode toward them at a confident pace. His stately poise emanated an air of authority and sharp intellect. Richly embroidered with white and yellow designs, a dark grey outer coat squared his shoulders and strengthened his confident appearance. The crisp collar of his shirt was embellished with geometrical stitchery, while a purple robe trimmed with ermine fur trailed behind him. Upon the chest of his outer coat was an emblem of a splayed bundle of goldenrod and thistle, with a white quill pen in the center.

Eyoés threw his arms wide and embraced his friend. "Andíamas Radem, Neifon! It's been too long!" he exclaimed with a laugh.

With an easygoing smile, Neifon released Eyoés and bowed his head. "For Sword and Crown, my friend," he said. Though friendship shone in his eyes and was evident in his words, his formal demeanor belied it.

Neifon paused as his proud eyes peered over Eyoés' shoulder. Haeryn's iron gaze gripped Neifon's with the strength and confidence of a keen personality. The resemblance to his own acuity brought an amused smile to Neifon's face.

Eyoés stepped aside, catching Neifon's glance. "We received the summons and came as quickly as we could," he said, glancing at the soldiers standing at attention.

Neifon nodded. Stepping toward Haeryn, he took a knee in the respectful greeting of the Court. "You must be Haeryn Irongaze," he said. Hesitantly, Haeryn bowed in the fashion of Taekohar. Seeing the boy's brow drawn in confusion, Neifon stood. He laid a hand on Haeryn's shoulder and drew him closer to whisper in his ear. "Welcome to Edeveros, Haeryn Wynrence," he whispered. "I hope you find your new name to your liking."

Haeryn gave a wavering smile. He clasped his hands behind his back. "It has not yet been decided," he answered quietly.

Sensing conflict, Neifon dropped the matter. He released Haeryn and turned to the waiting sentries. "Ancorsti, gos timas. Depart, sons of honor," he declared. As the soldiers clashed their gauntlets against their shields, they marched back down the hall in tight formation.

Neifon started down the hall and motioned for the two to follow. "Let us speak in private," he said. "There are things to discuss that these halls must never hear."

9

Neifon opened the door to his personal chamber and slipped inside. As he held the door, he watched the hall and gestured for his companions to enter. Eyoés and Haeryn hurried into the room, and Neifon briskly shut the door behind them. The clink of the iron latch eased their tense nerves. Eyoés nodded his thanks to his fellow Hero.

The warm and pleasant appearance of the room clashed against the austere white of Castle Mithlon. Shining wood panels ribbed with crafted ridges covered the cold marble walls. An archway of dark chestnut rose above their heads. The smell of fresh-brewed tea drew them into the neatly ordered parlor. A red Amiranooran carpet warmed the floor, and red velvet chairs offered a place of rest. Eyoés and Haeryn wandered into the great room. At the far end of the room, a stone alcove boasted latticed windows. Haeryn felt his nerves ease at the welcoming sound of a crackling fireplace. Despite the elegance of the chamber, the pleasing ambience reminded Eyoés of his humble origins.

With an unconscious smile, Eyoés looked up at the bronze chandelier dangling from the ceiling. "You must be quite at home here," he said, appreciating the warmth of a well-tended home.

Neifon gave a nod of thanks. "I was raised in the warmth of the Eastern Edeveran sun, and I find the dreary weather of the West quite dull. I sought to bring the warmth of my childhood here as a refuge against the cold," he replied, walking to a nearby table. Setting aside three white and blue lattice-painted teacups, he took up a steaming kettle. "Would you care for tea?" he inquired. The two nodded their assent, and Neifon poured each one a cup. He placed a small saucer beneath each cup and lifted them with the utmost care.

Eyoés and Haeryn accepted the teacups with earnest thanks. After blowing gently to cool it, Eyoés took a tentative sip. The tea was fine, floral in flavor, with accents of vanilla and imported citrus from Amiranoor. Eyoés relaxed into the chair as the tension of travel fell away.

Reclining in a velvet chair, Neifon folded his hands and sighed. "Your arrival in Mithlon is most welcomed —more than you realize," he confessed. The relief implied by his idle comment brought an impression of uncertainty into the room. He furrowed his brow, engaged in afflicted thought.

As he sipped his tea, Eyoés observed his friend over the rim of his cup. Neifon's stare unnerved him. He considered the utter stillness of his fellow Hero and the weight carried in his few words. He sat upright in his chair, anxious to understand. "Something is wrong," he said. Haeryn shifted in his chair, his grip tightening on the armrests.

Neifon sagged into his chair and squinted into the light of the nearby windows to gather his thoughts.

"Baron Galeras Estworth has remade Edeveros into the very image of vanity. His Baronship has oppressed the commonfolk with taxes. The people now resent both their leaders and each other. Under his corrupting influence, the officials of the Court have become vain and extravagant beyond all reason! Though wrought in secret, our concerted efforts to hinder his erratic uses of power have had little effect. Galeras exploits the people to finance his lavish living, contrary to the benevolent tradition of his ancestors!" he exclaimed in an angry whisper. Neifon closed his eyes and took a deep breath to regain his decorum. The revelation exhausted him.

Haeryn flinched as he set aside his tea, nearly spilling on the soft carpet. He concealed the surprise in his demeanor. "House Estworth is divided?" he asked.

Eyoés shared a knowing glance with Haeryn.

So, the fox upon the Estworth flag really is an indicator of conflict. Perhaps a badge of disgrace?

Neifon said nothing. He stood from his chair, taking an idle sip of his tea and leaning against the mantle of the fireplace. "Haeryn was not summoned simply for the people's comfort. He could be the final push we need to turn the public against Galeras," he said, glancing back to Eyoés with foreboding. "Eyoés, Gwair spoke to me of Rehillon's near collapse. I can assure you, the fall of Edeveros is on the horizon. Should this territory fall, it will not be long till the rest of Alithell follows its example."

Standing from his chair, Haeryn's face darkened, and he opened his mouth to speak. Eyoés shook his head and silenced him with a warning glance.

It is the natural state of man to seek out his own pleasure and self-interest. And it only multiplies when the baron is leading the charge. Excess and selfishness has lured them into weakness—just as in Taekohar.

Eyoés paused, regarding his fellow Hero steadily. Despite the revelation of Edeveros' frailty, he could sense the burden of something yet unspoken still weighing him down. "That is not all you have to reveal," he said.

Neifon's eyes darted toward the door and he pulled Eyoés closer. "A new threat is abroad. One that may indeed plunge Edeveros into a reign of terror," he whispered. "One of my spies overheard Galeras conspiring with an unsavory mercenary—a villain simply known as Lòfroy."

Eyoés frowned. "A single mercenary should not worry you," he said. "He has ulterior motives?"

Neifon's brow furrowed. He leaned against the arm of his chair, swirling the remainder of the tea in his cup. "My informant gathered that this Lòfroy is on the hunt for a certain man living on the outskirts of Anfon in the south. A Huntsman by the name of Fedrik," he said.

He clasped his hands behind his back as he strode to the windows and gazed out over the castle grounds through a mist of fine rain. "Had this Lòfroy been alone, I would have judged him a lesser threat. Perhaps even a trifling distraction. But he most assuredly is not

61

alone. There are men with him—and my spies have brought word of a significant advantage at his disposal," he continued. Eyoés stood, and Neifon turned, his face grave. "A griffin," he said.

Stunned, he transfixed Neifon with his stare, frozen to his seat. "Are you certain?" he asked, his concern palpable. A mercenary backed by a band of rogues was fearsome enough—but a griffin was a weapon few managed to attain.

Neifon nodded his assent with absolute certainty. "Our forces are ill-prepared for such unexpected threats. And as you know, ballistas and trebuchets do not easily pluck a griffin from the sky," he said. His eyes pinned Eyoés where he stood. "We need you," he said. "You and Gibusil are worth your mettle in battle. Perhaps even more than I have heard. Galeras will undoubtedly use the griffin for his own wicked ends— that is, if Lòfroy's presence goes unchallenged."

Eyoés rose to his feet, eyes roving about as the request unnerved him further. Tears welled in his eyes at the remembrance of Gibusil's dire impediment. He shook his head. "Gibusil is not ready to hold his own against another of his kind. His blind spot makes him vulnerable," he declared, staring at the wall. "It is only a matter of time till he is outmatched." His voice trailed away, and he bit his lip.

Neifon placed a hand on Eyoés' shoulder. "You know Gwyndel came to Edeveros for the Forester Assembly, do you not?" he asked, watching as Eyoés nodded in the affirmative. "I spoke to her when she arrived. Lord Belos Stonneter of Anfon invited her to a private hunt at his estate. It was only after she left that I learned of Lòfroy."

Eyoés' head shot up at the mention of the town. Gripping Neifon by the shoulders, he shook him. "Where the mercenary is headed? She could have walked into danger, Neifon! You did not go after her?" he said, his voice rising.

Neifon shook his head and broke away. "I wished I could have!" he replied with regret. "Crucial evidence against Galeras was uncovered before I could leave. The King placed me in Edeveros to safeguard his subjects—and I cannot lay down my duties lightly in the midst of Edeveros' turmoil." He extended an imploring hand at Eyoés, his reserved manner cracking to reveal his true concern. "But now that you are here, you can! Even if Gibusil is ill prepared, *someone* must come to Gwyndel's aid before she finds herself in the crossfire!"

Closing his eyes, Eyoés strained to calm himself. With a sigh, he set an apologetic hand on Neifon's shoulder. "As members of the Five Heroes, we both yearn to remedy the state of affairs we find ourselves in. Yet, we know that we alone cannot alter our circumstances—we can only change what lies in our control. You were given two opportunities—to either save Gwyndel or to save Edeveros with this new evidence you've uncovered. You needn't choose between the two. I will pursue Gwyndel," he said.

Haeryn rose up from his seat and strode forward, breaking the men apart. "What are we waiting for?" he asked. The youth's eyes looked imploringly at Eyoés and Neifon.

"I depart in the morning," Eyoés declared. Glancing at Haeryn, he pulled Neifon aside. Haeryn remained standing, watching them in desperation. Eyoés pointed firmly to a nearby chair, and Haeryn obeyed.

Eyoés leaned close to Neifon. "I entrust Haeryn to you in my absence," he whispered. "The boy has a strong sense of justice, Neifon. His upbringing in the harsh land of Norgalok conditioned him to achieve it by whatever means necessary."

Neifon met his friend's eyes, and the earnest light in them set Eyoés at ease. "I will not let him act rashly. You have my word that I will keep him safe," Neifon replied.

Eyoés patted his fellow Hero on the shoulder. Turning to Haeryn, he opened his arms wide. The youth, though fifteen years of age, embraced his father, his jaw set as he wrestled with his own helplessness.

Eyoés squeezed his eyes shut, and patted his son's back in reassurance. "I *will* return," he promised.

10

4th of Rotanos, 2209 SE

Haeryn strode beside Neifon ensnared. Ensnared in the thoughts clutching his heart and dragging him deeper into the quagmire of his emotions. Through the haze of his melancholy, the ornate tapestries and marble halls of Castle Mithlon became vague, their grandeur lost on him. Though servants hurried about in preparation for the night's banquet, he paid them no heed. Only the memory of his father's urgent departure remained, persisting despite his attempts at distraction. He stared ahead, his outward appearance putting on the image of fortitude despite his discouragement at his father's absence. He had been eager to share the momentous occasion with Eyoés.

His thoughts turned to Gwyndel, and he clenched his jaw. Straining against the worry welling up, he forced himself to focus on the slight cracks and imperfections in the marble walls. As he lay his sadness aside, Haeryn realized the exhaustion his inner turmoil had caused him. His eyes flickered as he reluctantly emerged from the seclusion of his reflection.

Neifon sensed the tension in Haeryn. As he wrapped an arm around the youth's shoulder, his reserved features softened with the pain of empathy. "I feel anxious for Eyoés and Gwyndel as well, but the Guide will guard your father's path," he said.

Haeryn's stride faltered. With a hesitating nod, he studied the floor and thumbed the edge of his tunic, feeling the ridges of Taekoharan embroidery under his finger.

The Guide is only a wise sage. A wise man cannot be everywhere at once.

Still, hoping in the Guide's protection for his father was preferable to wasting away under his own troubled thoughts. Haeryn looked at Neifon with a conflicted half-smile. The quiet, unassuming, and well-controlled personality of the Hero comforted him.

As the hallway came to its end, Neifon stopped and pulled Haeryn aside. "This banquet is for your arrival, Haeryn Wynrence. Because you are the descendant of the founders of Edeveros, you hold a prestige many in this court envy," he whispered. "Lord Raulin Estworth and his wife Lady Roseen will introduce you." An amused smile tugged at the corner of his mouth as he glimpsed the alarm in the boy's expression. "A messenger pigeon from Asdale brought word of your coming. Fear not. I will not abandon you to the mercy of the celebration. Let us both find some enjoyment," he said. Nodding his understanding, Haeryn swallowed.

They rounded the corner. An oak door barred the way, and the guards watching over it fixed their helmeted gazes upon them. Their gauntleted hands clutched halberds, and extravagant shields nearly hid them from view. Recognizing Neifon, they lifted their halberds in salute and clashed their gauntlets on their shields. One of them seized the ornate doorknobs and heaved the doors open with a quiet word of welcome. With a nod of courtesy, Haeryn passed by Neifon and entered with a boldness that strove to make up for his growing uneasiness.

The banquet hall's expanse yawned about them with a grandeur that complemented the pomp of its patrons. The din of idle conversation resounded off the high ceiling and vast walls, and the size of the crowd seemed to double by sound alone. Servants kept to the outskirts, going about their duties with the quiet humility of their position. Only the sound of clinking utensils and plates hinted at their presence. Pillars at the corners of the banquet hall supported the cathedral roof. Deep green designs were painted upon the white walls to enliven them with the same beauty that pervaded the rest of the castle. A massive fireplace was inset into one of the walls, emitting a steady wave of heat into the room.

Haeryn stared at the lavish outfits of the guests. The men boasted richly stitched outer coats, some trimmed with a strip of fur around the cuffs. The women's long dresses draped to the floor. Haeryn blinked as his eyes struggled to take in the complexity of the intricate embroidery and stitching. Elaborate, beaded headdresses were strapped precariously to the women's heads, shaped like inverted crescents or wide fans. Suppressing a smile at their exaggerated hats, Haeryn cleared his throat.

The doors to the banquet hall closed, and the guests turned in greeting. At the sight of Haeryn, they hesitated. The youth before them appeared too young for the heroic scion they had envisioned. Under their intense scrutiny, Haeryn stiffened, his iron gaze intensifying as he fought to keep from blushing. With a glance of pity, Neifon gestured toward the boy. "Behold, Haeryn Irongaze—the last heir of House Wynrence!" he proclaimed. The men genuflected in respect, and the women curtsied with demure smiles. At Neifon's signal, they rose, and a deafening applause reverberated through the banquet hall. Ears turning red, Haeryn smoothed the front of his tunic and swallowed to ease his dry throat. He had fallen into the trap his birthright had set for him, and he squirmed in its grip. The very thought of the Wynrence name seemed foreign to him—as if he didn't belong among its prodigious ancestry.

Neifon leaned close to Haeryn's ear. "Because of Edeveros' rich history of heroism, such martial gestures of respect and honor have become tradition. Kneeling is required in the presence of nobility," he explained.

Haeryn hesitated, the applause ringing in his ears.

They revere me, a former waif, as a noble?

Glimpsing insecurity in Haeryn's eye, Neifon sought to reassure him. "Be thankful, Haeryn, that you do not bear the burden of nobility as I do. My status as the Chief of Court is dearly paid for by unceasing labors," he whispered.

The din ceased at the tinkling of a servant's bell, and all turned to the tables prepared for them. With words of delight and exaggerated propriety, the guests dispersed to their tables of choice.

Haeryn's heart raced as he searched for some indication of the appropriate place to sit. Neifon motioned for him to follow. The youth walked in his shadow, glancing about awkwardly. He undid the topmost button of his shirt in an attempt to cool himself down.

Such formality is a waste of time. And an embarrassment.

Neifon headed toward a prominent table placed before the large fireplace and elevated on a dais. At their approach, two figures stood in respect. One was a woman, clad in a maroon velvet dress trimmed with tawny fur. A deep blue caul covered her ears, topped with a plain circlet. A light veil descended down the back of her head to her shoulders. Her willowy body gave her the appearance of total weakness, yet her rich brown eyes shone with determination. Her lips were pressed in a thin smile.

Beside her, a tall, broad-shouldered man overshadowed her small figure. The crest of the Estworths was sewn on his blue linen tunic, accenting his hardened frame. His stance exuded decisiveness. Haeryn's eyes widened as he saw the man's right arm ended at the elbow in a shrouded stump. But as he took in the man's friendly face, his shock faded. Neifon ascended the dais and motioned for him to follow.

Ushering Haeryn forward, Neifon gestured toward the two nobles. "Lord Raulin of Gahidros, Grandmaster of the Knights of the Lance," he said with ease. "And my sister, Lady Roseen." The rapport in his voice revealed his admiration.

Hands clasped, Roseen cooly studied Haeryn. Behind the poised aura she exuded, he detected a certain shrewdness that spoke of retribution. Roseen inclined her head. "Well met," she said.

Raulin smiled warmly at Haeryn. Though his face was hardened with the lines of struggle, it held a subtle gentleness and honor at odds with the image of a famed warrior. Haeryn's face flushed as he regarded the man with a new respect. The thought of his meeting the Grandmaster of the legendary Knights of the Lance humbled him.

Raulin clasped Haeryn's forearm in a warrior's welcome. "I heard you are a squire of Taekohar," he remarked.

Haeryn beamed with pride. "Yes sir," he replied, his chin held high. With a good-natured laugh, Raulin clapped the boy on the shoulder.

The servants upon the dais seated them. From his elevated place of honor, Haeryn found himself provided with a sweeping view of the guests. His eyes wandered across the long table in front of him, its grand length covered in a vast green silken tablecloth. He fingered the carved flower patterns upon the utensils before him. A ring of painted yellow designs covered the edges of his pearly white plate. Despite the surrounding beauty, Haeryn felt a fiery displeasure settle in his chest. Being thrown into the midst of outrageous vanity and formality after overcoming his melancholy gnawed at his nerves.

How can anyone find solace here?

After dismissing the servants with a kind word and a smile, Neifon glanced at Haeryn, his spirits dampened by the boy's hardened, restless manner. Laying a hand on the back of Haeryn's chair, Neifon leaned over to him, "Sometimes one can find himself isolated in the midst of a bustling crowd. Don't let the exuberance of the people here force you to wear a facade. I too understand the solace of solitude—"

A loud clang silenced the guests, and all eyes riveted to the open doors.

11

Several soldiers marched into the chamber, their halberds held high in procession, and their sleek, spotless plate armor shimmering in the light of Gesadith lanterns. They paid no heed to the murmurs of the crowd.

With a shouted command, the warriors ground to a halt, lowering their halberds at once and parting ranks. Haeryn's eyes narrowed as he observed a lone man walking through their midst. His purposeful stride and exaggerated walk gave clear evidence of his arrogance. An outer coat of golden velvet was buttoned up to the neck, and gaudy red embellishments spread across his shoulders and arms like creeping vines. His blue cape billowed behind him, while a servant held the hem off the ground to keep it from being soiled. His wavy black hair seemed a mane about his head, combed back to frame his face. Gleaming, wide-set eyes accented his striking appearance.

The man stepped out from the ranks of his escort, lifting his chin and throwing his arms wide with a grin. Applause roared through the crowd as they knelt in welcome. Haeryn's lip curled, and he recoiled at the blatant show of vanity.

Braggart. A fop deserves reproof.

Turning to Neifon, he hesitated. The Chief of Court did not stand and applaud like his fellows— instead, Neifon endured the spectacle from his seat with a plastered smile. Recalling his casual acceptance of custom and formality, his refusal to celebrate this man's arrival startled Haeryn.

He looked back to where the man stood, basking in his applause. As the man turned in his direction, Haeryn scrutinized him. Sewn onto the front of the man's overcoat was the profile of a fox, stylized and surrounded by a ring of holly.

Neifon shook his head. "Meet Galeras Estworth, Baron of Edeveros," he said, his voice barely audible to Haeryn. "He is known as the Fox throughout the territory."

Haeryn's brow furrowed. "For his cunning?" he inquired. Despite his question, he struggled to believe that such an extravagant, attention-seeking figure could bear anything similar to artfulness.

A quiet laugh escaped Neifon's watch, which he promptly stifled. "No—for his pompousness. A man once jested that the flowing beauty of the fox's tail paled in comparison to the baron's lavish clothes," he answered. "What cunning Galeras does have comes from the books he reads. Including the works of Stannard of Auxwood."

Haeryn smiled to himself. "I've heard he instructed tyrants. Or sabotaged them, depending on your perspective. You've read his writings?" he asked.

Neifon met his gaze with a smirk. "Quite," he replied.

Gesturing for the guests to return to their seats, Galeras Estworth headed for the dais table. "Let the food be served! The Wynrences have returned!" he declared, his voice nearly childish in its flippancy. A wave of hollow applause rippled through the crowd as pride in Edeveros' roots stirred their own self-esteem. As the baron ascended the steps, Haeryn looked away to avoid attracting attention. He bit his tongue as Galeras seated himself beside Neifon.

The baron's demand for food was not taken lightly. Servants moved among the tables, distributing platters of delicacies to the guests within moments. Haeryn suppressed a sneeze at the pungent spices that filled the air. Large trays of food were placed before those on the elevated dais. The fragrance of the pungent soup nearly turned Haeryn's stomach. To his relief, the spiced meats arranged before them proved appealing to his tastes. Bowls of pears were served in puddles of syrup, and as soon as the guests had devoured their portions, the servants scampered away to fetch more. Steam rose in wisps above cups of sweetened tea, and fine wine flowed into tall, slender goblets. Musicians lingered in the banquet hall, filling the air with music.

Haeryn wiped his face with the elegant linen napkin and laid it in a disheveled wad beside his plate. Sudden bursts of laughter drew his attention. Away from the tables, several guests danced to the music to the merriment of their companions. Haeryn listened to the musicians, recognizing the lute, lyre, and drum— but he cocked his head as his eyes alighted on a strange sight. Elevated on a wooden stand was a wide, trapezoidal instrument. The man behind it held a hammer in each hand loosely between his fingers, striking the doubled strings with them. Sharp, echoing notes rang out. Though he had never seen one in person, Haeryn recognized the hammered dulcimer from one of the drawings in his books.

Haeryn watched Galeras, and his nose wrinkled in revulsion. The baron indulged himself with food, speaking in idle conversation with the women who thronged about him with flattering words. All formality had given way to rash amusement. Haeryn clenched his fists and turned away. He flushed indignantly, remembering Neifon's words to Eyoés.

Galeras exploits the people to finance his lavish living, contrary to the benevolent tradition of his ancestors!

Haeryn's eyes drifted over the platters of food that crowded the tables. Such bounty was not gained idly.

Galeras rose from his seat and raised his goblet of wine. He stumbled, and Haeryn noticed the redness in the man's face. Livid, the youth looked to Neifon, seeing a shared disgrace at the baron's drunkenness. Steadying himself with his other hand, Galeras raised his goblet again, spilling some on the table. "Let us raise a toast, my friends, to the grandeur of Edeveros and its wonderful bounty!" he proclaimed, sweeping an arm across the room. Haeryn's ire no longer could remain silent.

"You misspoke, Galeras. You meant *tribute*, not bounty. Or have I misunderstood?" he said curtly. The musicians brought their song to sudden halt. The silent guests gaped in disbelief. Feeling their horrified stares fixed upon him, Haeryn clasped his hands and awaited the baron's pitiful defense.

The smile faded from Galeras' face, and he spun to face Haeryn. He slammed his goblet to the table, spilling wine on the tablecloth and the floor. Haeryn met the baron's eyes with righteous confidence. Galeras started, swallowing uneasily. His bloodshot eyes darted about rather than meet the youth's potent stare. Neifon froze in his seat and shot a warning glance at Haeryn. The youth caught the glint of fear in the Chief of Court's eye. Whispers rose from the crowd, and Haeryn glimpsed two men rise from their seats and start for the dais.

Roseen deliberately rose, clasping her hands. "I beg you pardon the boy. He is a guest at Mithlon, and does not know the proper airs of the court," she said in a measured tone. Though her words were cordial, the challenge in her stare would not be questioned.

Nodding in agreement, Raulin stood. "My beloved Roseen is right, brother. He's only a boy," he declared. Unlike his wife, the man glanced back at Haeryn in apology. Though he sought to excuse the youth's actions, Raulin's look of admiration made it clear he did not see Haeryn as a mere boy.

Galeras' face contorted in scorn, and he threw his goblet to the ground. "You defend this little fool?" he slurred, glaring at Haeryn.

Neifon had heard enough. Raising a hand in peace, he met the alarmed looks of the guests. "My friends! As Chief of Court, I am obliged to intervene when it is in the Court's best interests to do so. Such private disagreements will not be accepted among the company of friends," he declared. "Rash action shall prove the ruin of Edeveros if we do not keep our decorum." His brow furrowed as he shot scolding glances at both Haeryn and Galeras, as if reproving troublesome children.

Swaying unsteadily, Galeras snorted in disgust, his face reddening. "Whatever you say, *Hero*," he snapped, snatching Neifon's goblet and overfilling it. "For the Wynrences!" He lifted the goblet high in a toast. At his sudden change of mood, the guests, eager to forget the embarrassment of insult, quickly accepted the baron's suggestion. Music rose again with renewed fervor, and conversation resumed.

Turning back to Neifon, Galeras spat at his boot and briskly sat. The women around him flocked about to soothe his nerves with words of vain praise. Neifon considered his soiled boot in silence and returned to his seat. "You should be thankful, Haeryn. Not all who trod upon Galeras Estworth's pride avoid the executioner's blade by a favorable word," he said. "The Wynrence name saved you—for now."

12

Haeryn strode into the parlor of Neifon's quarters and threw himself into one of the chairs, the strain falling from him like a weary traveler's burden. A gentle night rain pattered on the windows. Closing his eyes, Haeryn let his head fall back against the top of the chair. Even after spending the remainder of the banquet in nervous apprehension, his convictions remained steadfast.

I could not remain silent. Galeras disregarded the hard labor of the commonfolk in bringing such goods to his table. He acted disgracefully!

Neifon entered, his expression strained from the exacting duty of keeping the peace. But as he glimpsed Haeryn's exhaustion, his features softened, and a pained expression passed over him like a shadow. Though he disapproved of the youth's brashness, Neifon shared his nearly intolerable frustration at the baron's arrogant and overbearing manner.

Neifon turned as the door to the room was bolted fast behind him. Standing in the entryway in polite silence were Roseen and Raulin. Neifon shook his head to clear his mind and motioned for them to enter the room.

From his seat, Haeryn opened his eyes and sat up. At the sight of the two guests, he quickly stood. Words of thanks welled up as the recollection of the incident reminded him how close he had come to peril—perhaps even execution.

Roseen sat in one of the chairs and adjusted her caul. Raulin strode to the seat beside her, glancing at Haeryn with a friendly smile. Haeryn gestured to his own chair with a bow of gratitude. Raulin paused, glanced at the chair, and inclined his head in thanks as he sat. The youth smiled in return, his heart warmed by the man's affability. Haeryn watched with curiosity as Raulin scooted the chair closer to the fireplace with ease, despite his missing limb.

Neifon knelt before the fire and stoked the coals. As he added fresh kindling, his eyes turned to Haeryn with a calm, controlled manner. "I believe you have come to a fuller understanding of your error, Haeryn, so I will not speak of it again," he said.

The fireplace crackled to life. Wiping ashes from his hands on a nearby towel, Neifon took a seat in a spare wooden chair in the corner of the room. "Haeryn, I believe it is time that you understood the matters at hand," he sighed with an expectant glance at Raulin. "Start from the beginning, and leave nothing out." Raulin pressed his lips together, his expression drawn and weary with the story demanded of him. Roseen's brow wrinkled in misery.

The two who had rescued Haeryn from Galeras with their proud and powerful presence now cowered at Neifon's seemingly harmless request. He pitied them in their discomfort.

Raulin stared into the fireplace. "It began in childhood. Our father, Renoutos Estworth, challenged all his sons to strive for honor and distinction. The same way our ancestors did. As the eldest, I endeavored to the best of my ability to grow in martial skills, as did my brother Rodmer. Galeras, the youngest in the family, had little aptitude for combat, or any honorable endeavor, save for oratory," he began. "Our father tried his best to encourage Galeras in his pursuits —yet each time he attempted this, Father struggled for the right words. Each encouragement, once spoken aloud, sounded more akin to rebuke than exhortation. Rodmer and I watched our father's faulty attempts at encouragement crush Galeras. It was not long afterward that Rodmer joined the Phantom League. His eagerness for power led to impatience when our father would not grant it, and he abandoned his family to become a murderer."

Tears welled up in Raulin's eyes, and he stood, moving toward the fireplace and leaning against the mantle. "In the years that followed, Father and Mother grew old, stricken by sorrow. Galeras and I had become noblemen in our own right, set to inherit what lands were bequeathed to us. Since I was the firstborn, I was to inherit the Baronship once my father had passed. As Grandmaster of the Knights of the Lance, I desired to prove my prowess to the public in a contest of arms. The Fest of Heroes was my chance. So I entered the annual joust," he said, looking down at the stump of his right arm. "My opponent's lance missed its target and impaled my arm. The surgeon was forced to amputate. There is an old law that demands the baron be able-bodied if he is to inherit his title. I was rendered inept—an illegitimate heir in the eyes of the law! Upon the death of our parents, Galeras took the throne of Edeveros in my stead, as the law had prescribed. I was lowered to the rank of Lord."

Roseen closed her eyes and clamped her jaw shut. Her hands wrung a wad of her dress. With a trembling breath, she looked up into her husband's eyes. "The truth became known to us not long afterward. Galeras had orchestrated the 'accident' in hopes of stealing Raulin's birthright!" she said through her teeth.

Then, as if doused, her anger abruptly ceased. Her chin quivered as she wiped away tears. "In my horror, I unleashed my frightened outrage upon all who seemed suspect, enemies of the Estworths and the Vassaros' as well as those who found themselves in the path of my blind despair. I cared little about who I had arrested and imprisoned—only for my vengeance. As word spread of my reckless retaliation, the people of Edeveros began to feel anxious because of me," she revealed. "Only when the Guide visited me did I realize my error. It took me many years to heal the wounds I had caused, and those whom I had imprisoned were set free." Wounded by the memory, Roseen fell silent, staring out the window into the darkness of night. "Our son Ancelet has a tyrant for an uncle. We'd hoped to raise him in a harmonious family."

Pinching his lips in a tight frown, Neifon wandered away from the fireplace and shook his head. His eyes were grave. "We have been trying with all our might to hinder Galeras and bring an end to his Baronship legally. The Lords of Edeveros dislike him. Even the haughty Lord Stonneter seeks a way to be rid of him," he said. "But the people are afraid of Galeras. He is unpredictable, and his passionate emotions quickly spiral out of control. The law also proves an obstacle. In the past, it has saved worthy Barons from false accusations. But it was because of the law that Raulin found himself stripped of his rightful title as Baron. In this dire time, we must find a way to utilize the law to our advantage in order to oust Galeras from his throne."

Brow wrinkled in thought, Haeryn listened and considered the situation at hand.

Old wounds remain tender in the face of hardship.

The image of his Kinsfolk pendant and his coat of arms flashed before him.

Edeveros deserves justice. I must bring it about.

Haeryn's expression hardened, and he leaned forward in his chair. His firm, formidable gaze met the eyes of all those present. "Laws that hinder the pursuit of justice have no purpose. They must be ignored. Oust Galeras from his throne, and give no thought to petty formalities!" he insisted. At the declaration, his face flushed, and he eagerly searched for approval. He was sorely disappointed.

Neifon shook his head in objection. "If the people of Edeveros hear we have broken the laws of old to remove Galeras, the door will be opened for more blatant transgressions. It would be the ruin of Edeveros

—the very thing we fear now," he argued. He stood, strode to the table, and poured himself a cup of tea. "Plans for a Baronic Trial have been arranged in secret, and a witness' testimony will speak volumes. The Lords have pledged their cooperation, and we have all gathered here to attend the Council. We are prepared to construct a document detailing the accusations against Galeras. This document will be given to the Court Magistrate. Should he approve or reject it is beyond our control. The Treasurer must also go over all financial records of those involved to assure that no bribes were taken or given," he explained, holding his teacup and saucer in his hand. "Tea?"

Roseen nodded, striving to regain her poise. "I have met with the Lords in our attempts to hinder Galeras' Baronship. We call ourselves the Knights of the Throne, for it is the Baronic throne of Edeveros that holds the key to the stability of our people," she said, accepting her cup of tea with a smile of gratitude. "But the Baronic Trial process has been corrupted before, and it can be corrupted again."

Haeryn frowned. "Can we find a witness?" he remarked.

A triumphant smile tugged at the corner of Roseen's mouth. "There is one woman who could prove the key to Galeras' downfall—and she's here in Mithlon, waiting for us," she said.

13

4th of Rotanos, 2209 SE

Eyoés huddled upon Gibusil's saddle, fighting off the lingering chill of his rain soaked garments. In the distance, the roll of thunder echoed through the expanse of moorlands below. Each flap of Gibusil's wings propelled him further into the veiled expanse of grey.

Gritting his teeth against the cold, Eyoés guided the griffin to a lower altitude as he struggled to survey the landscape. Before his departure, Neifon had spoken of a cabin lying several miles to the east of Anfon. A past conversation with Lord Belos Stonneter had revealed this as the location of his Huntsman's cottage.

While he searched, Eyoés felt his mind drift to his adopted son.

Is Haeryn endangered by the strife of Mithlon?

Shaking his head, he clenched his jaw and strove to keep a calm head despite the anxious tension in his chest. Comforting words from the Proverbs rose to his memory. The wise sayings soothed his mind, and he returned to his search.

Gibusil pierced through the thick mist and fog like a knife. Eyoés glimpsed the dark green of sparse conifers mixed among the few groping branches of barren deciduous trees.

A small farm sat exposed upon the gentle slope of the moors. At the sight of the cabin, Eyoés patted Gibusil on the neck. "We made it," he said with a weary smile. The griffin rumbled at his approval.

Beside the cabin, a stable and shed huddled together in the rain. A miniature overhang sheltered a stack of firewood from the elements. Surrounded by a fence, a vegetable garden was nourished by the rainfall.

The air whispered under Gibusil's feathers as he glided down to the opening before the cabin, claws digging into the soft earth. Unbuckling himself from the saddle, Eyoés dismounted. He wiped his wet face with his sleeve and approached the cabin. Eyoés stopped as he heard the griffin's footsteps following him. He turned and gestured toward the surrounding fog. Gibusil hesitated, ears perked as he glanced from Eyoés to the grey, endless mist. Like a wraith, the griffin soared into the fog and vanished from sight. Eyoés pressed his lips together. He knew the sight of a griffin would be threatening to anyone, and that it would be best if Gibusil stay hidden in the forest.

Turning back to the cabin, Eyoés approached the door and knocked. His hand fell to the sword hidden beneath his cloak. There was no certainty he had found the right place. His heart raced as the scraping of chairs sounded from within. Eyoés blinked the rain from his eyes as the door opened.

He was greeted by the familiar face of his sister. At the sight of her brother, the tension in Gwyndel's expression fell away in disbelief. The Sword Imperishable vanished in a wisp of blue. She rushed

85

forward and embraced her brother. "Eyoés!" she exclaimed. "What are you doing here?"

Eyoés released his sword and pulled her close. His heart warmed at the sight of her. "Haeryn and I came to Edeveros on business, and Neifon told me you were here," he replied. He glimpsed movement from inside the cabin. A prodding within warned him to reveal no more.

She was expecting danger. If she fears immediate peril, caution is of the essence.

Releasing her brother, Gwyndel turned back to the cabin's welcoming light. "Come in! There is much to tell you," she said. Eyoés followed Gwyndel into the comfort of the cabin. Should danger beset them, the griffin would prove a capable watchman. Eyoés shut the door fast behind him.

The cabin's interior was simple, save for the quilted blankets hanging upon the walls. Within an alcove inset into the leftmost wall, two beds and a cot were divided for privacy by a thick wool curtain. The beds were neatly made, and several loose household items lay upon them. A crackling fireplace warmed the space with comforting heat. Before it stood a rather small table, surrounded by several chairs.

Wiping his boots upon the doormat, Eyoés accepted the towel offered him by Gwyndel and dried his plastered hair. He removed his boots at the threshold. Stooping before the fireplace, a woman eyed him timidly, her round and plain face hearkening to the simple life she lived. Smoothing out her apron, she cleared her throat and gave a shy smile. Gwyndel moved to the woman's side. "This is Eyoés, my brother," she said, turning to him. "Kerensa is an excellent cook, given the rough and humble provisions at hand."

At her compliment, Kerensa blushed and turned back to the pot bubbling over the fire. "I do what I can," she said, with a sheepish grin. Eyoés smiled at the woman's humility. The creaking of a chair caught his attention and he turned toward the sound.

A man rose, his long dark hair hung down to his shoulders in wavy locks. Mottled shocks of grey and hollowed cheeks aged him beyond his years. A coarse beard, though roughly trimmed, lined his hardened jaw. It was his eyes that struck Eyoés—the weariness and hard, piercing longing he read in them. He saw a lifetime of grief and regret bottled within.

The man stepped forward, studying him. "You must be Eyoés," he said, his deep voice slightly hoarse. "Fedrik." He extended his hand, and though his features remained stoic and weary, his gesture of welcome broke through the veil of melancholy. Eyoés met the man's eyes with his own and took Fedrik's extended hand.

Kerensa wiped her hands and stirred the pot with a long ladle. "Our son Erling is out tending the flocks. He will return before nightfall," she remarked.

Eyoés nodded, his eyes roaming about the cabin. "Thank you for allowing me into your home," he said, wrapping his towel around his shoulders to warm himself. Fedrik gestured toward the fire, and ushered

Eyoés to the comfort of the flames. Kerensa pulled out one of the nearby chairs.

Eyoés muttered his thanks and sat. A shiver ran through his body as the warmth washed over him. "What happened at the Forester Assembly?" he whispered, leaning close to Gwyndel and glancing furtively to where Fedrik helped his wife with their humble dishes.

Gwyndel's shoulders slumped. Rubbing her forehead, she sat beside him with head bowed. As she stirred her memory to recollection, a numbness settled over her and obscured the fire's warmth.

She stared into the fireplace. "I have never seen such a divided Assembly in all my years of service. The arguments, the strife—the Foresters of Edeveros were the source of it. I cannot understand! I heard of the baron's injustices not long after my arrival, but seeing the havoc it has wreaked upon the common folk, and the Foresters themselves..." she wondered, shaking her head. "I met Fedrik not long before the Assembly's abrupt conclusion. He brought a summons from the Lord of Anfon, inviting me to accompany him on a private hunt at his estate. I was eager to leave the discord behind me. However, it became clear that Lord Belos had heard rumors about the Keeper of the Sword Imperishable—and desired a favorable prophecy. I dismissed him. Despite my refusal, he took me on a boar hunt as he had promised, though begrudgingly."

Gwyndel rubbed the wrinkles from her brow. "I saved Fedrik from a boar, and he invited me to meet his family. But we were followed. The woodsmen who had accompanied us on the hunt were enemies in disguise. When Fedrik and I arrived here, they ambushed all of us—but the Sword Imperishable was enough to ward them off," she recalled. "They were arguing among themselves. Sounded like the vagabonds had disobeyed orders by attacking us."

As he listened, Eyoés twisted the corner of his towel between his fingers. The throb of his heartbeat drummed quicker in his chest as he came to an unsettling conclusion, staring into the flaming fireplace. "Neifon found out after you left with Lord Belos that Fedrik is the target of a mercenary named Lòfroy. Baron Galeras Estworth gave this mercenary his approval to carry out the murder," he whispered.

"Are you sure?" Gwyndel asked, leaning closer to her brother.

Eyoés nodded. "I came here to protect you all," he said.

The cabin door burst open, and he leapt to his feet with sword drawn. Fedrik flinched at the sight of the glinting blade, and Kerensa clung to him, staring in shock. Gwyndel seized her brother's hand to stay him. Their nerves were still raw from the earlier attempt on Fedrik's life.

A young boy shut the door behind him. Undoing the brooch at the base of his neck, the boy removed the fur-lined cloak from his shoulders and hung it on a nearby post. "The flocks are penned away for the night, Father—I hope I am not too late for supper," he said. He turned and stopped as his eyes fell upon Eyoés. Clearing his throat, he wiped the wet, curly locks of brown hair back from his forehead. The boy's face still displayed the roundness of childhood, and his slim frame grossly accentuated his growing height. Despite his pounding heartbeat, Eyoés cracked a smile as he recalled the same awkwardness he had once felt as a boy.

A slight smile brightened Fedrik's hardened features and brought a happiness to his bearing that seemed foreign—even strange. He leaned against the table and gestured toward the boy. "This is my son, Erling," he said with pride in his voice.

Eyoés sheathed his sword. "I'm Eyoés," he said, glancing between Erling and Gwyndel. "I assume you already know my sister, Gwyndel."

With a nod, Erling snatched a nearby towel from its peg and dried himself the best he could. He wiped his face and hung the towel back in its place. Removing his boots, he turned to Fedrik. His expression darkened with a swiftness that startled Eyoés and Gwyndel. Fear glinted in his eyes, and he reached into his satchel. "While I was guarding the sheep, I discovered a carcass," he began, removing an object from his pocket. "I found this." He held up a piece of bone, picked clean of flesh. The edges of the bone were broken and gnawed, and across its surface was a deep, jagged furrow.

Fedrik took the bone from his son's hand and examined it closer. "Groundclaws, no doubt," he muttered, glancing up to study his son. "How fresh was the carcass?"

Erling met his father's gaze. "Only a day old—and it was picked clean," he answered.

Fedrik mumbled a curse to himself and handed the bone back to Erling. "The pack is within a few miles for certain," he declared. Eyoés and Gwyndel shared an uneasy glance.

Lòfroy was not the only danger prowling the moorlands of Edeveros.

14

The numbness of sleep lost its grip on Eyoés as he stirred, opening his eyes. Midnight had descended upon the cold lands of Edeveros, and the rushing of a windstorm outside met his ears. At the sound of a crackling fire, he blinked away sleep from his bleary eyes. Heat permeated the room, and presence of a fresh fire confused him. Morning was still far off.

The sudden thought of Lòfroy gripped him, and he cast aside his blanket. As he sat up, Eyoés caught sight of a figure sitting before the fire. He stopped.

Fedrik stared into the flames, angled away from the crowded sleeping quarters. His head hung down to his chest, and in the firelight, Eyoés caught the glint of tears upon the man's cheeks.

Eyoés swung his legs off the edge of his bed, looking at Gwyndel lying blanketed on the floor. A smile warmed his heart as he remembered how she had surrendered the better bed to him, knowing how far he had traveled.

A quiet muttering drew Eyoés' attention back to where Fedrik sat. He studied the man from the shadows. Even from a distance, he could see Fedrik's hands shake. Eyoés cocked his head and scooted closer. A sudden sob stilled him.

Fedrik clenched his fists. "I tried to restore our honor through *honesty*. And my reward was a beating?" he whispered, chin quivering. "I made him pay for his slander, but I too paid dearly." Eyoés shied back, his eyes shifting about as he sought to understand.

Fedrik wept silently, shoulders heaving. "Fordarre was right. I am nothing but a piece of filth. I made myself a fiend by my actions. Just when I thought I had left it all behind, violence returns to punish me! And yet I cling to hope?" he mourned, pressing his knuckles against his mouth. "I treated them both with such—*hatred!* What if I fall into the same pattern again?" His head fell into his hands.

A desire to comfort the man urged Eyoés to rise. He tiptoed to avoid waking the others.

What has he done? What has been done to him?

Eyoés flinched as the fearful cries of sheep broke through the silence of the night. Fedrik leapt up. Woken abruptly from sleep, Erling sprang from his cot and threw aside his blanket. Gwyndel sprang to her feet and woke Kerensa. All motion in the cabin ceased. They listened—and a blood-curdling shriek wailed on the wind. Erling's face blanched, and he slipped on his boots. "Groundclaws!" he gasped. Seizing a farm axe and Gesadith lantern, he threw open the door and dashed into the darkness.

Kerensa screamed. Fedrik paled and rushed forward to pursue his son. "Erling!" he cried, his eyes wide in horror. Intercepting him, Eyoés raced out after

Erling and drew his sword, encouraged by the light elven footsteps of Gwyndel behind him.

They followed Erling's bouncing lantern through the dark, anxious for the flame to withstand the howling winds. The cries of the flock echoed in the vastness—and some cut off into grim silence.

Shapes moved in the blackness. A sudden choir of shrill screams rose and fell, followed by clicking growls. White eyes gleamed in the lantern light as Erling slowed his pace not far ahead. Within an enclosed corral, long limbs and slashing claws were exposed in their wrongdoing. Eyoés' heart skipped as Erling lifted his lantern and brandished his axe with wild cries—and the white eyes riveted on him. Gwyndel shuddered.

An immense shadow swept through the pack of advancing monsters, and the Groundclaws fell back from Erling with screams of pain. A roar shook the earth in reply. Erling toppled into Eyoés' arms as the final scream was cut off. Only the bleating of the sheep remained. Shaking, Erling clutched his axe. The pure lantern light glimmered in the eyes of the sheep huddling at the far end of the pen—and revealed a mangled form lying in a heap.

The Groundclaw dragon's narrow jaws were agape in a final threat, exposing several rows of teeth. Deep gashes proved the rough, barbed scales impotent against a greater strength. Six scythe-like claws were robbed of their harvest. Long, bowed arms curled in on themselves, and the hind legs were coiled to spring. The dragon's lack of wings made its body appear misshapen, as if fate itself had cursed its kind to scour the earth in disgrace. The creature's only beauty lay in the two horns curling back from the base of the skull. Eyoés knelt before it to better realize the creature's size. It would be necessary to burn the carcasses before long.

Erling held the lantern aloft, illuminating ten more of the creatures, mangled and strewn about. He stepped back, eyes wildly searching the darkness as a whoosh of air raced across him, and heavy footfalls shook the ground. Erling dropped his axe and raised his quaking hand to ward off the menace. Rising to his feet with a smile, Eyoés laid a comforting arm around the boy's shoulders. He gently took the lantern from Erling's hand and held it aloft. Two large eyes gleamed as an immense silhouette was revealed. A beak glistened in the light, and two wings spread above their heads.

Eyoés beamed. "This is Gibusil," he said. At his voice, the griffin gave a whining trill and nudged him with its beak.

Gibusil lowered his head with a rumbling chirp. Erling's fear melted under the griffin's gaze. His hand relaxed, and he stroked the smooth black beak with his fingers.

Even while they lived in fear, an unseen guardian had watched over them.

15

The warmth of the sun pierced through the overcast skies of Edeveros at the coming of mid-morning. Bright light streamed into the covered balconies of Castle Mithlon, tossing the shadows about. Birdsong rose upon the gentle breeze, and the sunlight warmed the air. Haeryn felt the tension of the past day strain against the tranquility.

As he walked beside Neifon along the wide veranda, their footsteps rang against the tall, arched ceiling. Flecks of moss were tucked into the seam where the walkway met the base of the marble wall. To their left, small archways separated by clusters of pillars led out into the open air.

Haeryn let his gaze wander along with his drifting mind, taking in the green, branched designs upon the ceiling. His eyes alighted upon the painting of a fox on a nearby archway. Haeryn gave a loud sigh. The reminder of Galeras Estworth galled him.

Neifon raised an eyebrow, sensing the youth's disgust. "I know you desire action, Haeryn. It shall be taken, I assure you—but the Courts of Edeveros exist in a fragile balance. The swiftness you desire would lead to anarchy," he chided. Before Haeryn could retort, Neifon turned to the left and passed through another pillared archway. At the edge of the balcony, Haeryn looked out over the crimson forest.

Turning back to where they had come from, Haeryn placed a hand on his dagger. "This place is not secluded enough. What if we are overheard?" he asked.

Neifon leaned against the veranda railing, contemplating the landscape with confident assurance. "My scouts are watching over all possible entries to this place. We passed them not long ago. Dressed as servants," he said with a subdued laugh. "Besides, Roseen and Raulin's guest quarters are nearby. As honored guests, they could demand complete privacy on this entire level if they wished. But they have decided to forgo such extremes to avoid attracting Galeras' unwanted attention. A brief time will suffice for our private discussion." Haeryn peered at the Chief of Court with resignation.

Footsteps echoed behind them. They turned to see Roseen and Raulin approaching, a gleam of victory in their eyes. Though dressed down since the banquet, their attire was still bold in its complexity and beauty. Their aura of defiance struggled against the tyranny that Castle Mithlon had come to represent.

Another woman trailed behind them, observing from lowered brows. She wore a dark red dress trimmed with lace and sequins, and edged with ample ruffles. Her rich blonde hair hung in curls about her round face. Thin lines of kohl outlined her eyelids. Despite her bold dress, she approached with timid steps, her shoulders caving under an unspoken burden. She clasped her hands to keep from fidgeting.

Roseen urged her forward with a reassuring smile. "As the old saying goes—'to know a man is to know his enemies *and* his friends,'" she began. "This is Aalys. She is one of Galeras' former ladyloves—and overheard him plan Raulin's jousting 'accident'. By relocating to Gahidros she distanced herself to avoid suspicion." Roseen withdrew and gestured to Neifon and Haeryn. "Tell them your story," she entreated.

Glancing timidly at Roseen, Aalys swallowed, a glint of fearful determination flashing across her face. "I was combing my hair in Galeras' bedroom when I heard voices outside the door," she began in a weak voice. "At first, I thought it was nothing. But then I heard him laugh—an unpleasant, harrowing laugh that chilled me. I rose and opened the door a crack to see several men gathered around him, all dressed in servant's clothes." She shivered. "Galeras commanded them to kill Raulin in the joust. I heard it from his own mouth!" she said in a harsh whisper. "I indulged his needy ego and penchant for excess, but to think I kept company with a murderer..." She blushed and looked away.

Raulin looked down at the stump of his arm with a humorous smile. "It appears the plan failed," he noted. A wide grin broke out over Haeryn's face, and he suppressed a laugh. Neifon and Roseen, intent on the woman's testimony, ignored the comment.

Aalys lifted her head. "I left him. And I haven't seen him since," she said. With the burden of the declaration off her shoulders, she withdrew behind her escort.

Haeryn paced about the balcony.

The path of justice lies before us. We have only to take it!

He spun around to face the others. "We have the evidence we need. There can be no more tarrying! Let's send the Fox fleeing into the brambles!" he exclaimed, his voice trembling with eagerness.

Raulin shook the stump of his arm in rebuttal. "The Court of Edeveros will not believe mere word of mouth. There are precautions that must be followed to provide a sufficient argument against Galeras and to maintain order simultaneously," he insisted. Haeryn muttered under his breath and turned away to look out over the horizon.

Roseen nodded her agreement. "The Council of Lords is to take place tomorrow morning. I discussed the matter with the Lords before we fetched Aalys and returned to Mithlon. When the Council is summoned, the accusations can be made, and Galeras' hold upon Edeveros will crumble," she said.

16

6th of Rotanos, 2209 SE

The halls of Mithlon were still, save for the sputtering of scented candles. As Haeryn and Neifon hurried to join the Council of Lords, the silence quieted their troubled minds as if to prepare them for the confrontation ahead.

Foreboding unsettled Haeryn. While the baron's vanity had engraved the image of a petty noble into his memory, he realized the very present threat of Galeras' passionate outbursts.

There is no controlling such a man. Death is the fruit of such a temper.

Haeryn hurried his pace as he remembered the ruffians that had leapt up at Galeras' bidding during the banquet. The crooked baron might not shed blood himself, but it was clear he had no qualms about others working violence on his behalf. Haeryn mustered his courage.

He spotted the open doorway ahead. Since the Council had yet to begin, the doors remained open until privacy was demanded, though two armor-clad soldiers kept a strict vigilance. Leading Haeryn inside, Neifon shut the doors behind him. The sugary scent of hot scones made Haeryn's stomach growl. Several noblemen in crisp uniforms spoke among themselves, and he swung wide to avoid intruding upon their conversation. Stepping up to the round table, Haeryn leaned against a chair, his fingers digging into the soft upholstery. At the sight of the silver teacups placed before each seat, he smiled to himself at the irony. Although the matters at hand were far from amiable, the atmosphere sought to lighten the occasion. Tea among friends was rarely a time for hostility.

At Neifon's entry, the noblemen cut their discussion short. Removing their circlets, they bowed in mutual respect. The Chief of Court flashed a pleasant smile and muttered a few words of greeting.

From the far end of the room, Raulin noticed Neifon and Haeryn's arrival and moved toward them. His wife restrained him with a dissuading hand. Casting an attentive glance to where his brother Galeras idly read a book, Raulin assented. Roseen strode forward and pulled Haeryn and Neifon aside. "All is prepared, but we must not cause Galeras to be suspicious," she whispered. "Aalys is under guard in an adjacent room."

Neifon nodded. "Excellent. I shall start the proceedings," he said. Roseen and the Chief of Court approached the round table. Neifon took up a small bell and rang it. As the nobles concluded their small talk and seated themselves, Haeryn wandered to the edge of the room to observe. He held himself with dignity, despite the questioning looks from the Lords. Naive sentiment brought his Wynrence ancestry to mind and goaded him to take an active role in the proceedings, but Haeryn thought better of it. He knew his place.

Galeras reclined in his chair with hands clasped behind his head, his gaze wandering among the Lords with indifference. "Well, then," he sighed. "You summoned the Council, Neifon. Shall we discuss the peasantry, trade, or taxes, as usual?" He flashed a disarming smile.

Haeryn ground his teeth at the man's flippant tone.

Galeras is more than negligent. He expects the nobles to carry his load.

The Lords shared an irritated glance, and Lord Belos hung his head to hide his reddening face. Though they had borne the brunt of Galeras' years in power, they continued to feel embarrassment and exasperation at their baron's negligence.

With a hard smile, Neifon tapped his fingers on the table as he strove to regain his composure. He turned to the indolent Baron. "This Council has much to discuss with you, Galeras," he said curtly. "In fact, we are *eager* to speak with you." His words were sharp, with a hint of challenge lying underneath.

Galeras leaned forward with brow raised. "What a pleasant surprise! Pray, what is the matter of your inquiry?" he asked with a slight bitterness. It was clear Galeras was not quite the fool he appeared to be. The contempt in Neifon's words had not escaped his notice, and a scathing look passed between them.

Roseen swallowed a sip of tea and placed the teacup on its saucer. "Your crimes," she declared.

Galeras flinched under the accusation. He gripped the armrests of his chair, and he met the face of each of the Lords with eyes narrowed. "I have committed no crimes," he snapped.

Raulin leapt to his feet and glared at his brother. He raised the stub of his arm. "Explain your handiwork! What about my 'jousting accident'?" he roared. He lunged toward the Baron, and Roseen restrained him.

Gritting his teeth, Galeras glared at his brother. "I had no part in your pitiful misfortune," he snapped. But as he spoke the words, his eyes broke away and darted about the room.

From where he observed unnoticed, Haeryn shook his head, noting the baron's discomfort. The weight of his dagger at his waist called to him.

Galeras knows his injustice—and the punishment he deserves. As the last Wynrence, I will see him pay the price.

His thoughts were cut off as the door to the chamber opened. Several guards entered, and Aalys accompanied them, quivering as she struggled to muster her bravery. Galeras' eyes locked on her, and he leapt up from his seat with a puzzled glance at Roseen.

As Aalys came to stand before the Council of Lords, Neifon rose from his seat and faced her. Through his weary and angered expression, a slight smile came to his face at her courage. "Aalys of Toldan, do you consent to speak your testimony before these witnesses, through your own words and through the utter truth revealed by the White Flower?" he inquired according to tradition.

Swallowing the knot in her throat, Aalys nodded. "I do," she answered. Neifon motioned for her to begin, and returned to his seat. Aalys stared at the wall, unwilling to meet the black look of Galeras. "I was in the bedroom in the baron's quarters, combing my hair. I overheard heated voices, and I cracked the door open and peeked through to see him speaking with several other men. They were scheming to kill the Grandmaster in the upcoming joust," she said. "I—could see the eagerness in Galeras' eyes. He told them to 'stick Raulin like a pig.'"

As her words faded away, Neifon motioned to one of the nearby guards. With a nervous glance at the Baron, the man stepped forward, cradling in his arms a small, wooden box engraved with floral designs. Neifon stood and took it from the guard with a gracious nod. He unlatched the bronze clasp and lifted the lid. Nestled within the box's red velvet interior was a clear bottle, filled with a whitish liquid. Neifon set the box aside and removed the bottle, and Haeryn felt a twinge of pity as Aalys took it with trembling fingers. Her bravery and commitment to justice had aided them greatly.

Aalys stared at the bottle. She undid the cork and downed the liquid. Her eyes closed tightly shut, and she swooned within moments, falling back into the arms of the soldiers behind her. Her glazed eyes stared upward through the haze of the White Flower's influence.

Brow drawn in pity, Neifon grasped her by the wrists and pulled her upright. "If you have deceived us, your lies will be exposed—did Galeras Estworth conspire against Raulin, his brother, and instruct men to kill him in a jousting accident as you have told us?" he asked. All present held their breath as they awaited her reply.

Aalys nodded weakly. "Yes," she sighed, sagging into the soldiers' waiting arms. At a swift command from Neifon, the soldiers carried her out of the Council chamber.

The wrathful glares of the Lords fixed upon Galeras in silent demand for punishment. Sweat trailed down the baron's forehead.

Neifon casually sipped the remainder of his tea and set it aside. "We accuse you, Galeras, of two High-Crimes—treason against the people of Edeveros and conspiracy against your peers with intent to murder," he declared, glancing at the scribe lingering in the corner, writing down a transcript of all that occurred. "A document detailing these accusations against you will be presented to the Court Magistrate as demanded by the law. The Baronic Trial will determine your fate."

17

Twilight fell upon Castle Mithlon to the tremor of a thunderstorm. Against the canvas of darkness, the clouds turned to splotches of grey, blurred by the rain pattering on Galeras' windows. Gilded in gold and bronze, rose and fern embellishments blanketed the room to testify to the cultured opulence of its occupant. An inconspicuous door concealed the bedroom from prying eyes, and the light of several dangling chandeliers illuminated the suite.

A hammered dulcimer's lament filled the chamber, ebbing and flowing in and out of a grand theme. Galeras Estworth gazed out of the towering arched windows as he let the hammers fall upon the strings with expert precision. Dark notes rang out in accordance to his black mood.

He watched the misty grey sky choke the evening light. Enduring bitterness hardened him to the accusations lodged against him. With a grim twist to his mouth, Galeras released his rancor upon the instrument.

My people may dislike me, and the Lords might despise me, but I refuse to surrender the throne of Edeveros.

As Roseen's triumphant face returned to haunt his memory, Galeras cursed in the solitude of his chamber.

After years of suspicion, it was now clear to him what trap laid in wait for him. Roseen, Raulin, and Neifon sought his ruin, but he was determined to rob them of the satisfaction.

The song ceased as his mind faltered. A frigid calm settled over him. Galeras smirked as he began his song once more. The troubles that beset him would pass.

The doors to his chamber clanged open, and Galeras briskly stood, turning to welcome his guest.

The two black, vacant slits of an iron helm stared back at him. The man's gauntlets clinked as he flexed his hands. His armor was polished spotless. Behind him, a flowing cape rippled with a splendor that earned Galeras' envy. Though his face was hidden, he strode forward with a fortitude that conveyed supremacy.

Galeras smiled. "Ah, Lòfroy," he said, spreading his arms wide in welcome. "I was expecting you."

Lòfroy did not slow his stride. Crossing the distance between them, he loomed over the baron with an unsettling silence. Under the man's imposing gaze, Galeras absentmindedly tugged at his collar.

Satisfied by the show of submission, Lòfroy fell back and wandered about the chamber with the coolness of a conquerer. "You resolved to accept my proposal, then," he said, eying the lavish decor with disinterest. "My men were satisfactory?"

Galeras nodded. "When that *child* slighted me, they were quick to act. Not many of those under my authority are so willing to obey," he remarked with a smirk, puffing out his chest.

Lòfroy stopped, his armor clinking. "You remember my terms," he declared. "If I am to give you my services, you must assure me that, if my activity is discovered, you will turn a blind eye."

"It is done," Galeras said, pulling a folded parchment from the pocket of his outer coat. Briefly examining the papers with a curious glint in his eye, he extended them between his fingers. "What did this Fedrik do to you? " he asked.

In an instant, Lòfroy crossed the distance and snatched the papers from the baron's grasp. "You will not ask me further," he snapped. The finality in his voice hung between them as an unspoken threat. Galeras hesitated, the triumphant light in his eyes snuffed out as he backed away from the unflinching helm in submission. Lòfroy did not let him yield so easily. "What is the first move to be made?" he inquired, taking a step forward.

Galeras retreated another step. An embittered sneer contorted his features. "Kidnap that wench that dares to witness against me. I expect Raulin and Neifon will take her to Gahidros to assure her safety," he growled. "I assume you know of my confounded plight? Of the accusations?"

Lòfroy nodded. "I know *everything*, Galeras. Even as I awaited your summons, I have not been idle," he declared, lowering his iron helm to stare deep into the baron's eyes. "But kidnapping is not enough—this witness must die. To leave her alive is to invite her rescue. The dead do not tattle." A pained look crossed Galeras' features.

Grabbing him by the shoulder, Lòfroy sought to enlighten him. "You may have loved her once, but she betrayed you! A woman who betrays you does not deserve mercy," he said. "She will not receive mine."

Despite himself, Galeras nodded and dispelled his misgivings. "Very well," he sighed, "I defer to you in these matters. But leave no trace."

With a satisfied nod, Lòfroy released Galeras and started back toward the grand doorway. "My vendetta has waited years. It can wait a while longer," he said. Rolling his eyes, Galeras waved a hand in dismissal. Even with the wealth of Edeveros ripe for the taking, the mercenary had demanded no other price than the death of a mere commoner.

A trifling price Galeras was more than willing to accept.

At the grand doors, Lòfroy paused, glancing back at the Baron. "I am at your command. But tread carefully, Galeras, and don't let your arrogance fool you into crossing me," he said, his gauntleted fist clenching with a clink. "Even Barons bleed."

18

5th of Rotanos, 2209 SE

The crackling of the fireplace overwhelmed the light patter of rain upon the roof of Fedrik's cabin. Kerensa knelt before the fire, tending a pot of porridge. Sitting quietly in a nearby chair, Fedrik cradled a piece of wood in his hand, carving and whittling it into a cup. His hard face was afflicted with the lines and wrinkles of a weary soul.

Eyoés found it difficult to pull his eyes away from the man. The wretchedness emanating from the haggard face stirred him to sympathy, reminding him of Fedrik's secret musings.

I am nothing but a piece of filth. I made myself a fiend by my actions. And yet I cling to hope? I treated them both with such—hatred! What if I fall into the same pattern again?

Eyoés looked away to hide his pained look. Remorse for past wrongs was familiar to him. Squeezing his eyes shut, Eyoés felt a sharp pain skewer him as the memory of Asdale's destruction returned like a thunderclap. Screams of terror and the roars of dragons echoed in his head, and the odor of smoke met him afresh. Eyoés opened his eyes and sank into a chair. The recollection faded like a wisp of smoke, leaving only a racing heartbeat in its wake. He was no stranger to remorse and shame. The recollection of Asdale's fall brought him to sympathy. Eyoés glanced at Fedrik. He hesitated.

But what if he truly is a villain?

Rising from his seat, he snatched up a nearby cup and walked to the keg of fresh water against the wall. He removed the cork stopper with a hollow pop and poured a modest amount. Eyoés stood behind Fedrik, watching him work in silence. There was little evidence in the man's words to piece together what crimes he had committed. Despite his own unsettling speculations, Eyoés longed for the man's restoration.

Remorse without hope of redemption chokes the life of the sorrowful. Fedrik yearns for forgiveness and restoration, and I must help him find it.

The cabin door creaked open, and a cool draft of air drew Eyoés' attention elsewhere. Closing the door behind her, Gwyndel entered and set aside her bow and quiver. A light sheen of rain wetted her clothes and curly red hair. Blowing into her hands, she removed her boots and strode to the fireplace to warm herself.

With a contented sigh, she reached out to warm her hands by the flames. "It seems Gibusil slew the only Groundclaw pack in the lands around Anfon," she said. "I scoured the surrounding area and found no fresh sign. Only a herd of stags and the remains of a wolf kill."

With a firm nod, Fedrik ceased carving and set his dagger on the table. "All the better," he said, tracing the cup's rough surface with his fingers.

Taking a drink, Eyoés set his cup on the table. "Any sign of the ruffians who attacked you and Fedrik? Although time has passed, they may be lingering out of sight to await another chance," he remarked. Wincing, he muttered an apology as he saw the glint of worry on Fedrik's face.

Gwyndel sensed the anxious gazes hanging on her words, and the inquiring look of her brother urged her to reply. Her brow furrowed. She snuffed out the desire to lie, and her eyes flashed blue in defiance of the dishonest inclination. As the Keeper of the Sword Imperishable, she knew she must give them the truth.

Gwyndel looked to her brother, the knowing look in her eye betraying his suspicions. "I pursued them the morning after the attack and their trail ended a few miles into the nearest forest," she began. "The Groundclaws found them before I did. I stumbled upon the aftermath."

Fedrik sank into his chair, squeezing his eyes shut and swallowing the knot in his throat. "We truly are safe then," he declared. Kerensa left her place by the fire and stroked his hair with a quiet look of relief.

"I am not sure," Gwyndel said.

A glint of fear flashed in Eyoés' eyes. His face hardened as the threat of Lòfroy returned to him. "What do you mean?" he asked.

Gwyndel met Fedrik's startled expression. "In the wake of the attack, I did not think it appropriate to mention it. You and your family were still in shock. But where the Groundclaws had killed the other two men, I discovered another trail breaking away to flee into the forest," she revealed. "It appears that one of the men escaped the demise of his fellows. I fear he may have fled to secure aid from unknown allies."

Fedrik stood, nearly upsetting his chair as the danger of Gwyndel's statement fully settled into his mind. Arms around her husband, Kerensa stared at Gwyndel in dread. "Who are these men? What do they have against us?" she cried, chin quivering. Gwyndel did not reply—she knew no answer.

But Eyoés, seeing the dread on their faces, could not bring himself to reply. Neifon's voice once again spoke into his ear, hushed with secrecy.

My informant gathered that this Lòfroy is on the hunt for a certain man who lives on the outskirts of Anfon in the south. A huntsman by the name of Fedrik.

The realization of the poor family's peril pierced Eyoés like a blade, cutting through his own doubts and fears to the duty he was entrusted to. Only he and Gibusil were the only ones capable of ending Lòfroy's prowl. Neifon's hands were tied by the duties of his office. Eyoés' face hardened.

Lòfroy may be surprised to find himself not the hunter—but the hunted.

19

Tranquil was the song of the moorlands. Droplets of dew clung like notes to the knolls of scrub-grass to anchor the clouded sky to its melody. The steady dripping of rain provided a constant, driving rhythm—subtle, yet demanding in its tempo. Fog masked the landscape with its furtive refrain, drawing Erling deeper into its beauty as the dimness of evening unfolded before him.

Erling leaned back against a lofty hillock and gazed over his flock. Legs crossed and staff laid upon his lap, he watched the white shapes of the sheep drift like wraiths through the fog. The mist seeped through his skin to shroud his thoughts in serenity, sending a lightness through his bones that revived him. He inhaled a draught of the crisp air, intoxicated by the vitality it stirred in him. As the gentle rain trickled down his face, he welcomed its cool, vivid touch. Erling smiled as a gust of wind tossed his curly brown hair and combed it with invisible fingers. His fondness of the ancient tales sparked anew, inspired by the muse of his ancient homeland. "Evening's gloaming, with sword a-gleaming, o'er moorlands and vale, dread foes did assail, Edeveran heroes of old, conquerers both noble and bold, charging into mists of the North," he quoted. The lilting poetry and imagery in the words cheered his heart with their vibrancy. Eyes glistening, Erling embraced the sentiment. He longed to be worthy of honor.

The peacefulness within him receded as his thoughts left the calm moors and returned to his warm home. Erling's smile lost its warmth. He recalled the times he had slighted his parents through disobedient speech and action. A heaviness gripped him like the finality of a judge's decree. As he looked down at the staff in his hands, Erling slumped.

My father believes the only mercy for him is what he may gain by virtue. I have heard his night rantings. If forgiveness is something he must earn, why should I be any different?

Burdened by the verdict, Erling retreated into his thoughts for guidance. He envisioned Perren Alcarthon, Eryndál Amberster, and the other warrior heroes of his fantasies standing before him. Erling straightened as he imagined their voices rising as one, urging him to live by the honor they shared. With his resolve rekindled to life, he stood and pressed his fist over his heart in reverence.

I choose to be like them. I will earn the praise of others, and my misdeeds will be nullified.

Taking up his staff, Erling reached for the dirk at his belt. With a warm smile, he drew it and held it before him. Carved in the likeness of a stag, the handle curved to fit snugly into his hand. The broad, tapered blade featured a narrow groove inset halfway down its length. Erling squeezed the weapon in his palm, remembering the somberness and reluctance with which his father had given it to him. In a way, the blade had become a manifestation of his father's love.

Sheathing the dirk at his side, Erling looked out over the highlands, glimpsing his flock huddled together in the fog. The vague edge of a shadowed forest caught his eye, rousing his wonder as the crooked branches beckoned him. Pursing his lips, Erling searched the surrounding fog for sign of imminent danger. Seeing no predators or thieves in sight, he indulged his imagination.

He sprinted across the highlands, his curly locks bouncing about his ears. With the naivety of youth, he cast aside the worries of responsibility and left his sheep to the protection of the fog. In moments, he stood before the forest's edge. He looked back with an uncertain frown, shuffling his feet. From where he stood, the shapes of his flock were only illusions of the mist. Shoving his staff into the ground to avoid losing it in the brush, he stepped into the forest.

The dim evening light was choked into shadow. Blinking to accustom his vision to the darkness, Erling took a few careful steps forward. As his eyes adjusted to the gloom, he glimpsed tall pines loom above him like giants. A few leaves were scattered about the forest floor with the coming of autumn. Ferns curled about his boots. The familiar, soothing presence of the arcane forest enveloped Erling. As his eyes roved the surrounding scenery, he inhaled the fragrance of damp wood and moist vegetation. Erling continued into the woods in a quiet serenity.

A low moan startled him. Erling yanked his dirk from his sheath and scoured the trees, eyes wide with fright. The shadows that had once been inviting and mysterious turned cold and monstrous before him. His blade flashed as it shook violently in his grip. He listened, gulping down a trembling breath.

The guttural groan echoed again through the dim forest. Erling's heart pounded, urging him to flee as thoughts of monsters raced through his mind. As he stared into the forest, he trembled. Scrubbing his ashen face with his sweaty hand, Erling stifled his terror and wiped his damp palms on his shirt.

A true hero doesn't run from danger. What would others think of me if I fled like a coward?

Erling swallowed. With every muscle clenched in anticipation of escape, he darted forward before his fear could regain its hold. As the moan resounded in from the dimness, he barged through a thick cluster of trees and into a glade. He stopped, his dagger mid-air.

A large, rotten pine stump greeted his bold entrance, covered in downy moss as if to preserve its decency. Leaning against it, a lone man flinched at Erling's sudden appearance and dropped his short sword. He scrambled to stand, and with a curse, fell back against the stump, moaning in pain. Erling sheathed his dagger and studied the man.

The gambeson he wore struggled to contain his broad, stocky frame, and a tattered peasant's hood failed to cover his balding head. Two small eyes set close within a square face, and a thick, ragged mustache drew unwelcome attention to his ugliness.

Scars streaked across his face and hands, testifying to a life of violence.

As Erling scrutinized him, his eyes were drawn to the unnatural angle of the man's leg—and his skin crawled at the sight. Caught in a tangle of roots, the man's ankle was mangled and bloodied beyond treatment. Erling looked up at the man with a flash of pity, noticing the signs of hunger and thirst in the man's wide face.

The fright in his eyes waned at the sight of Erling. With a sigh of relief, he adjusted his position and roughly gestured for the boy to approach. "Come, boy! Lend me your aid!" he commanded. Though he spoke with authority, his voice quaked.

Moved by the man's pitiable state, Erling stepped forward—then hesitated, drawing back toward the trees with a frown. "Who are you?" he demanded. As he studied the man's face, a wary quiver in his stomach warned him.

With a bitter, trembling laugh, the man swore to himself and bared his teeth. "You little whelp!" he snapped, his whispering voice growing louder as he spoke. "Just get me free of this cursed stump! I fear there may be Groundclaws about!" Gritting his teeth, he attempted to rise, only to fall back to the ground, gasping in pain.

As Erling stared at the man, a sudden recollection struck him with a potency that made him reel. The man's face returned to his mind, his pleading look transformed into a sneer of wrath. The cries of his mother and father echoed in his memory, and the gleam of the Sword Imperishable pierced through the nightmare. In a moment of clarity, rage seized Erling.

He clenched his fists, and resentment twisted his heart like a ragged cloth. "You tried to kill my father outside our home," he said through clenched teeth. He drew his dirk from its sheath, heart pounding in his chest. But conviction stayed his hand.

What hero of old would slay a wounded man? Hasn't he already paid for his evils?

The man stared back, and spite twisted his unsightly features. His recognition of Erling was unmistakable. Hindered by his injury, he seized handfuls of the mossy ground as he attempted to claw his way to the boy. He ground his teeth at the searing pain in his ankle, and his nose wrinkled in rash derision. "Should have killed the old man and done away with you too," he snarled.

His mind clouded by anger, Erling shoved his dirk into its sheath. Gritting his teeth, he turned away in silence and went back the way he had come. There was no mercy for such a man.

And as the man's desperate cries echoed through the forest's expanse, Erling stopped his ears. The murderer had earned his just punishment.

2◊

Kerensa gingerly placed a bowl of hot stew before Gwyndel. Placing the wool napkin in her lap, Gwyndel scooted her chair aside to allow more room for Eyoés. She took up the hand-forged utensils and watched as Fedrik and Kerensa dug into their meal. While Eyoés and Gwyndel appreciated the hospitality of their hosts, the tension of their unstable predicament had separated them with a tangible silence. Save for a few shallow discussions, no words of encouragement had managed to break through.

Eyoés studied Fedrik as he ate, intrigued by the mystery of his reserved manner. He wiped his mouth with his napkin. "Is Edeveros your native land? It seems you have a long relationship to the people of Anfon, to become the Huntsman for Lord Stonneter," he remarked. Gwyndel eyed him with a sharp, reproving look. Knowing the somberness with which Fedrik held himself, she remained unsure as to what such a prying question would unveil.

Fedrik didn't notice. A momentary pause interrupted his feast as he considered the question. "Actually, I was born in North Rehillon in the town of Andieff. Joined the Northern Guard against the will of my parents. After over thirty years in the service of the High Marshal, I got in an altercation with one of my

120

superiors. I decided to make the best of my exile by making my home in Anfon," he replied.

Eyoés stared down at the stew before him. His brow furrowed as the man's secret confession continued to ring through his thoughts.

Perhaps his exile from the Northern Guard is what he regrets. Maybe I have been too hasty to assume the worst of him.

Yet even as he considered the notion, he was dissatisfied. Eyoés took a bite of his stew. Being exiled for insubordination would not produce such a burden of remorse—and the hastiness with which Fedrik spoke suggested a false story.

Unsure, he set aside his questions and returned to his meal. Kerensa, unaware of the curiosity hidden in Eyoés' inquiry, interjected. "I met Fedrik not long after his arrival. This homestead used to be my aging father's farm—I grew up surrounded by these walls," she said, her unfocused gaze pondering the haven she labored to preserve. "We fell in love, and upon my father's death, took this home as our own."

Fedrik smiled at his wife and planted a kiss on her cheek. "And a fine home it has become," he said. With a kind look, Kerensa smiled in return and leaned up against his strong shoulders.

Erling sat motionless in his chair. Staring at his stew, he hung his head. Gwyndel's brow furrowed as she glimpsed his trembling grip on his spoon. Her vision sharpened with the discernment of the Sword Imperishable, and she flinched as Erling's stress became her own. Though Eyoés ate in silence, his gaze had settled upon the boy with the same questioning look. Gwyndel caught her brother's eye with a shared glance of unease.

Hidden guilt rots the heart and mind from within.

Swallowing a bite of stew, Gwyndel leaned forward. "Is everything all right, Erling?" she asked, looking fixedly at the boy. Compelled by her kind words, he swallowed. He said nothing in reply—yet the tortured pleading in his eyes spoke for him. Gwyndel's eyes softened, and with a slight smile, she nodded silent encouragement for him to speak his mind.

Erling swallowed. He glanced uneasily at those gathered around the table and cleared his throat with a grimace. "I abandoned my flock today to explore the forest for a time," he began, voice cracking.

Fedrik wiped his mouth with his napkin. With a stern glance of disapproval, he shook his head. "Foolish," he said, washing down a mouthful of stew with a cup of water. "You're lucky the local pack of Groundclaws is no more. They might have slaughtered the sheep—or worse, *you.* " With that, Fedrik let the matter rest and returned to his meal. Kerensa regarded her son from under lowered brows. Gwyndel caught her suspicion as she watched Erling shift uncomfortably in his seat.

The boy could no longer suppress his guilt. Pushing away his bowl, he hung his head in his hands. "I found a wounded man," he confessed. Anticipation lingered in the silence.

Eyoés studied Fedrik and Kerensa, and a knot wrenched his stomach. Though her son's nervousness sowed anxiety in her heart, Kerensa mustered an encouraging smile. But as Fedrik stared, an growing unease haunted his expression.

Erling sighed and lifted his head. "He was one of the men who tried to kill us, Father. So I left him to die," he said. Eyoés felt his heart skip. As the narrative began to take shape in her mind, Gwyndel's heart broke.

Fedrik leapt to his feet, his chair clattering to the floor. His face contorted in a storm of emotion that heaved the entire room into confusion. Staggering back, he sank against the wall of the cabin in utter anguish. He seized his hair in handfuls. "NO! It cannot be!" he yelled. Fedrik seized Erling by the shirt. "Do my wrongs pass down to stain your hands? Why?" he cried, voice breaking in grief and anger.

Erling suppressed a sob as tears flowed down his cheeks. His face contorted in bitterness and grief. "He tried to *kill* us! And I hated him for it! But now, I only feel regret," he answered. Wrenching himself free, Erling collapsed into the nearest chair and wept. Eyoés and Gwyndel could only watch as father and son wept in shared sorrow.

Tears welled up in Gwyndel's eyes as the sharp agony of their grief became her own. Looking to her brother, she met his gaze in a silent plea for help. Though the desire to comfort her two stricken friends blazed in her throbbing heart, she struggled to find a way to comfort them without encouraging further conflict.

Before Gwyndel could act, Fedrik lifted his head and fell to his knees before Erling. The horror on his face fell away as he realized his harmful treatment of his son. With a choked sigh, he embraced Erling and kissed his forehead. "I should not have despaired. I'm sorry," he said. Erling returned his father's embrace, and no more words were needed.

Eyoés stood and snatched up his cloak from where it hung. His eyes softened. "There may still be a chance to save this man's life—but we must hurry," he said. "Show us the way, Erling."

Throughout the dark expanse, the wind whispered to the crickets nestling within the underbrush as the moon's gleam trickled through the forest canopy. Holding a lantern aloft, Eyoés searched the darkness unafraid. The flames within it flickered as he leaned against a conifer, the coarse bark pressing into his palm. Footsteps crackled like sparks as Erling and Fedrik stopped beside him. Kerensa joined the three of them, gripping her spare lantern in trembling hands. In the light of the burning Gesadith, her stiff, wide-eyed expression was painfully vulnerable.

Gwyndel scouted not far ahead of them, her bow at the ready. Her features tightened in a hard smile at her negligence in leaving Fóbehn behind in Asdale.

Eyoés smiled to himself as he considered the company he kept. Though troubled over Fedrik's heart wrenching outburst, he admired the family's dedication. They remained faithful to one other despite their trials—even if it meant facing the night and its terrors.

A resounding thump pulsed in his ears, and Gibusil's vast shadow soared above the forest canopy. If the creature sensed an unseen threat, there would be sufficient warning. Eyoés motioned for Erling to come alongside, and the boy hurried forward through the underbrush. Though Fedrik's unsettling outburst had been laid aside, Eyoés could tell the wound still stung.

Eyoés laid a comforting hand about the boy's shoulders. "Show us the way," he said. His voice barely disturbed the night.

Too absorbed in his own guilt to detect the kindness in Eyoés' voice, Erling stopped, shaking as he scanned the forest ahead. Without a word, he dashed forward into the forest. Fedrik gasped and bolted after his son, towing his wife behind him as he traversed the uneven ground with a Huntsman's skill. Gwyndel glided past Eyoés like an elven shade with soundless footsteps, and he followed carefully.

Erling skidded to a stop as the ground underfoot sloped downward. Kerensa and Fedrik held their breath, while Eyoés and Gwyndel tuned their senses to the surrounding woods. The wind chilled them with a sudden gust, and the forest enveloped them all in its magnitude.

No moans of pain. No muttered curses. Only the caw of a distant crow.

Erling ran his hands through his hair, his stomach knotting as his mind raced to wild conclusions. Shaking his head in disbelief, he rushed into the trees opposite, and the others followed his swishing trail through the underbrush. As soon as they broke through the cover of trees, a small glade came into sight. Eyoés and the others came to an abrupt stop behind Erling. The boy stood rigid, staring into the darkness. Fedrik and Kerensa moved beside Erling and held him close. Steeling himself, Eyoés swallowed and moved around them, holding his lantern aloft as he stepped into the glade.

The man lay slumped up against the old stump, staring up into the canopy of boughs above. His ankle was mangled and twisted as Erling had mentioned. As Eyoés moved closer, he noticed a pool of blood surrounding the man's body—and he sucked in a quick breath at the sight of claw marks. His stomach lurched.

Brow furrowed, Gwyndel passed her brother and crouched to examine the area around the body. After many years in Forester service, she had become less unsettled by the sight of death. She felt about the mossy forest floor, then stopped, scrutinizing the ground for a brief moment. "Lone wolf," she said, kicking a short sword from where it lay. "Not all the blood is his own. It appears he tried to fight it off."

Erling retched violently into the nearby bushes. In the moonlight, the haunted look on his pale face was clear to see—the childhood innocence that once brightened his face was dulled. Wiping his mouth, he wept aloud, comforted by the embrace of his parents.

Eyoés exchanged a furtive look with Gwyndel, then turned back to the body lying before them.

This had to have been one of Lòfroy's men.

Time was fleeting—and there was no telling how much remained.

21

9th of Rotanos, 2209 SE

With a click of his tongue, Haeryn moved his horse alongside Neifon and Raulin as they journeyed to Castle Gahidros with Aalys. A seamless grey sky hung over the Hero Mountains as the company passed through the Vale of Teuthros. The jingle of metal bridles and armor cut through the steady drone of wind. Surrounding the three travelers, an escort of mounted soldiery surveyed the valley with precision, drops of rain trickling down their plate armor.

Seated upon a jet black horse, Neifon fixed his gaze on the path ahead, unfazed by the moist weather. Edged with a checkered pattern, a long saddlecloth draped across the horse's sides and front. Emblazoned upon it was the emblem of House Vassaros—a black X with engrailed edges, set upon a white background bearing a golden bundle of thistle and goldenrod at its center. Though the crest and its bearers had long been relegated to minor nobility, Neifon held his shoulders square like a nobleman on parade.

As Haeryn caught the dignity in his friend's proud, yet thin figure, he smiled.

He is a relic from another age. Both confident and humble. Daring and yet firm in his lawfulness.

At the recollection of Edeveros' stringent laws, Haeryn's expression turned dour. The triumphant face of Galeras rose into his thoughts, only to be cast aside in bitter disgust as Haeryn gripped the reins of his horse and shook his head. Galeras may have been a fool, but he was a wily one, using the laws to shelter himself while simultaneously achieving his own ends.

Why should one adhere to any law that is blatantly being manipulated for evil purposes?

He looked up at Neifon. Though reserved, and even withdrawn at times, the man exuded a poignant authority that rivaled Galeras' extravagant ardor. Neifon's opposition to the baron and his knowledge of the law's manipulation was beyond doubt. Yet even in the face of corruption, he remained faithful to the edicts of his homeland. Haeryn stared into the distance, squirming as he recalled Neifon's insistence that things be done according to tradition. Even though Galeras misused the law, the Hero continued to cling to it. Contrary to what Haeryn expected, Neifon's lawfulness had not endorsed the baron's misdeeds in the slightest.

Perhaps a code of moral standards truly is just.

Haeryn shook himself from his daze, and as his mind cleared, his convictions returned with greater resilience. He stirred himself to indignant determination.

As a Wynrence, I owe the people of Edeveros a debt of honor. No law will protect Galeras from my efforts.

His thoughts were interrupted as the abrupt whinny of a horse broke through the sounds of their journey. A gilded breastplate girded Raulin's chest, bearing the coat of arms of House Estworth—minus the fox emblem that his brother Galeras had so brazenly added. Glancing at the two riders on either side of him, Raulin raised his eyebrows at their somber expressions. "Why so stone-faced?" he asked with an amused smile. "The capital is behind us, and my brother cannot reach us here. He acts like the King of Alithell, but he can barely command his stubborn butler!" A bemused smile broke Neifon's calm demeanor.

Haeryn accepted the distraction gladly. Turning in his saddle, he looked back to where Aalys rode behind them, surrounded by her armed escort. She stared at her saddlehorn, frightened by the bold presence of the warriors around her. With a twitch of pity, Haeryn turned back to Raulin. "How is she?" he asked.

Raulin's smile lessened. Glancing back, he shook his head. "She has not spoken a word since we left Mithlon," he said.

Neifon met their compassionate gazes and smiled in earnest. "Aalys will be alright once she settles into her accommodations in Gahidros. The fright of her confession and the danger of her plight will not easily be forgotten," he said. Despite his companion's assurance, Haeryn hastily suppressed an uneasy quiver in his stomach. He turned his attention to the valley surrounding them.

The Vale of Teuthros lived up to its name—the vale of clutter. On either side of the valley, broken shards of rock littered the steep slopes. The distant howl of wolves echoed on the winds, and the caw of crows joined in harmony. As Haeryn surveyed the road ahead, the wild terrain made their strategic retreat to Gahidros seem like banishment.

As they passed through the final stone corridor, the rocky hillsides veered into a wider course before falling away altogether into a tract of open heath. Ahead stretched endless fields of faded green, dotted with specks of purple heather. Farms began to appear on the horizon, clustering together in ever-growing villages. Raulin gave a sharp command, and the party of horsemen stormed across the plains, leaving the mountainous vale behind for the highlands that lay ahead. Haeryn's eyes sparkled as he glimpsed the outline of a distant structure coming into view.

Nestled within a semicircle of trees, Castle Gahidros rivaled the splendor of Mithlon with an ancient grandeur that stood the test of time. Gahidros spread across the ground like the roots of a birch, clinging to the ancient heritage birthed in the soil. Before its high walls, the shimmer of a deep moat caught Haeryn's eye, and tall spires rose skyward like royal flags in procession.

As they drew near to the castle, Raulin drew a horn from its place at his side and blew a blast of greeting. The echoing welcome of horns rang out from the ramparts in return. With the sharp clang of metal, the drawbridge bowed in homage at the approach of the Lord of Gahidros. No sooner had the bridge dropped into place, than the party of riders galloped across like a flash through the arched gateway.

Pulling back on the reins, Haeryn slowed his steed to a trot along with Neifon and Raulin. The courtyard grounds were unusually spacious. According to history, the warrior founders of Gahidros had purposely arranged the castle to accommodate their unwieldy lances.

Within the confines of the castle walls, a large, round building rivaled the size and grandeur of Gahidros' keep. A circular roof sloped above it, and drops of rain glistened as they rolled off its edges. The structure's wide doorway swung open, and Haeryn stared, mouth agape as mounted knights sallied forth to patrol the moors, their tapered banners fluttering in defiance against the light rain.

The knights ushering forth were unmistakable. Their kite shields boasted traditional Edeveran knightly crests—flora and bright artwork, set against contrasting shades of light and dark. In the overcast daylight, their plate armor glowed, yet few were free of the scars of conflict.

Seeing Haeryn's smile, Raulin laughed and sidled beside him as the Knights of the Lance paraded. "Gahidros is loyal to the traditions of the past," he said. "I do not believe an enemy could escape our vigilance."

A whinny from Neifon's horse broke through the haze of Haeryn's wonder. Glancing about, the Hero of Alithell nodded in the direction of the keep. "I fear a vigilant eye is not enough in our predicament," he remarked. He caught Haeryn's uneasy glance. "You have both the vigilance and keen mind we need, Haeryn—the Guide will lead you to use it well," he encouraged, glancing up at the ramparts hemming them in. "But we must hurry inside. Should we be followed, I do not wish to give our foe an opportunity to spot us."

But the eyes of their enemy had already riveted upon them.

22

Throughout the halls of Castle Gahidros, the crisp pelting of rain echoed off the vaulted ceilings. Surrounded by their escort, Haeryn, Neifon, Aalys, and Raulin strode past stained glass windows, inset in individual alcoves along the length of the rightmost wall. Red Aggas wood pillars stood watch, covered in bold high-reliefs.

As Haeryn relished the dignity of Gahidros, an invigorating reverence for this home of heroes filled him. The castle itself reflected the manner of the great heroes—practical, yet possessing a beguiling charm.

He paused as Raulin laid a hand upon his shoulder and pulled him and Neifon aside. Glancing between them, Raulin nodded down the corridor. "I have commanded some of the garrison to position themselves along this hallway tonight," he said.

Neifon stroked his chin. "But are they prepared for a skulking enemy?" he inquired in a hushed whisper. "Assassins adhere to the fewest scruples." By the caution in his voice, it was clear he did not wish to unsettle the soldiers around them.

Raulin considered the matter, scrutinizing the hallway with a critical eye. "Perhaps. Hopefully our foe may be dissuaded by the vigilance of a commanding armed presence," he replied with a nod of affirmation.

Their escort halted. With a brisk command from the Captain of their escort, the soldiers turned to face the single door to their left. Crafted from oak, it was painted with elegant ivy motifs in matte gold and red. Glimpsing a slight movement, Haeryn glanced back to where Aalys stood.

She withdrew back among their escort, looking at the door with mistrust. In Mithlon, Aalys had understood the danger of testifying against her former consort. Now, the consequences of her actions stood before her in waiting. Wrinkles tugged at the corners of her eyes as she wrestled with the necessity of her captivity. To reject protection would invite a dangerous alternative.

Raulin grasped the door handle—and Neifon seized his wrist to stop him. The Hero of Alithell looked to the Captain of their escort and nodded toward the door. "Send your men in first to search the room. Replace whatever food and drink lay inside—not even perfume is safe from poison. And check the closets for any hidden surprises," he commanded. With a crisp bow, the Captain assented to the Hero's demands.

Minutes passed with the thud of moving furniture and the clinking of folderol as the soldiers rummaged through the room. Several bottles of wine and perfume were carted away. As a plate of tea cakes passed by, Raulin shook his head. "I sent word from Mithlon with news of Aalys' coming. It seems that the servants' attempt to make her feel welcome will have to be redone," he sighed. A twinge of regret pricked Haeryn at the thought of the kindly cooks having to make another batch of tea cakes under outside supervision.

Neifon turned to Aalys and set a hand on her shoulder. She lifted her downcast eyes to meet his soft, understanding gaze. With a smile, he motioned toward the room. "I apologize for such considerable precaution —I can see it disconcerts you. We only wish to ensure your complete safety. Your courage to testify against Galeras has given us hope," he said, glancing at Raulin. "The Lord of Gahidros will restore your quarters to their previous state."

Raulin smiled warmly at Aalys. "You will get your tea cakes—you have my word," he said.

Suppressing a laugh, Haeryn turned aside. He considered with fondness the man's humor and gracious nature. Raulin's care for the people rivaled Roseen and Neifon's.

What a shame that his good heart suffered the brunt of Galeras' scheming.

The Captain emerged from the room, bowing to Lord Raulin and Neifon with equal respect. "The room is cleared of possible poison, and no one hides within the lady's closets," he declared, standing at attention. Raulin stifled a smile at the thought of an assassin cooped inside a small wardrobe. Taking Aalys' hand, he nodded at the Captain and entered the room, with Haeryn and Neifon following behind.

The circular bedchamber was pocketed by small alcoves, and arched vaults supported the roof, coming up to form a large star at the pinnacle. On the far end of the room, grey light streamed through glass tracery windows. The stone windowsills were set at wide intervals from one another, while wooden accents emphasized their architecture. A small curtained bed stood to the left of the door, while a simple bookshelf reinforced the subtle and plain grace of Castle Gahidros. Silent, Aalys sat on the edge of her bed and stared out one of the nearest windows.

Raulin swept a hand around the room. "Roseen and I planned for this to be our son Ancelet's room when he came of age," he reflected. "However, it also proves ideal as a safe haven against unwanted visitors." Turning aside to Neifon and Haeryn, he said, "And the size allows for maneuvering in case of conflict."

Neifon examined the room with a critical eye. "Haeryn and I will sleep on the floor to assure the night passes peacefully," he said, stepping toward the jovial Lord of Gahidros. "Raulin, I'm afraid you will have to sleep in your usual quarters."

At this, Raulin's smile weakened, and he shook his head in stubborn refusal. "I will sleep outside the door if need be," he said, determined not to abandon his friends in their time of need.

But to Haeryn's surprise, the Hero held his ground. "You are Lord of Gahidros and Grandmaster of the Knights of the Lance—you are nearly as promising a target as Aalys. If you were taken captive or slain by an assassin, Gahidros would be left leaderless and susceptible to Galeras' corruption," he replied.

Haeryn laid a reassuring hand on Raulin's arm. "It will be fine, my friend. Neifon and I will keep a strong vigil. If anything happens, we will fight to the death to protect Aalys," he promised. But as he spoke the words, he realized the gravity of his oath. He swallowed. Aalys' life was key to Galeras' defeat. Without her testimony, the Baronic Trial would never come to pass.

Night would come in time. And with the coming of the moon, men of darkness prowl freely.

Stifled screams woke Haeryn from the fog of sleep, and terror bolted through him. He seized Neifon by the shoulder. They leapt to their feet, drawing their weapons at the sight of the fallen guards in the open doorway.

Aalys lay partially dragged from her bed by the gauntleted hand around her neck. A silent figure enfolded in a blue cape faced Haeryn and Neifon as Aalys pulled at his armored arm in vain. The two, vacant eyes of Lòfroy's iron helm dared them to defy him. A second figure lingered in his shadow, brandishing two daggers.

Lòfroy tightened his grip on Aalys. "With so many soldiers about, Gahidros is a hard place to hide. But I am not easily cowed, Neifon Vassaros. Your precautions only strengthened my resolve," he taunted, reveling in his supremacy.

Neifon sprang. Dropping Aalys' limp body, Lòfroy barely dodged Neifon's streaking blade and savagely kicked him back. Lòfroy's dagger clattered to the floor as he knocked his arm against the bedpost and stumbled forward. Haeryn's training took over as he parried the mercenary's dual blades, shoving him into a nearby bookshelf. It toppled with a loud crash, crushing the man underneath.

Glass shattered as Lòfroy punched a window out, and Neifon pinned him against the windowsill, fighting to plunge his rondel dagger into the eye slit of the helm. Haeryn dashed forward with his sword.

Lòfroy was not so easily taken. Seeing the boy's rush, he twisted Neifon's wrist and backhanded Haeryn with his gauntlet. With a grunt, the boy fell against the wall, and Lòfroy swept Neifon's legs from under him. Seizing Aalys by the hair, Lòfroy shoved her out the broken window. Haeryn caught his breath as her body tumbled out of sight to the cobblestone below. He and Neifon lunged.

Lòfroy leapt out the window and into the night.

And as the air pulsed with the thump of beating wings, Haeryn stared in horror at Aalys' broken body on the cobblestone below.

23

10th of Rotanos, 2209 SE

Darkness permeated Galeras Estworth's bedroom, broken only by the light of two candles upon the nightstand. Lying fast asleep under the blankets, Galeras slept, his breathing smothered by the thunder's roar and the rain's drumming. Through the curtained window, a flash of lightning illuminated the room. The shadow looming over him did not stir.

Lòfroy shook his head as he stared at the sleeping man's vulnerability. Even Galeras Estworth had moments of weakness.

Ever since his youth, the potent musings of Lòfroy's mind had proved the greater power. He reveled in the depth of his thoughts and the emotions they stirred to life.

He clenched his jaw. The iron helm upon his head stifled both his breath and his mind. His hands involuntarily moved to remove the helmet—then stopped, falling to his sides in resignation.

My features remain the one thing that I can call my own. Dare I make vulnerable the last vestiges of myself? Never.

Lòfroy released a quiet sigh. He curled his lip in disgust as he regarded the sleeping Baron. For years, he had been the master, the schemer—now, a milksop commanded him like a child playing with his toys.

The kingdom I was promised will come in time. I must endure this disgrace.

Looking away to curb his wrath, Lòfroy gritted his teeth. He lowered his head and leaned against the nearest bedpost for support. With a heavy sigh, he regarded the sword and dagger upon his belt, and the smooth armor upon his arms and chest.

What have I become? My mind once proved my strongest weapon. Now I am a brute who instead crushes his enemies into submission? Yet only ruthlessness will succeed against the one who beat me till I yielded.

Shaking his head, Lòfroy gathered his senses. Upon the nearby nightstand, an empty glass sat beside a tall pitcher of drinking water. Pushing away from the bedpost, he grabbed it. With a smirk, Lòfroy dumped the pitcher over Galeras' face.

Galeras sat up with a gurgled cry. Gasping for air, he pushed the wet hair out of his eyes and looked wildly about. He caught sight of the looming shade at his bedside and jumped in fright. As he recognized the iron helm, Galeras scowled. "You?" he asked, his cracking voice revealing his wounded pride. With a growl of indignation, the baron looked down at the nightshirt plastered to his chest with water.

Leaning close to Galeras' face, Lòfroy placed a hand against the bedpost. "She is dead," he said. "I embark on my errand with five of my men, and leave the rest with you to do your will. There is no time to lose—my scouts have not given me any report on Fedrik."

Scooting away from Lòfroy, Galeras swallowed and raised a hand to stay the mercenary. "There is more to be done first—if you are willing," he added, gripping his bedsheets. "The Court Magistrate and Treasurer must be turned against the Baronic Trial. I will pay you double your rate." A shiver raised the hairs on his neck as he recalled this mercenary's sinister words.

Tread carefully, Galeras, and don't let your arrogance fool you into crossing me. Even Barons bleed.

Lòfroy paused, tapping his finger on the fauld of his armor. With a muttered curse he nodded his assent. "Very well. I doubt either the Court Magistrate or the Treasurer will reject my offers," he said.

He backed into the veil of shadows and motioned with his gauntleted hand. At the command, a figure emerged at the foot of the baron's bed. Though taller than Lòfroy, his thin, death-like frame made Galeras shiver. An array of daggers hung carelessly from his belt, like a collection of relics from past victories. Two piercing amber eyes peered out from a head of wavy red hair. Pointed ears revealed his race. Galeras shuddered. The elf knelt before Lòfroy, and Galeras caught a flash of spite in his eye. But the iron helm stared back undaunted, and the elf lowered his gaze in surrender.

Lòfroy gestured toward the kneeling figure. "This is Gawter, my second-in-command," he said. "During my absence, you will treat him with respect. Understood?" he asked. His words dared Galeras to defy him.

Warily eyeing Gawter and Lòfroy in turn, Galeras swallowed. "Agreed," he replied, his words choked by the knot in his throat. Without a second glance at the unnerved Baron, they withdrew, shutting the door with a firm clang.

In the outer hall, Lòfroy shoved Gawter against the wall, his gauntlets digging into the elf's shoulders. With a smile, Gawter welcomed the pain. "Until I have his full trust and cooperation, you will not touch him," Lòfroy snapped. "Or I'll scourge you myself."

Gawter grinned.

24

Bruised and bested, Haeryn and Neifon trudged to Raulin's quarters as morning rose over Gahidros. Hands limp at his sides, Haeryn hung his head in defeat. A bruise marred his youthful face as a testament to Lòfroy's brutality—yet the greatest bruises he bore were invisible to the eye.

Haeryn's heart thudded dully in his chest as he envisioned Aalys' broken body, and hot tears welled in his eyes. Mindless of Neifon's presence, he held his head in his hands. He desired to flee and hide his shame in solitude. He had failed in his knightly duty, and now he was to deliver the news to Raulin.

Chin quivering, Haeryn wiped away tears and lifted his eyes. As he searched Neifon's face, he saw a shared sorrow. And as they shared a look of understanding, the kinship of struggle drew them together. Haeryn's heart thudded at the sight of Raulin's door. He faced it in silence, brow drawn inward as he strove to muster his fortitude.

Noticing the concern on the youth's features, Neifon laid a comforting hand on Haeryn's shoulder. "I will deliver the news. Do not burden yourself any further," he said. "You fought valiantly—the mark on your cheek affirms it. You have been trained well."

Though these words lightened Haeryn's heart, he struggled to believe them.

How can a well-trained squire prove so helpless in a single attack?

Neifon stepped up to the door and hammered upon it. The hollow knocks thudded in Haeryn's chest in tandem with the beating of his heart. Urgent footsteps approached the door, and with a crisp click Raulin opened it.

His face fell as he took in the bruises and dejected looks upon their faces. He closed his eyes, leaning his forehead against the doorframe, "She is gone." Folding his hands, Neifon nodded and hung his head.

Haeryn raised his hand and touched his wounded cheek. "I did all I could," he said, pressed by the solemn bond of a knight's charge. He said no more, silenced his own simple admission.

Raulin opened his eyes and regarded the youth with a tender smile. He pushed away from the doorframe and embraced him. "I am sure you did. And as Grandmaster of the Knights of the Lance, I applaud you for your efforts," he said, holding the youth at arm's length. Haeryn's reddened eyes flashed as he looked to Raulin with pride.

"We woke to the sounds of her struggle," Neifon whispered. "It was Lòfroy."

Raulin's face hardened. His hand slipped from Haeryn's shoulder. With a quick glance down the hallways, he backed into his quarters and motioned for them to enter. As Haeryn and Neifon withdrew into the privacy of the room, Raulin hastily shut and locked the door with a resolute click.

Ribbed stone vaults soared over Haeryn's head and the room widened as he entered. A curtained bed of deep brown oak awaited the next nightfall, and a stained birchwood chest sat at its end. Spread across the breadth of a barren wall, a vivid tapestry brought the thrill of a boar hunt to Raulin's chamber. Haeryn let his eyes roam across the scene—men on horseback surrounded by baying hounds, fighting to control their steeds. The boar's snarl failed to hide the gleam of bestial fear in its eyes. Haeryn studied the scene, finding an unexpected respite from his inner hurt.

"A riveting scene, isn't it? Taken from the Grandmaster's escapades, no less," an unfamiliar voice remarked. "The honor of men can be found in the thrill of the hunt, as well as the danger of battle." Haeryn turned, noticing a previously unseen figure.

The man's combed hair and trimmed beard framed a freckled face with youthful zeal. His hand laid causally upon the hilt of his sword, and at the collar of his blue outer coat, Haeryn glimpsed concealed chainmail. A golden emblem of a cat passant was sewn onto his shoulder.

As the stranger extended his hand, Haeryn shook it. Inclining his head, the man bowed in a gesture of respect. "I am Marcas, son of Wilnor. Squire of the Lance," he said. "You can call me Marc."

Haeryn stood tall, squaring his shoulders. He returned the shallow bow. "Haeryn. Squire of Taekohar," he replied. He studied the man with excitement. "My aunt Gwyndel told me stories of a young man named Marc. He joined the forces of Captain Beydan in Rehillon years ago," he said.

A grin brightened Marc's face, shining through his eyes. "The very same," he replied. At this, Haeryn grinned.

Clearing his throat, Neifon strode to Marc's side and briefly embraced him. "Pardon my interruption, but there are matters we must discuss," he said with an amused smile at Haeryn. "Marc is like a son to me."

Raulin paced across the hardwood floor with head bowed. He pressed his palm to his forehead with a forceful sigh. "Without Aalys' testimony, the Baronic Trial cannot continue—she was the sole witness to Galeras' scheming. I must send a letter to Roseen to inform her," he muttered. "She should receive the pigeon's message before nightfall." He glanced at Haeryn, hoping his comment had not pricked the youth's guilt. Haeryn's smile faded, and Raulin's spirits waned with it.

Striding past Raulin to a nearby shelf, Neifon pulled out a book and flipped through it. The crisp flap of the pages cleared his thoughts, and the familiar touch of parchment soothed him. "Galeras may have Lòfroy's aid for the time being, but that will not last for long. Lòfroy is clearly strong-willed, and determined to get what he desires. I presume that, if he feels manipulated by Galeras, he will betray him," he mused. "But let us not occupy ourselves with possibilities that are beyond our influence. Galeras will not be content with this single act of murder. Since

Aalys' death cannot be traced back to him by hard evidence, he will be emboldened to attempt greater, more daring actions."

Haeryn's thoughts wandered back to the drunkenness of the Baron, and as he observed Neifon, he remembered the Hero's words.

Be thankful, Haeryn, that you do not bear the burden of position as I do.

Haeryn's face grew taut with worry, and he swallowed. "Galeras has his eyes set on you. As Chief of Court, you have challenged him publicly," he said. "You may be his next victim." Marc's hand fell from his chin, and Raulin's pacing steps ceased. All eyes turned to the Chief of Court.

The crinkle of turning pages stopped. Neifon's eyes locked with Haeryn's—but his expression was unreadable. "I do not fear him," he said. As he spoke, his eyes briefly flashed with inspiration, then dimmed in a sudden change of mood.

Raulin stroked his square jaw. "Galeras will surely have his eyes set upon the other chief courtiers—the Court Magistrate, the Treasurer, and the Chancellor. There is little knowing his intentions for them. We must act quickly," he insisted.

Roaming across the room, Haeryn cocked his head, his gaze bouncing back and forth as he sought for a solution. It would take a dilemma Galeras could not ignore.

His eyes wandered to a large shield hanging above him, displaying the Estworth coat of arms for all to see. As he contemplated the sight, a triumphant half-smile spread across his face. Turning to Raulin, he pointed toward it. "Edeveros is the oldest territory of Alithell. The people must be proud of this," he said. The beginnings of an idea began to form in his mind.

Raulin shot a quizzical glance toward the familiar crest. "They are," he agreed with an uncertain frown. Catching the glint of victory in the youth's eye, he held his breath, hopeful.

With a gleam in his eye, Haeryn held his hands loosely behind his back and strode toward the Lord of Gahidros. "You are the Grandmaster of the Knights of the Lance. You can stir the people's pride—and spread word of a rogue mercenary that prowls the moors and forests in search of victims. Make known Lòfroy's name," he declared.

Neifon frowned in disapproval. "Such a false statement could sow mass hysteria across Edeveros," he warned. The insistence in his voice was lost on the youth.

Haeryn inclined his head. "Or, perhaps they will pressure the baron to deliver them from Lòfroy's menace," he countered. "Galeras most certainly will not want to bring Lòfroy's wrath down upon himself. If he is goaded to hunt down his ally, he may ignore the issue. His unwillingness to pursue such a blatant threat to the peace would arouse suspicion."

As Raulin considered Haeryn's words, he nodded, his widening grin shining through his eyes. "But as Baron of Edeveros, Galeras *must* personally lead his armed troops against Lòfroy," he said. "Should Galeras refuse, the people will demand an explanation—and if one is not given, they may rise up against him. In time, Galeras' alliance with Lòfroy will be exposed, and he will be deemed an unworthy baron in the eyes of the law." He lifted his eyes to the heavens with a hearty laugh of relief. "Thank the Guide!" he exclaimed. "I will instruct my Steward to begin arrangements for a parade. Once the people's love of country is stirred, word of Lòfroy will be spread."

Shaking his head, Neifon bowed in surrender. "I suppose there is no alternative for such a wily foe. Haeryn and I will journey back to Mithlon tomorrow. Perhaps the Court Magistrate, the Treasurer, and the Chancellor will aid us in our cause," he said. He spun on his heels and moved for the door, with Haeryn following.

"Wait," Raulin said, holding up a hand to stay them. As his companions turned, he strode toward them with an air of decision. "I will return with you in secret. As long as Roseen and my son are entrenched in Mithlon, Galeras has only to lift a finger to command his men to harm her. I will not stand by if Lòfroy has his eyes set on my family," he insisted, his brow furrowed with fierce concern.

Laying a hand on Neifon's shoulder, Raulin turned the focus of his unease on the Hero. "As Haeryn said, Galeras would most certainly welcome your demise, Neifon. Your life is too precious to leave undefended. Marc will serve as your bodyguard." At this, Marc stood at attention and bowed in a solemn gesture of allegiance.

Lost in a moment of thought, Neifon regarded Marc with a pained glance. He flashed a smile to briskly conceal his troubled expression. "Very well. You are skilled beyond many of your peers, Marcas, and I trust you. I doubt an assassin could escape your vigilance," he said.

25

12th of Rotanos, 2209 SE

The curtain of mist withdrew from the Vale of Teuthros like a veil, rippling on the breeze as it revealed the sun. The light warmed the sky as if to hearten the company of riders weaving along the valley's winding path. Under the scrutiny of the daylight, the slopes of the vale lost their guise of bleakness.

Lingering behind his companions, Haeryn idly guided his horse along the stone path. He withdrew into the solitude of his thoughts, deaf to the clinking of armor around him as he contemplated Aalys' death. The clear highland air failed to cleanse him from the wrenching guilt that haunted him. He envisioned her wild eyes darting about as she struggled, clawing for breath. In a terrible twist of fate, those charged to protect her life proved inept. The shock had crippled them—mocked their warrior's hearts. Haeryn hung his head, wearied by the somber thought. He recalled the words his father had spoken years ago, when he was no more than an adopted waif.

Death is not the end. The Kingdom above the stars awaits.

The further he considered it, the more Haeryn found himself doubting. As a yearning strained at his heart, calling him to believe, his childhood stirred him to question the sentiment. The memory of the Kinsfolk gods and the traditions of Norgalok set his teeth on edge. Olthroc and the gods had proved themselves powerless to save their priests and shrines.

But the Guide—he saved us all in Ellokon. And I spoke to him face to face.

He hesitated. In the past, Eyoés, Gwyndel, and Vakros had spoken of the Guide with awe shining on their faces. The sight had sparked a longing in Haeryn that, even when besieged by doubts, would not release him from its grip. Because of its persistence, his iron heart had lost its edge—and it frightened Haeryn more than his doubts. Squinting as he delved deeper into his thoughts, he fingered the reins. As he struggled to bear the fresh burden of Aalys' death, Haeryn struggled to accept the Guide's methods. The abuse he had endured in Norgalok continued to work its destruction through the skepticism it instilled in him.

Death is a fact of life. But why does the Guide not openly fight evil?

No answers rose to rebuff his questions. Too absorbed in his doubts, Haeryn was oblivious to Neifon's troubled gaze. The Hero fell back from Marc and Raulin to ride beside the youth. He was stricken by Haeryn's grief. "Does Aalys' death still trouble you?" he inquired.

Torn from his thoughts, Haeryn looked up at Neifon, despondent. "We were charged with her protection, Neifon. Yet we failed. Even as a Hero of Alithell, you could not stand against Lòfroy," he said.

"I am bound by my oath to fight and defend—and Aalys died on my watch." He looked away, striking the saddlehorn with his fist and gritting his teeth as he fought back tears.

Neifon paused, drawing himself up. His brow furrowed. Turning ahead, he nodded in understanding. "You were not the only one charged to guard her life," he said, guiding his horse around a section of cracked and broken roadway.

Haeryn's ears reddened. He lowered his head. "I did not mean to slight you," he apologized.

Neifon brushed the youth's apology aside. "You didn't," he insisted. He smiled. "You were bold to confront Lòfroy. And you nearly shared Aalys' fate because of your boldness," he pointed out. "Even the most experienced of warriors suffer defeat. Lòfroy caught us both off guard. You fought well. I shall send my commendation to your Master Knight, Sir Thrynnis. He taught you well." Haeryn grimaced as the Vale of Teuthros stretched out ahead.

Failure was not worthy of praise.

26

12th of Rotanos, 2209 SE

Evraxis Sarall, Treasurer of Edeveros, woke to the crackling of his fireplace. Squinting, he yawned, greeted by the red curtains of his bed. They were drawn and tied to the bedposts to admit the fireplace's warmth. In the darkness, the marble walls glowed. Suppressing another yawn, Evraxis closed his eyes and lingered in bed. A light clinking sounded above the crackling of the logs. His brow furrowed, and his eyes searched the shadows. A bitter taste lingered on his tongue.

Perhaps Merilda needed a drink of water.

He rolled over in bed to where his wife lay. His heart skipped. Bound hand and foot, she lay motionless, her tears staining her pillow. A bundle of cloth nearly choked her, and she looked up at her husband with a whimper. With a gasp, Evraxis threw off the covers and leapt from his bed.

Shrouded in the flickering firelight and shadow, an armored figure stood, as if merely waiting to be noticed. Evraxis' horror turned to wrath as he stabbed a finger at the figure, warily edging toward it. "Who do you think you are? How dare you hurt her!" he exclaimed.

Lòfroy's laugh rang in the prison of his iron helm. The thud of his boots on the wood-covered floor unnerved the Treasurer as he approached. "You and your wife are unhurt, though quite drowsy due to the alocress. It saved me the trouble of you both sounding the alarm," Lòfroy said, casting a disinterested glance to where one of his men held a knife to the woman's throat. "I have more important things to attend to tonight. I will have your silence—or she'll have my blade."

Several men emerged from the corners of the room and surrounded Evraxis. The Treasurer looked into their masked faces with a bewildered stare. Reveling in the man's confusion, Lòfroy smiled underneath his helmet. He removed a leather sack from his belt, holding it before the Treasurer and shaking it to allude to its jingling contents. "I am only here to ask for a favor," he said. "You received the financial records involved in the charges against Galeras Estworth, did you not?"

Evraxis nodded. A creeping suspicion raised the hairs on his neck. As Treasurer, he had been entrusted with the records for the Baronic Trial. With such responsibility came fear—though Evraxis had quickly dispelled his misgivings. Bribes were no stranger to the courts of Edeveros, and as he regarded the bag of coins, he realized the predicament he was in.

Even so, he wrinkled his nose in disgust. "I may enjoy the comforts of Galeras' Baronship, but I have my convictions. I vowed to myself to uphold my grandfather's legacy, and the records of Galeras' accusers were in order," he retorted. The whimpering pleas of his wife were lost to him.

Lòfroy tightened his grip around the sack of coins, and returned it to his belt. The cold stare of his helm transfixed the Treasurer. "So be it," he muttered. The men behind Evraxis seized him by the wrists and wrenched his arms behind him. Striding to the darkest corner of the room, two other men heaved an iron vat into the light with grunts of effort. With a clang, they set it before the Treasurer and lifted the lid. Evraxis hesitated as he saw the glistening liquid within.

Casually removing his gauntlets and setting them on the wooden chest at the foot of the bed, Lòfroy removed a flint and steel from his belt. As the Treasurer fought against those restraining him, the mercenary wandered toward the vat and struck his flint and steel into it several times. A cloud of sparks fluttered into the vat, and a whoosh of flames stilled the Treasurer's struggle. In the light of the wild flames, Lòfroy returned his flint and steel to its place and put on his gauntlets. "Drowning in water is torturous enough, Evraxis Sarall. But drowning in flaming oil is quite a spectacle," he remarked.

The Treasurer's eyes bulged. He flailed in the grip of his captors, trying to tear himself away. With venomous grins, they shoved him forward. Evraxis struggled to backpedal, his feet slipping out from under him. His wife Merilda's muffled screams compounded his suffering. One of the men drove his fist into Evraxis' stomach to force him to bend over, bringing his face closer and closer to the flames. Shrinking back, Evraxis felt the heat singe his dainty mustache. "Wait!" he cried.

His captors relented, yanking him back from the brink of torture as the other men covered the vat with its iron lid to starve the flames. Turning to the Treasurer, Lòfroy folded his arms across his chest. Evraxis gasped for breath as the men released him, and his knees shook. "I will accept your bribe," he said, a tinge of regret in his voice.

Lòfroy clapped in approval. "You have proven yourself an intelligent man," he said.

27

Eyoés closed his eyes as the gentle rain cooled his face, trickling down into his short beard. As he inhaled a draught of crisp, misty air, the quietude within him matched the stillness outside. Opening his eyes, he brushed his sodden hair aside and scanned the land around him. The stillness seemed so out of place in comparison to the strenuous days spent among Fedrik and his family.

Suppressing a shiver as rain trickled down into his shirt, Eyoés glanced sidelong toward the cabin door. He shifted where he stood, crossing his arms as the humble family's predicament weighed on him. They clearly cared about one other—perhaps even to a fault. But a tension pervaded over them like a bowstring about to snap, and every dawn brought the expectation of a new, crushing revelation or moment of weakness and despondency.

He recalled the startling image of Fedrik huddled against the wall, weeping at Erling's revelation. Eyoés lifted his eyes to the moorlands. It was clear that Fedrik's unstable moods and somber demeanor continued to unsettle those closest him. In an effort to ease the burden and bring cheerfulness to the modest family, Eyoés and Gwyndel had strived to aid in as many tasks as possible. Chopping firewood, tailoring old clothes, gardening—though they eased the poor family's load, much remained the same. Only in times of music and storytelling did a smile even touch Fedrik's expression.

But Eyoés did not forget.

His mind wandered back to Asdale's rising obsession with seeking pleasure rather than harmony through service. He had been overwhelmed by the tide of change. No longer. One man could not convince all to see the light. But when faced with the opportunity to brighten one man's life, Eyoés found his chance and took it.

Mind alert, he blew into his hands to warm them. Eyoés wrapped his fingers around the door handle, paused to gather his senses, and entered the cabin. Embracing the warmth of the fireplace, he shut the door and wiped his damp face with a nearby towel.

"Back so soon?" Fedrik inquired. He looked up, grasping a woodcarving knife in one hand and a newly hewn axe handle in the other. Before his guest could reply, Fedrik returned to his work, carefully whittling away the wood to fit the blade on the table before him.

Eyoés hung the towel and removed his boots. "I needed the cool air to refresh myself," he said, glancing around his feet to make sure he wasn't dripping water. He placed one of the chairs in front of the fireplace. "Are Gwyndel and Kerensa still picking watercress and brassolary from the garden?" he asked.

Fedrik nodded. Meeting Eyoés' look with a teary eye, he smiled. "You two have done much to aid us during your stay," he acknowledged. "I cannot thank you enough."

Eyoés smiled in return. "When I intrude upon another's home, I strive to be a relief, not a burden," he answered, leaning forward and extending his chilled hands toward the fire. "Are you going out in search for game?"

The scrape of Fedrik's carving knife came to an abrupt halt. Clearing his throat, he shot a wary glance toward the cabin door and shifted in his seat. "No," he said, his curt reply as stiff as his posture. Silent, he returned to his carving, ignoring the slight chill that raised the hair on his arms and neck.

Eyoés understood the man's unwillingness to venture out into the unknown. With Lòfroy and his men haunting the wilderness like revenants, all converging on Fedrik's poor soul, he did not blame the man for his unease.

But Eyoés knew it was not only his peril that burdened the man's mind. His pulse quickened as he collected himself, pushing his damp hair out of his face. Pursing his lips, he watched Fedrik out of the corner of his eye and curbed a sigh. "You are tormented, Fedrik—I have seen it, and so has Gwyndel. What troubles you?" he asked. "How can I help ease your burden?"

Shaving off a curled flake of wood from the axe handle, Fedrik stared across the room. His eyes glistened. He let his woodcarving knife slip from his limp fingers to the table. Averting his gaze, he shook his head with conviction. "One who brings suffering upon others will find *himself* suffering for his wrongs. My past life condemns me—there is no changing that," he said, slumping in his chair as he resigned himself to his fate.

Eyoés gently grasped Fedrik's hand and regarded the man with fixed attentiveness. "There is forgiveness for past wrongs—I know it well," he encouraged. The heartfelt certainty in his words and his behavior lightened Fedrik's look of defeat.

Looking into Eyoés' eyes with a weak smile, Fedrik shook his head. "Not for me," he replied, his hushed voice breaking. Blinking away tears, he hung his head and returned to his work.

Eyoés faltered, his hand pulling away and falling to his side. A desire to press the matter gripped him as he recalled the position of influence he found himself in— but an inner prodding restrained him.

Let him be. In time, his tears will dry, and his grief will fade in the light of a new deliverance.

At the Guide's voice, Eyoés pursed his lips and nodded in compliance. "Perhaps I should find Erling and assist him with the flocks," he said with a compassionate smile. Returning the chair under the table, he started for the door. The scraping of chair legs stopped him.

"Thank you," Fedrik said with a nod of gratitude.

Eyoés turned to Fedrik and flashed a smile. "The peace I bring is not my own. Should you need company, I will never turn you away," he declared.

Gwyndel's broom whisked the cabin floor, and her bright eyes sparkled as they roved across the mismatched wooden floorboards. With a contented smile, she strove to bestow a simple gift on her hosts as she swept the last traces of dirt and dust away. She straightened and combed her hair with her fingers with a smile of satisfaction. Setting the broom in a nearby corner, Gwyndel watched Fedrik mend a broken leather strap. "Is there anything else I can do for you?" she inquired, her face glowing.

Kerensa looked up from her sewing and blushed. "You've done more than your share. Rest for a while," she insisted. Pausing her work, she patted the chair next to her in an invitation to rest.

Gwyndel smiled, stretching her limbs. "I relish the work—it makes me feel useful. But a brief rest would be welcome," she said. Spotting the nearby keg of water, she retrieved a cup.

A sudden wave of dizziness overtook her. All around her sharpened into clear focus, yet as she looked around, a surreal distance set her apart from her surroundings. Gwyndel collapsed in a heap and the cup clattered to the floor. Kerensa and Fedrik sprang from their seats and rushed to her side. A shocked stare covered Gwyndel's paled face.

Fedrik seized Gwyndel by the shoulders and shook her. "Gwyndel! Are you alright?" he asked, his voice growing louder with panic.

As if startled from a dream, Gwyndel gasped and blinked, her curly red locks disheveled. Noticing Fedrik and Kerensa, she reached out a hand to steady herself. Swaying as she stood, she stared at Fedrik, her brow furrowed in disbelief.

So that is what is to come.

Haunted by the vision she had seen, Gwyndel swallowed and mustered a weak smile. "I'm fine—I just need a drink," she said.

Kerensa took her by the arm and seated her at the table while Fedrik picked up the fallen cup and filled it from the water keg. With a hasty nod, he set the cup before her. Gwyndel smiled in gratitude, clearly seeing the strain of worry tighten its grip on him. Taking the cup with shaking hands, she drank deeply. None dared to speak further of the matter.

The verdict had been decided.

28

19th of Rotanos, 2209 SE

The moon seized its throne, and the night haze sparked alight with an ethereal blue glow. Trees grew indistinct within the fog, stranded like islands upon on the rolling moors. The song of crickets thrummed in Eyoés' ears as he peered into the endless darkness. He made out a barren tree looming out of the depths, the dark, sodden wood standing black in comparison to the moon's glow. As he leaned back against the cabin, Eyoés' eyes traveled up its stiff, sprawling branches. The stillness of the night soothed his mind like a salve. In peace, he faced his thoughts anew. The distant bleating of sheep brought a brief smile as he thought of the shepherd who cared for them by day. Despite the trials battering his family, Erling clung to mercy and pitied his father's despair.

But for how long? How much more suffering can they withstand before they snap like twigs?

He opened his eyes, considering the gaunt, frail branches at the tree's top. Glancing to the cabin door beside him, Eyoés bit his tongue. Danger was brewing. He was certain. Something intended to shatter them. Whatever came, Eyoés was determined to remain by their side through it all, and deny Lòfroy his chance.

He blinked away the mist upon his eyelashes. Eyoés crouched, his arms resting on his knees. Neifon's words reminded him of his responsibility to both Edeveros and to those closest to him.

We need you. Galeras will undoubtedly use the griffin for his own wicked ends—that is, if Lòfroy's presence goes unchallenged.

Gazing up into the lambent sky, Eyoés envisioned the golden flicker of Gibusil's wings interspersed with the alternating shades of blue. Without his full range of vision, Gibusil would be hard-pressed to unleash his full strength upon the enemy. Lòfroy's griffin would surely exploit the weakness. There was no telling when the enemy would strike—and there was little Eyoés could do to prepare. As he pondered the outcome of the inevitable, he pressed a loosely clasped fist to his lips.

The realization unnerved him. With both his concern for Gibusil and his duty to protect his companions pressing in on him, his attention was divided across two fronts. Eyoés bit his lip, the sharp pain expressing his misgivings. Whether Lòfroy's aspirations were greater than a single murder was uncertain. Neifon had mentioned that the mercenary had met with Galeras Estworth, and from his experience in Rehillon, Eyoés knew those who kept such weak-minded company were likely set upon exploitation. Edeveros was desperate for champions in its trying time.

Standing, he rubbed his arms to ward off the cold. He took a final glance into the blue haze and turned for the cabin door.

A hand held him back, and Eyoés spun to snatch whoever had laid hold of him. His heart skipped. The moors about him were lifeless and desolate, save for the chirping crickets, and a tingling like sparks burned in his shoulder. As his heart thundered, Eyoés recognized the warmth that lingered.

What does the Guide seek of me?

He peered into the night with an uncertain frown. No white cloak appeared in the darkness. No gleam of light. The gloom continued, unbroken. Eyoés hesitated, eyes narrowed as premonition fell upon his shoulders like a sack of rocks.

A warning?

The distant peal of hooves caught his ear.

Gwyndel startled awake with a gasp. Drawing her dagger, she cast aside her blankets. Before she could shout a warning, a hand clamped over her mouth. "Don't speak. Gather our supplies and run for the moors," whispered a harsh voice. In the darkness, Gwyndel recognized Eyoés and fell silent, sheathing her dagger and gathering her things.

The rustling of blankets broke the stillness, and Gwyndel glimpsed Eyoés stooping over Erling's bed. Jostled from sleep, the boy nearly leapt out of his cot in fright. Placing a finger against his lips, Eyoés restrained him and looked pointedly at Erling to assure his understanding.

"What is the meaning of this?" Fedrik asked, his voice hoarse as he wiped the sleep from his eyes. By his side, Kerensa tossed in bed.

Turning to Fedrik, Eyoés gestured to the door, his eyes bright with growing apprehension. "Prepare to flee," he whispered. "I fear your enemies are catching up to you." The sleep vanished from Fedrik's eyes. He shook Kerensa.

Gwyndel shot an anxious glance to the door, as she stuffed provisions into her bag. She snatched her bow from where it lay. Eyoés noticed her ordinary weapon. "Fóbehn?" he asked.

With a disgusted snort, Gwyndel growled. "I didn't expect trouble," she replied.

Eyoés dashed to the open doorway and squinted into the night. He glanced back to where the family hurriedly dressed.

"Is there time?" Gwyndel asked.

Eyoés gritted his teeth. "Barely. But the fog will conceal us," he said. Gwyndel nodded for the others to follow as she dashed out into the night. Eyoés stepped aside to let them pass. Fedrik held his wife and son close as he shot a wistful glance at their cold beds. Erling clung to his father's cloak, his face pallid as Kerensa spoke unsteady words of comfort. They struggled to leave their sanctuary.

"If you tarry, you destroy all hope for a future— Erling's future," he urged through clenched teeth. His desperate tone broke through their daze. The small family ran out into the night, and Eyoés closed the door.

The haze of blue transformed them into phantoms. Underfoot, the gnarled moors rose to trip Eyoés as he ran after the others. Shielding Kerensa and Erling under the shelter of his billowing cloak, Fedrik broke away from Gwyndel's trail, briskly escorting his family behind cover. Bewildered by the unexpected change of course, Eyoés drew Gwyndel's attention with a small whistle. She gave him a puzzled glance as she noticed the missing family. He motioned to a hillock, and they dashed to where it lay almost hidden in the gloom.

"What are you thinking?" Eyoés asked the cowering family. Falling to a crouch, Gwyndel studied Kerensa and Fedrik.

Kerensa shook her head, eyes wide in panic. "We *must* hide!" she insisted. She pressed herself against the ground as if to bury herself. In her wild, harried appearance, Gwyndel recognized the senseless terror of the hunted. To move was to be seen.

Fedrik nodded in agreement. His eyes flared in obstinate refusal as he nodded toward the cabin. "I will not flee and let my livelihood be desecrated!" he snapped. He made no move to rise.

Squinting, Eyoés caught sight of the cabin, nearly lost in the fog. From a distance, it seemed insignificant, but the huddled family stared at the cottage as if it was encrusted in gold. The cabin was more than a warm home and a bed.

It stands for the life they have forged together—the battles they have won together. They are desperate to preserve it.

With a nod of surrender, Eyoés laid flat upon the hillock and waited. A long silence passed as they held their breath, anticipating the worst. Squinting, he glimpsed several horsemen approaching with stealth. As he looked sidelong at Gwyndel, he saw her fidget with a blade of grass. In an attempt to reassure her, Eyoés mustered his confidence.

The Guide is the one protecting Fedrik's life. Not Gwyndel. Nor I.

The riders halted before the lonely cabin, motioning wordless commands among themselves. As he watched them pull torches from their saddlebags, Eyoés clenched his fists, cursing his helplessness. Sparks flashed to life, and the indigo veil around the cabin dissipated as torches surrounded it like a pyre. Fedrik gasped, clutching Kerensa as she muffled her weeping against his chest. Nestled between his parents, Erling gaped at the violation of his childhood haven. Eyoés hung his head.

The thud of wingbeats stopped his heart, and as Eyoés lifted his eyes, the moonlight revealed a dark, soaring shape.

The griffin.

Eyoés shuddered, slinking back to assure his concealment behind the knoll. The creature's grey feathers were tipped with crimson, as if sprinkled with blood. The silvery scales upon its forearms glistened in the moonlight. Two gleaming eyes peered from under a crown of scarlet and grey feathers. Slighter in build than Gibusil, it swooped to the ground and landed with an astonishing swiftness. Like a stone-hearted effigy, the dark figure of Lòfroy sat rigid in the saddle.

Wrapping his reins around the saddlehorn, Lòfroy dismounted, and the men surrounding the cottage turned to him, awaiting his command. Eyoés held his breath. Lòfroy drew a torch from his saddlebag and set it alight with another man's flaming brand. He paused, transfixed. Then, with a laugh, he tossed it onto the thatched roof, and the others followed suit. As the fire surged to life, the thatch gave way and collapsed in a smoldering bundle. Fedrik hung his head, shoulders heaving. Erling looked away, and Gwyndel choked back tears. As the flames writhed under the walls, Eyoés shuddered at the resemblance to Asdale's fall.

A gust of wind surged and a shrill roar made Eyoés leap up. His face paled.

Gibusil cut through the mantle of smoke like a blade, colliding headlong into Lòfroy's griffin. With a shriek of pain, the creature thrashed as it struggled to recover. The cloud of smoke churned in billows, and Gibusil darted into the darkness. Startled, Lòfroy staggered back and shouted a desperate command. As the cutthroats scrambled together, Gibusil sped through their midst, scattering them like ants as they fell victim to his claws. The grey griffin screeched in wild fury, and Gibusil pounced, throwing the smaller creature into a pile of rubble. With a desperate roar, Gibusil tore into the ruins, heedless of the heat and flames. Fedrik rose to his knees, watching the violence with a haunted stare.

Eyoés' eyes widened.

Gibusil thinks we're still inside!

Gwyndel scrambled to her feet as her brother dashed down the slope, sword aloft. "Eyoés, wait!" she shouted, shrugging her bow off her shoulder. At the sound of her voice, Gibusil lifted his head, searching with his one good eye. As the grey griffin sprang up from the rubble, Gibusil lashed it with his tail. Whipping an arrow from her quiver, Gwyndel aimed at the scattered henchmen and let fly.

A whistling arrow cut one man down as Eyoés dashed into the chaos, smoke stinging his eyes. Dodging an erratic sword blow, he spun on his heels and cut the man down. He faced the burning wreckage, the silhouettes of warring griffins thrashing within the flames. "Gibusil!" he cried, shying back as foes dashed forward to overwhelm him. Arrows whizzed through the air, plucking off his adversaries one by one in quick succession.

Gibusil shot through the wreckage, plucking him from the ground. Wincing at the hot touch of his griffin's talons, Eyoés craned his neck back toward the cabin's ruins. Snarling insults, the grey griffin hung back, unwilling to pursue Gibusil. Dazed by the swift assault, Lòfroy caught sight of Eyoés and stiffened.

Gibusil's wings swelled as he reared back and placed his master atop the hillock. As Eyoés lurched to his feet, Gwyndel ran to his side, looking down on the scene of confusion below. "Gibusil cannot carry all of us," she said.

Eyoés shook his head. Placing a hand against her cheek, he leaned close to her. "The Guide warned me of this attack. He wills Fedrik to live—I am sure of it. We must get a horse," he said. "But only the Keeper of the Sword Imperishable can do it." There was little time to debate.

The last remaining horseman galloped toward them, chunks of sod flying in his wake. Setting her eyes on the approaching horseman, Gwyndel charged —and the Sword Imperishable raged to life in her hand.

Eluding a whistling blade, Gwyndel sheared it from its hilt and sliced the saddle girth, spilling the man to the ground. He tumbled down from the steady incline, coming to lay lifeless at its base. As quickly as it had come, the Sword Imperishable vanished in a wisp of blue. Gwyndel mounted the saddle and galloped back to her companions.

As she helped Fedrik into the saddle behind her, she saw his confusion. "It distinguishes between good and evil," she explained, heart pounding as Eyoés scrambled atop Gibusil with Kerensa and Erling. Gwyndel rode into the night, followed by the deep thud of Gibusil's wingbeats. The silence settled over the smoldering ruins, with only the crackling fire to challenge it. Lòfroy hesitated.

His prey was *not* helpless—and now he wanted revenge against three, not one.

29

13th of Rotanos, 2209 SE

The steady beat of Haeryn's footsteps rang out in the stillness of Castle Mithlon. Ascending the stairs alongside Neifon and Marc, he traced the wrought-iron banister to his right with his fingers. Haeryn leaned over the railing, stomach crawling at the great height. As thoughts of Aalys' cruel fall flashed in his mind, he stepped away and quickened his pace.

Clearing his throat, Haeryn tugged at the collar of his modest overcoat. At Neifon's insistence, the castle seamstresses had measured the youth after the banquet and sewn him a full uniform. Although the Wynrence colors of purple and slate-grey brought an unnatural flair to his pragmatic bearing, a growing sense of identity cemented his heritage with pride. He *would* be worthy of it.

Haeryn glanced to Neifon, and his pride was humbled.

He is a man of high honor. How can I boast of my heritage when he does not?

Beside him, Marc noticed him lingering in Neifon's shadow as they ascended the next flight of stairs. He smiled to himself and followed his friend's example. Lost in contemplation, Haeryn did not notice this attempt at fraternity.

Checkered stones drew their eyes ahead to the set of doors before them. Graceful floral designs in bold metalwork represented well the feminine strength of the Lady of Gahidros. Neifon knocked and fell back with hands clasped in patient expectancy. The doors swung inward to reveal a lady-in-waiting standing before them with a quick curtsy. With a brief word of thanks, Marc held the door for her, and Neifon and Haeryn entered. The scuffling of small feet brought a smile to the Chief of Court's face.

A small child scampered toward them, bouncing with each wobbly step. His long blonde hair curled about his plump face, and his eyes widened with curiosity. At the sight of Neifon, a grin brightened the child's sweet face. "Nuncle 'Ayfon!" he shouted with a merry giggle.

Neifon welcomed the little boy's embrace. "Hello, little Ancelet!" he said, sweeping the child into his arms and spinning about. Haeryn was caught unawares by the broad smile on his companion's normally reserved face. Neifon knelt and ruffled the boy's hair with a laugh. Straying from his uncle's side, Ancelet played with the nearby carpet, lifting it up to see what lay beneath.

"I am glad you have returned," a voice said. "If only it was with better tidings." Haeryn turned to see Roseen Estworth seated in a nearby chair. She motioned to the maidservant. "There are things I must discuss in private—but be sure Ancelet returns in time for dinner," she declared, catching her son's scattered attention. "Go play with Padia, and then we'll have time for a story!" At this, the boy's eyes widened in giddy excitement. With a quick bow, the maidservant took the child's hand and departed. Marc waved at Ancelet as he closed the doors behind them.

Neifon sighed and ventured across the room to where Roseen sat. "You received our message, I presume," he said.

With a heavy sigh, Roseen rested her forehead against her hand and stared out a nearby window. Her eyes seemed tired—tired of the tension and struggle that tore Edeveros apart. She stood, taking up a cup of steaming tea from a nearby table and letting the aroma clear her head. "We've lost our witness, and the court is compromised. Our challenge is impotent," she sighed, her head bowing under the verdict's weight.

Haeryn spun to face Roseen. He stepped toward her with brow furrowed, leaning forward as if to hear better. "How so?" he thought aloud, sharing a troubled glance with Neifon. Marc turned to Roseen with an expectancy that was unfazed by her rank. The crisp crackling of ensconced candles covered for Roseen's hesitancy.

Closing her eyes, Roseen gathered her senses. "Killing the witness was not Galeras' only move," she said, her expression grave. "The Court Magistrate, rejected the Lords' Charter of Accusation outright. He recalled how I imprisoned innocents in my frenzied search after Raulin's jousting accident. He determined the Charter cannot be considered trustworthy due to my involvement. Supposedly, I am 'unstable'," she said, shaking her head and looking back to Neifon and Haeryn. "Our case is dead."

Haeryn clenched his jaw. "Have any of the Lords' charges survived?" he inquired. He held his breath, hoping for the survival of their efforts.

Roseen flung her teacup to the floor in frustration. The sudden crash made Haeryn flinch. "Only a petty tarnish on his reputation, which will do nothing," she remarked. "The Lords have departed to return to their own estates."

Marc paced about, the firm tap of his boots exuding a strength of will. "The Guide will provide a way. If we act upon his Proverbs and obey the law, victory *will* come," he asserted. The conviction in his voice shone in committed hope.

Haeryn questioned his companion's optimism. He worked to suppress his indignation at their misfortunes. As he closed his eyes, he could feel the summons to action grip him. Despite the growing urgency, he held his tongue, irritated at his their inability to see reason. To his thinking, law was to be abandoned in such a crisis, not obeyed.

Why do we insist on a trial? Throw the fool from his throne!

Neifon pinched the bridge of his nose with a sigh of exasperation. "We have kept Galeras' corruption at bay for years, and now, he finally ensnared the chief courtiers! Upon our arrival today, one of my spies informed me that the Treasurer had been bribed— under threat of death," he declared. Haeryn's heart plunged at the thought of Lòfroy's brutal methods. He shuddered to think of the peril that compelled the Treasurer to turn traitor.

Blind to the tea stains on her dress, Roseen shook her head, and Haeryn caught the glint of bitter tears in her eyes. "How long before the Chancellor is bribed, or murdered, or threatened?" she said. "We must ride the storm and hope it will spare us." Neifon looked out the window as the patter of rainfall began, fighting to collect himself. The confidence that had come from being a Hero of Alithell suffered from this blow to their efforts.

The determination in Marc's eyes softened at the sight of Roseen's dejection. He wandered toward her with a kind smile. "You speak out of fear. I know how that feels," he said, the former strength in his voice now replaced with compassion. "It's easier to doubt honor than fight for it. But integrity is its own reward, and can change all who come in contact with it. We have every confidence in you, Roseen." Haeryn turned away, convicted as he wrestled to subject Marc's words to his own standards.

Neifon's hope rekindled. "We must consider the matter akin to a game of intellect, not as the triumph of our enemies. Galeras' schemes must be met with maneuvers of our own. As Trystem of Toldan once said—'If we play the game with skill, there is always a chance for triumph,'" he said, his confident smile driving away Roseen's somberness. "I will send a messenger to inform Raulin."

Roseen frowned. "A herald? Wouldn't it be quicker to send a pigeon to Gahidros?" she objected.

Haeryn interjected, "The Grandmaster returned to Mithlon in secret. He wanted to assure you were safe should Galeras' attempt—"

The locked door clicked open. Haeryn and Marc spun toward the open doorway, seizing the hilts of their swords—and Neifon snatched their wrists to restrain them. Flanked by two guards, a wide-eyed servant boy hesitated. Padia held Ancelet, the key to her mistress' room in her hand. "I apologize m'lady," she said. "Their business is urgent."

Closing her eyes, Roseen sighed with a quiet smile of relief. "Thank you, Padia," she said, turning to the messenger. "Speak."

With an awkward bow to the Lady of Gahidros, the servant boy turned to Neifon. "Neifon Vassaros, sir," he said, fidgeting under the expectant gaze of the Chief of Court. "Chancellor Leofas wishes to meet with you and Roseen in the Great Library of Mithlon."

Neifon raised an eyebrow. "Did he mention why?" he asked with a considerate smile to the young servant. Though the boy's sudden intrusion had unsettled the Hero, Haeryn could see patience in Neifon's eyes.

The servant boy's brow furrowed. "In addition to the summons, the Chancellor wished me to tell you that it pertains to the baron's 'obligations'," he answered, nodding in recollection.

Neifon straightened. Stifling an astonished smile, he waved to the guards. "Send the Chancellor my regards and tell him we will be on our way," he said. With a bow, the servant departed, and the guards shut the doors with a salute.

Discerning Haeryn and Marc's confusion, Neifon turned to them with a gleam in his eye. "Chancellor Leofas and Galeras have not been on speaking terms for over a year. The baron's insulting remarks concerning the Ambersters of Rehillon greatly embarrassed the Chancellor and ruined his efforts to bring about a military alliance," he explained, with a humorous smile at Roseen. "Before the Baronic Trial was arranged, there was another scheme the Chancellor and I began in hopes of triumphing over Galeras. It appears that our efforts were not as futile as we had thought."

30

13th of Rotanos, 2209 SE

With a sharp clink, the doors to Mithlon's Great Library swung inward. At the sight of Roseen and Neifon, the guard beside the entry inclined his head in courtesy. He glimpsed Haeryn and Marc and hesitated, shooting a questioning glance toward the two nobles. Neifon raised a hand to assure the man. "They pose no threat to policy. Both are guests of honor in my care, and as such have full authorization to enter," he said. The sentry bowed in compliance and gestured for the two squires to enter.

Haeryn coughed at the pungent scent of incense, and his boots sunk into the carpet. Inset in the far wall, a gated fireplace labored to preserve the comfort of the library's patrons. Between the ceiling's web of transepts, painted scenes instilled Edeveran history with a new life. Dressed in ornate finery, the many librarians scurried up the grand staircases to the multiple levels of bookshelves and study alcoves, organizing and cleaning as they made their rounds. Bronze pediments with decorative finials crowned each bookshelf, and carved signage indicated the subject matter for each section. Windows and chandeliers worked in harmony to illuminate the Great Library's glory. But it was the books themselves that proved the most striking adornment, their spines of brown, red, and tan like an earthy canvas. Haeryn gaped at the grandeur. The simple elegance of Asdale's modest library was overshadowed by the magnificence of Mithlon's Great Library.

Several librarians stood from behind a nearby desk, bowing to Neifon and Roseen in respect. Long, flowing dresses made them seem as if they drifted across the floor like loose pages in the wind. At the sight of Haeryn, the Head Librarian smiled, her status indicated by the owl pendant around her neck. "Welcome, Haeryn Wynrence," she said. "It is an honor to have you among these hallowed shelves." Haeryn smiled uneasily, feeling her gaze drift across his formal attire. From the flash of humor in her eyes, it was clear she noticed his discomfort.

Eyes narrowed in his single-minded quest, Neifon roved the multiple stories with his gaze. "Chancellor Leofas?" he inquired. Though he appeared composed, he clasped his hands tightly behind his back to curb his urgency.

The Head Librarian pointed to the nearest staircase. "He's in the furthest study alcove, on the uppermost level," she said. At Neifon's appreciative smile, she inclined her head with a good-natured twinkle in her eye.

Roseen shot an uncertain glance to the Great Library's closed doors. "Can we trust you to keep our presence a secret?" she said, choosing her words carefully.

Shaking her head, the librarian held up a hand to dissuade her concern. "The utmost discretion, my lady!" she insisted. "We never breach the trust of our patrons!"

With a gracious bow to the librarians, Neifon strode across the Great Library's expanse, with the others trailing behind. As their footsteps echoed upon the marble stairs, Haeryn squirmed at the fractured stillness. Several librarians moved aside to let them pass, bowing in respect for their guests before moving on. Haeryn peered off into the obscure corners of the library, flanking Roseen and Neifon with Marc. He remembered Neifon's private words to him upon their arrival.

A library is a haven for the burdened pilgrim. This is a place for searching, not hunting.

Though he understood Neifon's sentiments, Haeryn wasn't convinced. The untroubled atmosphere of the Great Library seemed fragile. He felt for the dagger concealed within his outer coat. Marc furtively glanced over his shoulder to study a librarian that lingered behind them. The shared foreboding was evident in his probing look. As they crested the stairs, Marc and Haeryn both moved in front of Neifon and Roseen to shield them.

Along the edge of the library's uppermost level, a walkway guided patrons down rows of bookshelves. Study alcoves were inset at various intervals along the walls, retreating into secluded havens for undisturbed study. Standing before a shelf, one of the patrons unknowingly strayed into their path, his head in a book. As they weaved around the man, Marc moved to shield Neifon, his hand on his concealed dagger. With a small lift of his hand, Neifon waved him off.

The small group stopped before an arched entryway of polished wood. As they entered the alcove, bookshelves encompassed them like a silent council. Antiquities awaited study with patience, chained to the shelves like prisoners on display. The pleasant light of latticed windows was darkened by a domineering shadow.

Standing with his back turned, the Chancellor held himself with a composure that rivaled Neifon's. Deep red robes of soft wool draped to his feet, and cuffs of dyed fur covered his hands. At his shoulders, a trimmed collar of ermine encircled his neck. Neifon hurried his pace, momentarily outpacing his bodyguards. Haeryn and Marc hurriedly matched his stride.

At the sound of their footsteps, the man turned with an eyebrow raised in curiosity. His wizened face was noble and clever, and his balding head was offset by a snowy white beard. At their approach, he bowed courteously to Roseen and nodded to Haeryn and Marc with a warm smile. "I received word you had returned to Mithlon, Neifon. I summoned you as quickly as I could," he said. His voice was deep, slurred with an unusual and rich timbre.

As he watched Neifon listen with rapt attention, Haeryn's curiosity was stirred. Leaning against a nearby chair, the youth regarded the Chancellor intently, trying to determine the nature of the man's news.

Reaching into the folds of his robes, the Chancellor withdrew a rolled parchment and handed it to Neifon. "I have received a message from Baron Falrey O'Dyre of Fenabor," he said with a triumphant glint in his eye. He shook Neifon's shoulder to drive home his words, "He's coming."

An incredulous stare broke Neifon's poise. He opened the letter and skimmed the terse script. Roseen frowned as she struggled to make sense of the matter, while Haeryn and Marc shared a puzzled glance. At Neifon's excitement, Haeryn attempted to read the message over Neifon's shoulder.

Clasping her hands, Roseen tilted her head. "I know nothing of this," she said. The thought of her brother withholding something so significant took her by surprise.

Neifon laid an apologetic hand on his sister's shoulder. "The matter was a risky one, but Leofas and I took it. We hoped that, by keeping it to ourselves, sensitivity of the matter would not compromise you or Raulin," he said.

The Chancellor smiled. "The heart of the matter is this—early in his Baronship, Galeras secretly signed a trade agreement with the Baron of Fenabor, Falrey O'Dyre to secure exclusive access to Fenabor's famous wines. The crucial element of the arrangement was that Galeras pay an exorbitant price—far above the usual," he said.

Neifon folded the message and stuffed it into the pocket of his outer coat. "Due to his lavish spending habits, Galeras hasn't been able to pay for all the wines he's imported. He indebted Edeveros to Fenabor without the consent of the Council of Lords. Therefore, Galeras' leadership has come into conflict with Royal Law," he said, lifting his chin with a pleased smile. "Leofas and I sent a letter to Falrey, asking him to come resolve the matter in person. He agreed."

Roseen thought to herself, mulling over her brother's strategy. "Galeras will be forced to choose between two unsavory options. He can either pay his debt—which by now must be enough to severely wound Edeveros—or have his debt exposed and his hold on the Baronship compromised. With such a blatant abuse of power, Galeras will be compelled to abdicate by order of King Fohidras," she mused. Turning to Neifon, she blinked away tears. "Edeveros is saved," she said. Neifon embraced her.

Haeryn smiled to himself, his thoughts surging in a tempest of emotion.

Galeras won't be so haughty when his throne is pulled out from under him!

Neifon turned to Haeryn, and he laid a hand on the youth's shoulder with a warm smile. "Galeras imperiled his homeland through impulsiveness, and if we are not careful, reckless measures could endanger Edeveros again. Prudence, not insurgency, is the best means of preserving liberty, for insurrection always comes at the cost of others caught in the crossfire. A true leader seeks not only for the security of his homeland, but for the well-being of his people," he said. Haeryn hesitated as his friend's words left a weighty impression in his thoughts. His certainty was shaken.

His elation stalled as he cleared his throat. "Haeryn, Marc," he said, wrapping an arm around Marc's shoulders. "I wish to discuss something with Roseen and the Chancellor in private."

Marc hesitated. "With respect, sir, your safety rests upon my shoulders," he protested, unmoving.

Neifon eyed the squire with a look that ended the matter. "It will be only a moment. Step a few bookshelves away, but keep me within sight," he asserted. "Galeras holds the Great Library with indifference. He finds little interest in the knowledge of books, save the few that inspire his juvenile schemes. We are safe here." With a nod of submission, Marc briskly left the study alcove, Haeryn following behind him.

Neifon's smile faded under a heavy heart.

31

15th of Rotanos, 2209 SE

Haeryn crept up the stairs in a half-crouch, arms spread slightly to quiet his steps. His boots sunk gently into the red and gold rug leading up the center of the stairway. Catching sight of a guard further down the hall, he slowed, ears attuned to the slightest sound of his footsteps. Haeryn laid a hand on the balustrade, unsure if the man had ascertained his presence. His eyes darted frantically, and he ducked into the night shadows.

The man didn't seem to notice him, rounding a corner in the hallway and vanishing from Haeryn's sight. Feeling his tension subside, Haeryn cautiously crept onward, hurrying his pace till he found himself running up the stairs. The smug face of Galeras branded itself upon his memory, and with each step Haeryn took, his pulse quickened. He glared down the hallway, envisioning Galeras cowering at the end of his blade. In such dire circumstances, Haeryn was convinced the baron would listen to him.

I have pointed out the law's ineffectiveness long enough. No one will listen. So I must prove myself.

Haeryn flattened himself against the nearest wall and chanced a glance around the corner. The two guards patrolling the halls casually whispered to each other, casting disinterested glances to the doorway they protected. It was clear they had more interest in small talk than in their duties. Haeryn loosened his dagger in its sheath. A rush of adrenaline focused his potent gaze upon the imposing doorway of Galeras' quarters. Its gold trimmings and intricate carvings reminded Haeryn of exquisite armor.

With a fanatic gleam in his eye, Haeryn crossed the distance and slipped a lock pick from his pocket. Grasping the cool bronze handle, he inserted the pick and leaned down by it. He bit his lip as he recalled the few poorly taught lessons given by one of his fellow squires. It would have to do.

Haeryn bit his lip, his breaths becoming quick and shallow. His hands shook. Muttering to himself, he took a calming breath and reinserted the pick into the lock. His obsession was checked as his repeated attempts continued to fail.

"What's this?" a voice inquired.

Haeryn's chest tightened, and he spun to face the two guards. Their visors were lifted as they regarded him with curious expressions. As he fumbled for a reply, they toyed with their halberds. The glint in their eyes revealed their amusement at the youth's discomfort.

Clearing his throat, Haeryn furtively dropped his lock pick into the decorative flowerpot beside him without attracting the guards' attention. "I'm lost," he said weakly. Though he strove to appear sincere, he winced at the awkward excuse.

The two soldiers looked at each other, suppressing laughs of amusement. One of them raised an eyebrow and studied Haeryn. "Of course," he said. Haeryn swallowed. The man's mocking tone did not bode well. Taking the youth by the arms, the two soldiers started down the hallway. As he was torn away from Galeras' quarters, Haeryn felt his heart sink. The soldiers restraining him laughed. "Until we find out what in Ramrow's name you're doing, boy, we have a comfortable cell for you to sleep in," one of them said.

Haeryn slumped against the bars of his jail cell, the coldness of Mithlon's dungeon settling deep into his bones. He wrinkled his nose at the stench, ignoring the jeers of common criminals that rang out in the dim expanse. As Haeryn stared at his feet, the barren granite walls and floor stared back, cold and unforgiving. The opulence and vanity of Mithlon did not reach into these forsaken recesses.

Cheeks burning at his plight, Haeryn shuddered, recalling the ease with which he had insisted the laws of Edeveros be broken. The reality he now found himself in fractured the illusion that had blinded him. Shaking his head, he grumbled to himself. Justice had seemed so simple. In his confidence, Haeryn had thought he could achieve what no one else could.

He struggled to make sense of it. The confidence that had endured Aalys' death and the trials of Mithlon had been shaken by a simple act gone wrong. As a squire, Haeryn had made simple mistakes, as had many of his fellows—but despite his reasoning, a heavy sense of failure weighed on him like the chains binding his ankles.

Is some greater power foiling my attempts?

Footsteps echoed against the dungeon's immovable walls, and the taunts of several prisoners called out in hostile greeting. Grasping the bars of his cell, Haeryn leaned out the best he could, glimpsing the light of a lantern bobbing down the corridor. As Neifon's long face was illuminated by the lamplight, Haeryn shrank back into his cell.

Clasping his hands tightly together, Neifon stood opposite the youth, separated by the veil of iron bars. As he took in Haeryn's sorry state, the Hero clenched his jaw and pressed his lips together in a hard line. The soldier beside Neifon handed him Haeryn's sheathed dagger. "We confiscated this from his person, sir," he said, shooting a suspicious look at the imprisoned youth.

Masking his alarm, Neifon turned to the guard beside him. "Leave us," he commanded. With a curt nod, the soldier hung the lantern on a nearby post and departed. Neifon shook his head with an irritated sigh. "A dagger, Haeryn? Even a child could guess your scheme. It is impossible for you to hide your indignation, and your straightforward disposition makes you predictable," he said. "Thankfully I was able to persuade the guards to overlook your zealous blunder. They are not too fond of the baron themselves.

You didn't think through the consequences of your actions?"

Gathering the shattered remnants of his former convictions, Haeryn clenched his fists. "Galeras must be reined in and vanquished. Law will not achieve that. A leader must take things into his own hands. Otherwise, the evil will always triumph," he retorted.

Neifon pinched the bridge of his nose in exasperation. "Look around you! A true leader knows when to advance, when to retreat, and when to stand still. Have you considered the possibility that your methods for seeking 'justice' serve to further your own self-interest? Instead of benefiting Edeveros' people?" he exclaimed. "If I had not been summoned in time, you may have been imprisoned for months. In Mithlon, petty criminals are held longer and without reason, since the Court Magistrate often has greater cases to decide before he can deal with more trivial complaints."

Haeryn grimaced at the stench of the dungeon. "So I am free to go?" he asked.

Neifon glared at the youth. "You will stay the night and be released in the morning. I have tried to warn you, but it seems something greater than a prison cell will have to convince you," he snapped.

He snatched the lantern away and stomped down the corridor before Haeryn could retort.

32

18th of Rotanos, 2209 SE

18th of Rotanos, 2209 SE

Haeryn Irongaze quickened his steps up a spiraling marble stairway in Castle Mithlon. His shimmering reflection upon the bronze railing trailed him as he ascended. Marc strode beside him, eyes fixed on the stairs ahead. As over the course of the last few days, Neifon had again slipped past their guard. Following a hunch, they had made for the Great Library, knowing his affinity for the place. Haeryn frowned, struggling to understand his friend's irrational behavior.

Is he trying to get himself killed? Mithlon is not a safe place.

They both quickened their pace as the stairs ended in a wide hallway. In the wake of Chancellor Leofas' news, the unwelcome memory of Aalys' death returned to Haeryn. Her death would not be in vain—not when Falrey O'Dyre avenged Galeras' wrongs.

Haeryn studied Marc's expression, reading in his friend's face both tension over Neifon's disappearance and triumph at Falrey's coming. Even though the stress of their present circumstance remained ever present, Haeryn felt the burden lighten at the mutual understanding. He was glad for the kinship they shared. They had much in common, despite their differences.

"Tell me, what is it like? To serve the Knights of the Lance?" Haeryn inquired.

Marc flashed a smile and placed a hand on Haeryn's shoulder. "You have more in common with the Knights of the Lance than you realize," he answered. "The battle of life is fought and won by virtue, regardless of where you hail from."

"Ethics and codes of honor are a hindrance," Haeryn said with a disgusted snort.

Marc shook his head. "Ethics are what moved me to save your Aunt Gwyndel from Beydan's temper. The best action is not always the most direct. Without guidelines, the abuse of power runs rampant."

Haeryn brushed the comments aside. "I prefer to act directly and decisively," he replied.

Marc sighed. "This is not an easy lesson, but it is a crucial one," he said.

A scream startled them. Haeryn and Marc dashed down the hall to the Great Library as a man bolted out the library's open doors, nearly colliding into them. As they rushed into the Great Library, the two of them were greeted by a crowd of frightened librarians. Recognizing Haeryn and Marc, the Head Librarian pushed through the crowd. "Hurry! In the rightmost study alcove—he's not responding!" she exclaimed. The panic in her voice made Haeryn's skin crawl. They raced up the stairs, heart pounding in their ears as they charged into a study alcove.

Neifon lay unmoving upon the floor—with a spilled wine goblet in his limp fingers.

Marc's scream of agony tore through the silence. They bolted to Neifon's side and knelt. As Haeryn looked into Neifon's pale face, sobs wracked his young frame, his iron gaze blurred by tears.

Marc wiped the corner of Neifon's mouth, flinching at the sharp scent of the spittle on his fingertip. His eyes grew livid. "*Poison,*" he growled, clenching his fist. "GUARDS! Noble blood! Noble blood!"

The words no Edeveran soldier wished to hear.

20*th* of Rotanos, 2209 SE

It was the mourning of Castle Mithlon that summoned the rain. The quiet keening lifted a song of farewell as the crowd gathered around the Chief of Court's coffin. The clatter of the storm upon the Noble Mausoleum's stained-glass windows rumbled throughout the expanse like drums accompanying the mourner's dirge. The floor of the mausoleum was illuminated with colored prisms of light, as Neifon Vassaros joined the other heroes of old entombed in undying stillness. A red tapestry was draped over it in honor, and all hung their heads in reverence.

Haeryn stood numb at the foot of the stone box, envisioning the body of Neifon lying motionless within. Beside him, Roseen stared, silent tears trickling down her face. Little Ancelet held his mother's hand, silent, not understanding what he witnessed. Marc wept without shame, leaning on his glaive for support. The candlelight flickered over his full suit of ceremonial plate armor. Though he was only a squire of the Knights of the Lance, he had borrowed an elder knight's armor for the occasion. Roseen's heart warmed at this show of respect for Neifon.

Dressed in his finest attire, Galeras stood at the coffin's head, hushed as he stared fixedly at it. Though his expression was solemn with feigned sorrow, some doubted his sincerity. Lifting his head, he addressed those gathered. "Neifon Vassaros was true to his ranking as Chief of Court and one of the prestigious Five Heroes of Alithell. His legacy will not be forgotten. An effigy will proclaim his greatness for the generations to come, so all will come to know of his nobility, intelligence, and tenacity," he declared. Haeryn's face darkened as he recognized the spite in that final word.

He stared at the coffin with a deeper pang of loss.

We've lost a great leader. A model of principle.

Haeryn winced, his throat raw from suppressed sobs. His eyes were hot and tacky with tears. Neifon had loved the Edeverans more than his own life. His senseless death could not be meaningless. Haeryn watched Galeras bow his head in a moment of silence. Anger pricked him, clouding his mind. Before he could entertain his outrage, Haeryn remembered Neifon's repeated challenge.

Prudence, not insurgency, is the best means of preserving liberty, for insurrection always comes at the cost of others caught in the crossfire.

Haeryn looked away to restrain himself, feeling an inexpressible desire to respect his fallen friend's integrity.

My rashness puts me in league with Galeras and his ilk. Neifon held to honor, even to death. I must follow his example.

At first, the thought galled him. Yet as he looked upon the stone coffin of his companion, Haeryn lifted his head in a silent oath of obedience.

21st *of Rotanos, 2209 SE*

Within the secrecy of Galeras' quarters, the brisk notes of the hammered dulcimer sang in conquest. Feeling the song flow from his own dark exultation, Galeras rejoiced in its echoes. The image of Neifon's tomb hung immovable in his memory, sparking a smile. The baron felt a thrill of relief.

I am finally rid of the cur! Who threw him down from his self-righteous tower? Lòfroy? Or perhaps that elvish fiend of his—Gawter? But what does it matter? Neifon's death is my gain!

Galeras' laugh lent an ugly twist to his features. The reward of the Chief of Court's demise had been difficult to conceal from those who grieved. In the emotion of the moment, they had been too blinded by their care for Neifon to realize the glorious future their baron had in store. Emboldened, Galeras gazed out the window with a smirk. In time, he would appoint a new

Chief of Court—and the Court of Edeveros would be wholly his. At his glee, drops of rain streaked the glass windowpanes in grief. As he caught sight of a folded paper upon a nearby chair, Galeras frowned. His twisted joy deflated at the details his spy had reported.

He had underestimated Raulin. At first, the news of the parade in Gahidros had alarmed him. With the people's pride stirred, and the word of Lòfroy's prowl spread among the people, the outcome had seemed unknowable. For a time.

A smart move on my brother's part—though I can only guess who put it into his head.

In a quick play of cunning, Galeras had imprisoned a random scapegoat and declared to the public the supposed capture of Lòfroy. He straightened, waking the song of the hammered dulcimer from its momentary slumber. No longer did the people consider calling for his abdication—now, they praised his name. To further solidify his hold on his subjects, Galeras had called for a festival.

A smirk of disdain entrenched his contempt.

What a pity Neifon perished before I could taunt him with yet another defeat.

33

20th of Rotanos, 2209 SE

Clouds laden with rain covered the highland sky, sympathizing with the burdened spirits of those who wandered. A light shower drizzled to stain the ground below with its moist touch. Moorlands rolled in all directions, stretching out ahead of the company of wanderers in alternating fields of rich green and brown. Hills rose from the highlands where they pleased, with their peaks hidden by the low clouds. It almost seemed that the landscape strove to ease the burden of the journey.

Gibusil adjusted his flight as Eyoés, Erling, and Kerensa huddled upon his back, eyes squinted against the rain. Below, Gwyndel and Fedrik rode on horseback across the moorlands, guided by the griffin above.

After the haste of their escape, a simple plan had been arranged. Being lured into a prolonged pursuit would leave them vulnerable and play to Lòfroy's advantage. The northern town of Fiwood stood as their best place for refuge. Eyoés had insisted they must weave their way ever northward to the capital of Mithlon in hopes of gaining the protection of Neifon and his powerful allies.

Gwyndel found little comfort in their plan of escape. As she galloped across the moorlands, the thought of Lòfroy spurred her to urge her horse to greater speed. She clenched her jaw as she recalled the fear that haunted their steps. As the Keeper of the Sword Imperishable, she felt her empathy draw her to sow hope.

Her curly red braid hung like a damp weight on her neck. Gwyndel glanced back at Fedrik huddled behind her, bracing himself against the back of the saddle. Gwyndel could feel dread closing in on him.

He is hopelessly caught in his own trap, as Eyoés once was.

Seeking her advice, Eyoés had confided in her regarding Fedrik's misery. From both her brother's words and her own observation, Gwyndel guessed the man saw himself as a tragedy, unable to gain forgiveness. Yet, though he had sought her aid in understanding the situation more fully, Eyoés had sworn her to silence.

Gwyndel shook her head as she wrestled with her conflicting desires. Her heart softened as she recalled the image of Fedrik distraught and sobbing at the news of Erling's misdeed.

His tattered heart is longing to be mended. There must be something I can do.

Gwyndel swallowed, then broke the stillness of the rain. "You feel condemned, Fedrik," she said. "Whatever your past may be—it is unchangeable. But the stains you feel so poignantly can be cleansed."

As she felt the saddle shift, the man's sharp gaze pierced her, and she held her tongue. "How do you know this?" Fedrik asked. The scathing in his voice was glowering—even murderous.

Gwyndel tensed in the saddle. She sought for a way to appease his suspicion. "It is evident in your manner," she replied. His firm hand gripped her shoulder, and Gwyndel swallowed.

"Then why do I feel you're lying to me?" Fedrik asked. Gwyndel wavered, resisting the urge to lie. Resolved to speak the truth, she began to reply, slowing her horse.

But Fedrik needed no answer—her brief silence had condemned her. Yanking his hand away from Gwyndel's shoulder, he gritted his teeth and stared up to where Gibusil soared. The anger in his expression turned to anguish. Gwyndel heard the ripping of cloth as he tore the collar of his shirt. "He told you, the liar!" he roared.

At the sound, Gibusil awkwardly landed beside them, impeded by his missing eye. Eyoés leaned out from the saddle with a look of concern. "What's the trouble?" he asked.

Fedrik unbuckled the saddle strap and dismounted with a growl of disgust. Glaring at Eyoés, he planted his feet and pointed an accusing finger. "You *told* her?" he questioned, demanding answers.

Eyoés glimpsed tears roll down the man's wizened face and into his greying beard. He looked at the two riders, dejected as he pieced together what had happened. The pain of fresh betrayal in Fedrik's eyes sparked a flame of pity in his heart. He turned to Gwyndel, and his face became like flint.

She ignored my request for discretion and took matters into her own hands! Just as she reprimanded me for doing in my days of confusion!

His brow furrowed as his sister looked away. Though silent, he gave her a reproving look, laced with a justified disappointment that Gwyndel felt keenly. Hearing Fedrik mutter curses under his breath, Eyoés turned back to him. "Fedrik, I sought her wisdom regarding the matter in an attempt to aid you the best we could," he said.

Fedrik laughed bitterly and shot a savage glance in Gwyndel's direction. "*False* wisdom, if you ask me," he snapped. "I will fly for the remainder of our journey. I tolerate you both only for the sake of my family's safety. I can't trust you."

Knowing that to oppose the man would only sow more conflict, Eyoés brought Gibusil to a crouch, and aided Kerensa to dismount. Fedrik hurried to help his wife to the ground and join Gwyndel on horseback. Stricken by her own error, Gwyndel held back tears as she gazed at Eyoés with regret.

Fedrik's wary heart had sealed itself off.

34

A measly campfire flickered in weak flames, clinging to its fragile life. As Eyoés gathered close for warmth against the chill air, he struggled to keep himself from coughing on the smoke. Fedrik and Kerensa sat huddled together, staring off into the darkness. Not far away, the snapping of branches rang out as Gwyndel and Erling collected firewood. They could not afford to let the fire die.

Forced into hiding by the ever present threat of discovery, the company had retreated into a copse of conifers at the coming of evening. The distant howl of wolves met their ears along with the keening of crows. The growing darkness transformed the boughs above their heads into a ceiling of prickly shadow, hemming them in with encroaching arms. Though they were glad for the refuge it provided, the forest stifled them.

The reflection of the flames in Eyoés' eyes brought life to his stare. At the sight of Fedrik, he winced. Crossing his arms, the man absentmindedly shook his head. The crisp, hard lines of his aged face were wrinkled with pain. Grief lingered about Fedrik like an old companion. Beside him, Kerensa leaned against him, head resting on his shoulder. She said nothing— neither a word in her husband's defense nor a word against him. Even in her silence, Eyoés could see the awareness in her demeanor. She seemed to know of her husband's struggle with despondency, and his inability to find relief. Shaking his head, Eyoés observed her out of the corner of his eye. Though she strived to be strong for Fedrik, he knew Kerensa faced the choice of supporting her husband's independence or guiding him to outside aid.

It will not be an easy one for her.

Eyoés warmed his hands near the flames. The snapping of branches continued from a nearby thicket. Shooting an angry look at the forest, he fought to suppress his irritation. He expelled a sigh. Though Gwyndel's rashness upset him, he was certain she had broken his trust in hopes of encouraging Fedrik.

Could it be that she spoke well, but Fedrik reacted unnecessarily?

He considered the thought. In truth, both he and Gwyndel were complicit in breaking trust. Harboring ill-will toward her would serve not to bring about reconciliation, but instead cause more division. Averting his eyes, Eyoés shook his head, vexed by his sister's impulsiveness. Though he understood her sympathy toward Fedrik, it could not justify her actions.

But I should be the last one to expect perfection.

Eyoés furtively peered at Fedrik, his muscles tense at the thought of confrontation. Despite his discomfort, he felt compelled to bring the matter up again. If left unaddressed, their strife would be the death of them. Eyoés exhaled, reluctant to meet the inevitable anger of Fedrik. "I apologize for her breach of trust—she did not intend to dishonor you in any way," he said, hoping his assertion would be enough to convince the man of his honesty and end the awkward matter.

Fedrik stirred and clenched his jaw. "You should make amends for *your* breach of trust before you do the same for hers," he snapped, snatching up a pinecone and crushing it in his grip. He winced as the sharp points dug into his hand. "I know the pain of betrayal. I will not let you subject me to it again!" he declared.

Turning to face Fedrik, Eyoés glanced at Kerensa, who listened in silence. "Even if you don't realize it, you still long for forgiveness, and you *can* lay hold of it. I will not betray your trust again, but I will not be silent while you continue in your misery," he replied.

Fedrik drove the heel of his boot into the ground, scattering bits of dirt into the fire. "I am beyond your encouragement. There is no hope for me. And if there was, I would not seek aid from the likes of you," he growled.

Eyoés lifted his eyes upward. "How can you expect forgiveness if you do not show it to others?" he said, exasperated.

Fedrik wheeled on him, bringing his face inches away from Eyoés'. "I do not expect it!" he shouted. "A murderer and traitor cannot expect such things!" With this, he returned to his seat, and Kerensa met his gaze imploringly in a silent plea for reason. From the sympathy in her manner, it was clear that she knew at least some of her husband's wrongs.

With a frustrated sigh, Eyoés cast the last piece of firewood upon the flames in a shower of sparks.

Gwyndel felt the branches prick her hands as she stooped among the thick undergrowth, gathering what dry wood she could find. The fading daylight alone guided her, streaming down through a break in the trees above. Crickets chirped in the shadows, silencing their song whenever she neared them.

Not far away, the murmur of raised voices could be heard above the crackling of the campfire. Turning away from the sound, Gwyndel bit her lip and blocked out the words in her ears. The pain in her heart lingered. In her attempt to heal, she had brought division instead. Hiding behind stray locks of her hair, she took a trembling breath.

Why could I not have waited for a better opportunity? Did I not learn my lesson in Ellokon?

Gwyndel straightened, readjusting her grip on the ever-growing pile of wood in her arms. She knew she had erred by confronting Fedrik outright. Gwyndel shook her head. Turning aside, she opened her hand, and the faint blue light of the Sword Imperishable glowed, waiting to be summoned. Ever since the King had bestowed the gift upon her, she had felt burdened to speak encouragement whenever she could. What once had been easy to hold back now seemed uncontainable. She still had much to learn in wielding it. The sound of nearby footsteps sweeping through the underbrush caught her attention.

Erling turned back in the direction of the camp. His shoulders slumped as the words of anger drew to a hasty conclusion. Lowering his gaze, he searched the forest floor—searching not for wood, but for his thoughts. Even in the darkness, Gwyndel could make out the dejection on the boy's face.

Sensing the elf's eyes upon him, Erling glanced up at her with a sigh. "I always wished to embark on an adventure—like the heroes of old. But I never envisioned it would be like this," he admitted. "I'd heard so many stories. I hoped that, maybe, I could learn to be noble like them. Then my mistakes would be trivial." He muttered something more, but his voice trailed off.

Gwyndel understood. Drawn to the boy's side by his longing, she felt his words ring hollow in her chest.

Fedrik's struggles have affected his son. And he is blind to it.

"I wronged your father by betraying his trust," Gwyndel confessed. The act of speaking the words aloud brought some relief, but also made her misdeed more tangible than before.

To her surprise, Erling nodded. "I know, and I forgive you," he said, glancing back toward the camp. "I only wish to bring an end to this bickering."

A slight smile came to Gwyndel's face at the boy's wistful look. "I have wandered moors and forests and seen distant seas, Erling. And through all of it, I have learned this—sometimes mercy and reconciliation can be just as daunting and heroic as traveling into an unknown land. Few minstrels have sung the praises of peacemakers—perhaps it is because forgiveness is a sacrifice too precious to put to words or song," she mused.

Erling looked at her, doubtful. "Father and Mother always said I was merciful. But then again, I also feel the desire to make things right once and for all," he replied.

Gwyndel shifted her load to one arm and embraced Erling. "Mercy is the strength of heroes, and judgement is the act of the impatient. Stand for what is right, but pity those deceived by evil. The beginnings of a noble hero are in you, Erling," she said, looking into his eyes with genuine conviction.

Erling lowered his gaze—embarrassed, but pleased.

35

Fedrik stared up into the blackness of midnight, his fingers bent and whitened as he clutched the hem of his blanket. All was silent, save the quiet breathing of his companions. In the murk, the boughs reached out like mangy devils. He curled up under his blanket, retreating into his thoughts.

How long will this grief over betrayal bind me? Would forgiveness bring an end to the pain?

Fedrik shifted about, yearning for the comfort of sleep. The simple solution was alluring, but he understood the price. Fighting off a sinking feeling in his stomach, he wrestled with his longing. Forgiveness demanded vulnerability. Vulnerability led to weakness. Weakness brought betrayal and shame, and gave birth to violence. And while sorrow was satisfied by violence, judgement was the penalty.

I'm caught in a hopeless pattern. Forgiving Eyoés and Gwyndel may return me to the mire that once ensnared me!

The battle for his mind began again. His heart desired freedom—but his mind knew it could never be so. Fedrik wept in silence, knowing his fate was determined.

The monster I am cannot be defeated. Why would Eyoés and Gwyndel risk their lives to protect me?

The notion was scandalous in its compassion. He envisioned his bloodstained hands washed clean, and the good they could accomplish. Yet, taking in a shuddering breath, Fedrik squeezed his eyes shut.

There is no escape for my atrocities. I am doomed by them, and to them I resign myself.

And with a final tear, he fell into a grieved sleep.

Fedrik suddenly found himself awake—a wakefulness that revived him with a immediate, peculiar peace. Every trace of his former depression was gone. He blinked at the pure white light, arms spread out to steady himself. Fedrik ran a hand through his hair as he looked around, bewildered.

He stood in a small glade. Mumbling to himself, Fedrik studied the ground around him. The sleeping forms of his companions were nowhere to be found. Springy moss covered the ground underfoot. No sound of life met his ears—no birdsong, no chattering of a squirrel. Only the faint sound of wind coursing through the pine boughs. Fedrik studied his surroundings again, disoriented.

He stood motionless.

A figure clothed in a pure white cloak appeared before him, face obscured in the depths of his hood. In his hand, he held a crook staff. Tendrils of steam curled before the man's mouth, and with every breath the figure exhaled, the air seemed cleaner to Fedrik's lungs. The urge to flee melted away, replaced instead by a desire to approach. Despite his hesitancy, Fedrik wandered closer to the peculiar figure, hands held out to shield himself.

"Who are you?" he asked.

"I see what is forgotten, what is present, and what is yet to be seen. I look into the hearts of men and judge rightly. And to those in need, I am help," the robed figure declared. Fedrik felt the voice vibrate through his very core.

Before Fedrik could inquire further, the white figure lifted his open hand. Fedrik's eyes widened as a golden chalice materialized in his hand, glowing with a radiance that stung his eyes. The robed figure extended the chalice toward Fedrik. "Drink. Be renewed," he proclaimed. Seized by sudden hope and great longing, Fedrik reached for the chalice. The scene cut to darkness.

Fedrik bolted upright and threw aside his blankets, eyes wide. The peaceful breathing of those sleeping around him brought clarity to his confusion.

What could this mean?

36

22nd of Rotanos, 2209 SE

The gentle breeze whispered through Gibusil's feathers as Castle Fiwood came into view of the company of fugitives. Through its humble presence, the town brought a peaceful haven to the dull landscape. Houses of wattle and daub lined the streets, and simple gravelled rock thoroughfares trailed throughout the town. Eyoés closed his eyes, enjoying the familiar comfort of the warm sun upon his back.

As Erling rested against his father's chest, Fedrik gazed out into the bright horizon, tears glistening in his eyes. Glancing over his shoulder, Eyoés caught a glimpse of hope on Fedrik's face. He smiled, content to leave the man's moment of rest alone. For a brief moment, the darkness of his past was lost in the dawning of the new sun.

I only wish Fedrik would seize the comfort available to him.

Eyoés looked down into Castle Fiwood. Positioned in the center of the town, the castle was surrounded by a diamond-shaped wall. A simple courtyard of packed sod lay within its confines, and the towered keep lay at the far end. As they drew near, Eyoés could see the glint of many windows lining the keep's walls.

Spotting the main road outside the castle limits, Eyoés guided Gibusil's descent. The griffin flapped his wings to steady his landing, and Gwyndel tugged her reins, sidling the horse to give room. Behind the Forester, Kerensa slumped forward in weariness, struggling to wake herself from her exhausted rest. As the griffin crouched, Eyoés slipped from the saddle, and Erling stirred from his nap, groggily dismounting as well.

Eyoés extended a hand to help Fedrik dismount. Eying the gesture with contempt, Fedrik shook his head in refusal. His expression hardened, and he slid off the saddle with little struggle. As Fedrik strode past him, Eyoés let his hand fall to his side.

This journey will be one of strife, due to my error and Gwyndel's poor judgement. I must work harder to regain his trust.

Taking Gibusil's reins in hand, Eyoés ventured into the town of Fiwood, and the others followed in the griffin's shadow. As Gibusil passed with rumbling footsteps, the nearby townsfolk gaped.

Rounding a bend in the road, Eyoés heard the faded song of minstrels, and he squinted down the street to see the colors of a market not far away. Removing Gibusil's reins and putting them in the saddlebag, Eyoés loosed the griffin to roam. Gibusil quietly took to the sky.

A sizable inn welcomed them. Three stories were stacked atop one other, each level jutting out past the previous one. The daub was stained with dirt, and the roof wore traces of moss. Emerging from the inn's stable with a bucket in hand, a meek innkeeper noticed them. He cast the bucket aside and dusted his hands together. "Welcome, friends! I do believe a warm bed and a meal would do you well," he said, noting their grubby clothing and exhausted faces. He glanced back at the porters assisting him, awaiting his orders at the entrance of the stable.

Eyoés nodded. "Two rooms, and lodge the horse in the stable with care. We will not stay long," he said, his eyes drifting about. They would not bring death upon this place of peace.

Disarmed by the darkness of midnight, the town of Fiwood was lured into sleep. The peacefulness of the day faded under the night's oppression, and the crescent moon curved like a scythe's blade in the sky. The light of a nearby lantern was smothered as wingbeats snuffed it out. Spreading its wings to steady itself, the dark shape of a griffin alighted on the sturdy, peaked roof of a guild-house. Its claws closed about the wood shingles, loosening some of them with a creak. The creature's eyes roved the gravel streets in search of vermin.

Lòfroy patted his griffin on the shoulder, breathless as his heart pounded. At the sight of the local inn, he leaned forward in the saddle, ruffling his griffin's feathers as he scrutinized the building. His mind envisioned his quarry lying abed in the peacefulness of sleep, and his lip curled in disgust. Lòfroy muttered a curse of spite and shook his head as the loneliness of his cause reminded him of his own deficiency. Alone he had once been, and alone he was now—yet this time, he could not confront his foe unaided.

Must this hunt end in failure?

He refused the notion. For years, the yearning for retaliation had grown, till the thrill of pursuit sustained him like bread. Tapping the saddlehorn with an idle finger, Lòfroy came to a decision.

Let them flee. I will stalk them like a wolf and deepen their terror of me. Fedrik will squeal for mercy at my threats.

He would find his opportunity.

37

23rd of Rotanos, 2209 SE

23rd of Rotanos, 2209 SE

With the morning clouds darkening the sky over the town, the company of fugitives huddled together as they drifted through the square. The morning crowd scattered about the plaza to patronize local farmers, craftsmen, butchers, and merchants for their daily provisions. The gentle tune of a young man's lute pleased the ears of passersby. The dirty attire of the humble crowds loosely emulated the fashion of the nobility.

Gwyndel savored the humble quiet of Fiwood. In the tranquility of the town, the ever-present strife that had plagued the Forester Assembly and Edeveros' people was put to rest. How long that peace would last was unknown. It seemed wherever peace came to settle, conflict would arise to undermine it.

A nearby butcher called out to her with a friendly welcome. As Gwyndel caught his eye, the man gestured for her to come near. Patting Eyoés' shoulder in an effort to mend their strained bond, she ambled toward the stall. Her eyes drifted over the bagged chunks of meat and bone, and a bundle of scented herbs hung on a post to freshen the air. Gwyndel raised her eyebrows as the man ducked to retrieve something from his supplies. Standing up, he held aloft a bag of dried meat. "Provisions for weary travelers," he said.

Gwyndel's heart warmed. "Thank you," she replied, exchanging a few spare coins for the man's wares. As another patron approached the butcher's stand, Gwyndel fell back, rejoining her companions. She noticed Kerensa at one of the booths opposite. The sparse provisions they had packed during their hasty escape would not last the distance.

Eyoés glanced back to where Fedrik walked in his wake, with Erling and Kerensa clinging to him. Gathering his family close, the man cast sullen looks at the crowd. His eyes were tight and harsh, and his jaw was flexed with the lingering hurt of Gwyndel and Eyoés' betrayal.

At the sight of the despair in his eyes, Eyoés felt a shared gloom—for Fedrik's pain, rather than their desperate predicament.

I wish he would allow me to share his burden, as the Proverbs say. To suffer alone is to die within.

Gwyndel covered their rear, vigilant for any sign of trouble. Glimpsing the glow of the Sword Imperishable in her palm, she tightened her fist around her bag of provisions. Since her return from Norgalok, her gift had materialized more and more frequently, sometimes bursting to life with little warning. The voices about her suddenly became clear and discernible. Caught off guard, she was gripped by the potency of Fedrik's hurt and the worry of his family. Gwyndel's peaceful expression faded into a sullen, sorrowful look as she was overwhelmed by their pain. She wiped away tears welling in her eyes.

A large shape caught her eye. Perched atop a distant building was a griffin's silhouette, and an iron-helmed figure overlooked the oblivious crowd. Gwyndel's heart raced, and her eyes darted among the crowd of townsfolk. Their presence had brought violence to Fiwood.

Gwyndel rushed to Eyoés and whispered in his ear, "Lòfroy is poised to strike."

Eyoés stopped in his tracks. His gaze hardened as he loosened his sword in its scabbard, casting wary glances at the aloof townspeople. "Cover Fedrik. We make for the empty streets," he whispered. Gwyndel nodded. They would not bring chaos to Fiwood's people.

Fedrik's sullen eyes flashed with horror as he perceived the fearful light in Gwyndel's eyes. Holding Kerensa and Erling close, he turned to speak—but Eyoés' reproving look silenced him. Crowding together as one, the group hastened through the town square, the lilting music fading under the pounding of their hearts. Gwyndel spread open her palm, feeling a warm assurance at the blue glow of the Sword Imperishable.

As soon as they entered the shelter of an empty alley, they bolted. Fedrik held Kerensa and Erling's hands as he ran, flanked by Eyoés and Gwyndel. Eyoés looked up to an empty sky, and his stomach dropped. No sounds of pursuit met his ears.

Where is he? Will Lòfroy allow our escape?

In quick dismissal, Eyoés whistled, hoping his griffin was nearby. Ushering Kerensa and Erling into the cover of a nearby recess, Gwyndel darted into the shadows in hope of evading Lòfroy's search. Eyoés ducked into cover alongside them—and noticed Fedrik was not among their number. A low growl drew his attention back to where they had come from.

Fedrik stood paralyzed, trembling as he fought to hold back a scream. Standing before him, was Lòfroy, his sword drawn.

He spoke no words of contempt. The stare of the iron helm alone struck terror into Fedrik's heart. From its perch, the grey griffin crouched to conceal itself. Stunned by the sight, Eyoés faltered—but Gwyndel did not.

Leaping from her seat with elvish agility, she crossed the distance in seconds, plucking up a fallen piece of wood and bashing Lòfroy's helm with it. The mercenary staggered back with a dazed moan. In a blur of gold, Gibusil plunged into the street, clipping a roof with his right wing and knocking some shingles to the ground as he landed in the narrow space. As they dashed out from cover, Eyoés, Kerensa, and Erling mounted on Gibusil's saddle. Leaping into the air, the golden griffin clumsily plucked Gwyndel and Fedrik up in his talons, struggling to ascend. Lòfroy scrambled to his feet and shouted a command to stay his griffin.

His head swam, and through his dazed vision, he watched his prey slip through his fingers—again.

24th of Rotanos, 2209 SE

Gwyndel tore off a chunk of dried meat to stay her tongue. Grimacing as burrs pricked her hands, she scooted back against the damp side of a knoll, eying Fedrik. She heard the splash of a nearby creek as Kerensa and Erling filled their water skins under the watchful eye of Eyoés. Being alone with Fedrik prodded Gwyndel to guard her tongue. After her misstep in speaking to him without thinking, she was content to keep her peace. In her careless words, she had wounded Fedrik.

I will not thwart the Guide's work again.

She studied the moorlands that spread ahead of them, before her view was obscured by low clouds. Below a stunted tree, a red grouse scuttled along the knobby ground. In the distance, Gwyndel glimpsed the orange coat of a fox as it nosed about for food. The stench of decomposing earth drifted on the wind, and daylight shimmered off the stagnant water of distant peat bogs.

Pursing her lips, Gwyndel glanced at Fedrik. She pulled her eyes away and looked down at her rations, taking a bite of coarse bread. There was no use making Fedrik uncomfortable with her probing looks.

"Is it true that the Guide cares for all who suffer? Even those unworthy of kindness?" Fedrik asked.

Gwyndel stopped chewing. Her eyes twinkled, and she held her breath as she met the man's inquiring glance. Swallowing, Fedrik squirmed under Gwyndel's gaze. He looked away, as if hoping to escape the awkwardness of such revealing conversation. The cry of hunting birds filled the silence in pity for his plight.

Gwyndel cleared her throat. She hesitated, her enthusiasm curbed by her previous failure. She gazed up into the sky, watching a flock of birds silhouetted against the clouds. "Despite my shortcomings, he continues to shelter me and help me grow," she said with a smile. "Don't worry, Fedrik. He will lead you to understanding without finding fault."

She opened her mouth to speak more, then thought better of it.

Where there are many words, wrongdoing is not far off.

Fedrik tucked away the rest of his midday meal, avoiding further discussion. Yet as she studied him in secret, Gwyndel glimpsed a tear in his eye.

38

25th of Rotanos, 2209 SE

The sharp crack of splitting wood echoed throughout the dawning forest. Setting aside his hatchet, Erling blew onto his cold fingers, watching his steaming breath curl in the dim morning light. The chill of the morning settled deep into his limbs. As he peeled the stubborn wood apart and stacked it, Erling balanced another piece on the fallen log before him. He shifted his position, the fallen leaves crackling under his feet. The hatchet blade descended with the crisp snap of wood, and Erling piled the kindling in a heap.

He sighed, the fresh scent of moist greenery invigorating him. Wiping the last remnant of sleep from his eyes, he looked back to where the campsite lay. The increased tension from their recent escape had taken its toll. He could only hope his parents slept in peace. The quiet chiming of reins met his ear. A kind family had given them a horse in exchange for a payment of gold coin. Having left their previous horse behind at Fiwood, there had been little choice.

Taking up another piece of wood, Erling felt the mossy bark compress in his grip. He remembered how his father had slinked away from Eyoés and Gwyndel during their evening meal the night before. Ever since the disagreement between his father and Gwyndel, his father had kept company with himself alone, growing less irritable with each passing day. Despite their sacrifices, Eyoés and Gwyndel received no praise from Fedrik.

How can they simply leave their mistakes behind?

Erling brought his hatchet down upon the piece of wood, expressing his troubled musings through the blow. As he considered the thought, his brow furrowed.

If forgiveness is not earned through the acclaim of others, is it something we can earn at all?

Wind whooshed over his head and the ground trembled behind him. Erling spun around, gripping his hatchet—and his eyes locked with the wild eyes of a griffin. Metal hands clamped over his mouth, stifling his screams. "*You* are my opportunity," Lòfroy whispered.

Eyoés drifted awake to Gibusil's shadow looming over him. With a chirp, the griffin nudged him out of his blankets, grabbing his shirt with its beak and yanking him to his feet. Stumbling to catch himself, Eyoés smiled in irritation. "What is it, Gibusil?" he asked, rubbing the back of his neck. The griffin leapt into the air, circling like a hawk over a nearby section of trees. Eyoés checked his sleeping companions. His brow furrowed as he noticed Erling's blankets were tousled and empty.

He rushed to follow at Gibusil's urgent growl. Leaving the campsite behind, Eyoés entered an open clearing. A small stack of chopped wood lay ignored beside a rotten stump. Eyoés' pulse quickened as he glimpsed the fallen hatchet, and Gibusil's snarl of outrage drew him to an indentation in the sodden ground. Eyoés knelt beside it, fingering its soft edges.

A griffin track. And surrounding it were several disorderly footprints, tearing up the fallen leaves and layer of moss.

Eyoés bolted through the trees, numb to the boughs pricking his arms. He burst into the campsite, the thud of Gibusil's wings hammering in his ears. "Wake up!" he shouted. Gwyndel sprang up. Fedrik and Kerensa staggered to their feet. "Erling's been captured!" he cried.

Kerensa's face fell, and she leaned against her husband for strength. Eyoés' mind stormed with visions of Erling's suffering, and he fought to steady his hands.

Fedrik moaned aloud, "It is my fault!" He knelt on the ground, head in his hands.

Eyoés glanced at Gwyndel. "What?" he asked.

Fedrik lifted his head, his grief written on his face. "I have run out of time. Fate has taken matters into its own hands and exacted punishment for my wrongs!" he exclaimed. Kerensa knelt beside him, blinded by her own sorrow.

Gwyndel shook her head, eyes soft with compassion. "Fate does not exact punishment. But whatever consequences may come, we will endure them with you," she said.

Fedrik shook his head. "As a young Rehil lord, my kin aided the indebted family of my best friend, Fordarre. But when I was unjustly accused of theft, my ashamed friend publicly slandered me and my family. When I tried to defend my name, he sent vagabonds to beat me. Even years after Baron Gaedal Amberster acquitted me of these false accusations, I endured the suspicion of others," he said, struggling to speak through tears.

Fedrik pulled back his hair to reveal a slight depression. "My skull was fractured!" he shouted. "You don't know how far I've fallen! Fordarre threatened the seizure of our land in his scheme to reestablish his status. So I killed him in secret. I broke every bone in his body. Since that day, I've drowned out my living nightmare with ale, taking out my misery on my woman and my son. I am of House Ravenstrong, a family that has worked to redeem the evil of our patriarch. I deserve punishment—and it has come to me."

The sack of supplies fell from Eyoés' limp hand. He ran his hands through his hair as the man's words rang in his ears. The face of Throst Ravenstrong flashed through his memory, and the man's smooth, beguiling voice returned to haunt him.

My father, Fedrik, and my mother never married, and I was their illegitimate son. Because of that, my father treated me like a servant. I was given a pittance for my clothing and food.

Eyoés recognized the horror and revulsion in Gwyndel's eyes. Ravenstrong—the name laden with suffering and manipulation. A name that still disgusted him. Convinced their shock was directed to his personal tragedy, Fedrik buried his face in his hands.

Overwhelmed by the barrage of misery, Eyoés turned to Gwyndel. "Gibusil can still follow Lòfroy's scent if we hurry," he said.

39

26th of Rotanos, 2209 SE

The wind and rain preyed on Erling's vulnerability, chilling him to the core. He hung his head, watching the griffin's saddle flex with each flap of wings. As he lifted his face, he huddled further in his seat.

Lòfroy paid him no heed, guiding his griffin with the reins as he peered into the mist ahead. Rain pinged against his helm like arrows against a breastplate of iron. The man's forbidding presence condemned his prisoner to silence.

Erling covertly struggled against the fetters that bound his hands to the saddle. Seizing the fear that troubled him, he bent it to his will, recasting it into anger. He tugged against his bonds in vain. As the griffin soared into a descent, the whistling of the air rang in his ears. The sharp scent of saltwater bit Erling's nostrils. He squinted, glimpsing the Edeveran coast through the mist. Whitecaps beat against the sheer cliffs as the Western Narrows proved its fury to the unrelenting rocks. Flat moorland crept up to the edge of the coastline in a dull green. Gulls glided on the air, squawking a warning as the griffin's vast wings cut through the wind. Lòfroy brought his griffin to a landing upon a small peninsula.

Dismounting, the helmed mercenary unfastened Erling's bonds and pulled him from the saddle. The ocean roared in the boy's ears as he searched the horizon for sign of civilization. His shoulders slumped as he saw nothing but rolling moors.

"There's nowhere to run," said a voice from behind. Erling turned to where Lòfroy shouldered a pack of supplies. The man studied the sea cliffs with nary a glance at the boy.

Erling's heart sunk. The indifference with which Lòfroy treated him made his skin crawl. Stiffening, Erling shied back, his pretense of bravery withering. If the brute sought his father's downfall, he would surely show no mercy to him.

Lòfroy shoved Erling forward. "There's an overhang this way," he snapped. He fell silent, starting across the moors with his griffin following along behind them. Erling obeyed.

The land sloped downward to reveal a hidden gorge, leading in steep ridges down to the seashore. Trickling over rocks, the ocean's waves intruded into the gully, foaming at Erling's feet. With only a quick glance to assure his footing, Lòfroy hopped across a narrow section of water to the bank opposite. The overhang of fallen rock that promised refuge was hardly welcoming. The grey griffin took refuge under a lonely, wind-blasted tree atop the overhang. The downpour of rain trickled to an end as Erling took shelter under the rock. Darkness lingered within the far corners, drawing back in aversion to the grey light streaming in to reveal sections of moss. Collapsing against the stone wall, Erling watched as Lòfroy set aside his gauntlets and gathered the makings of a fire.

Only when the crackling of flames filled the lingering silence did Erling muster his faltering courage. "Why?" he asked, voice breaking despite his efforts. "Why do you hunt us? Who are you?" Blinking back tears, Erling choked down the knot in his throat and bit his tongue.

Lòfroy paused—and perplexed Erling with a thoughtful nod. "Some say the life of an outsider like Fedrik has no meaning," he mused aloud. "But this is not always true. To some, an outsider is not what he seems—yes, to some, the life of an outsider is priceless. Would you agree, *Erling?*"

Erling stiffened. "How do you know my name?" he asked.

Lòfroy's smooth, disarming laugh rang out like an unsheathed blade to Erling's ears. "There are those in your hometown of Anfon whose eyes and ears belong to me," he answered. "But forgive me. I have only answered one of your questions. Allow me to answer the others." Lòfroy faced Erling, lifting his hands to his helm. The boy watched in apprehension as the man undid the strap and lifted the helm from his head.

The handsomeness of maturity endured on the man's features, traced with the lines of premature age. Erling's skin crawled as the man's features struck him as eerily familiar. His hair was pulled back and braided in the fashion of a warrior. His eyes held an air of power. Erling recoiled at the man's sunken and scarred left cheek. The stately features that had once been his pride now half-marred.

The man set aside his helmet and riveted his piercing gaze on the boy. Lòfroy held himself with poise. "You do not know me, Erling, nor do I expect you to. I am your half-brother, Throst Ravenstrong," he said. "Surely your father spoke to you of your family name. Even if he spared you the details."

Erling shook his head. The memory of his burning home flashed through his mind, entwining with the revelation of this unknown brother. An uncontrollable shudder swept through his body as the realization collided into his heart with a hard thud. Wrinkling his nose in revulsion, Erling cringed away from Throst.

This monster is my kin?

Seeing his brother's disgust, Throst flinched as if wounded. He knelt before Erling. With a pained look, Throst reached out to touch his brother's face. Erling flinched, and Throst pulled away. "I always wanted a brother," he said quietly. His words were met by Erling's sharp glance, and Throst hung his head.

Erling noted the brokenness in his voice, and a flutter of guilt softened his expression. He regarded his brother with skepticism. "You hunted us—you hunted *me*," he said, struggling to reconcile Throst's words with the dread of Lòfroy's dogged pursuit. "Why should I show you mercy?"

Throst lifted his head, face stricken. "I am not proud of who I've become. Or of the blood I have spilled. But I was *compelled* to avenge what Father did to me—what he has done to you!" he exclaimed, trembling. "The lies, the beatings! Surely you understand!"

Erling met Throst's eyes with a glare of challenge. "You do not know my father!" he snapped.

Throst froze, mouth slackened. The genuine love for Fedrik in Erling's eyes shocked him. "You are ignorant of his ways," he muttered, shaking his head. Turning away, he covered his face with his hands. Erling stared at his half-brother, his former fear replaced by disgust.

Throst let his hands fall from his face. The rage and hurt in his cold, raw eyes shook Erling with a greater fear than he had felt before. Throst clenched his jaw. "He used to beat me until I bled, calling me an ill-begotten cur. He treated my mother with the utmost contempt and abuse!" he snapped, tears coursing down his cheeks. Stepping back, Throst yanked his sword from its sheath with a feral shout. "My life was *hellish*, Erling!" he roared with vitriol. "And I *hated* him for it. My mother hated him for it. She left both of us to escape his madness. Before Father abandoned me, I planned to torture him—to make him beg for mercy as I once did!"

Sword poised in the air, Throst stopped, chest heaving. The storm of rage faded from his eyes, and he lowered his blade. "*That* is the father I know. When I discovered he had another son, I knew you would suffer the same abuse," he said. "I *saved* you, Erling. That is why I destroyed his home. That is why I tracked him across these forsaken moors. I once sought to reclaim what Father stole from me by chasing power and wealth. But I tell you this, Erling. Some say prosperity is a shield—but prosperity is not enough. Some wounds only *blood* can heal."

Erling stared at Throst in disbelief, envisioning his father's somber, quiet face—grieved, yet determined to be strong for those he loved. Even after hearing Fedrik's night ramblings, the image of his father being so callous struck him as foreign. But as he saw the conviction in Throst's look, he knew it to be true. Wetting his lips, Erling sighed. "I believe you. But you must believe me in turn," he said, leaning forward. "Father is no longer the same man."

Throst gritted his teeth and knelt before Erling. "A monster like Father doesn't change," he retorted, lip curled in distaste. "Fleeing from Rehillon was the greatest thing he ever did. His flight allowed me to rise to status and come within reach of the fulfillment he denied me. But then *they* came!" He spat on the ground in hatred, gesturing to his marred face. "Eyoés and Gwyndel cast me down before I could lay hold of wholeness. The Baronship of Rehillon was within my grasp, but they enabled that grey-haired Vikar Amberster to scar me for life!" he said.

His countenance softened. Laying a hand on Erling's shoulder, Throst mustered a weak smile. "Fedrik deceived you, as he once deceived me. But you are my brother, Erling. The raven lives in your blood as much as mine. Help me avenge Father's wrongs and bring peace to both of us," he pleaded.

Erling met Throst's pained and beseeching gaze with silence.

What a pity that such a wounded heart should fill itself with such bitterness.

Shaking his head, Erling held his brother's hand in his own. "Fedrik has his faults, as I do. As we *all* do," he said. "Peace is not found in brutality."

Throst's face fell. With a sneer of wrath, he swatted away Erling's hand and stood. He snatched up his helm from where it lay. "Your false friends will be looking for you, Erling," he snapped, his voice cold. "Fedrik *will* meet his death—and you are going to help me kill him."

4◊

28ᵗʰ of Rotanos, 2209 SE

Eyoés caught the sharp scent of saltwater upon the wind, and behind him, Fedrik anxiously scoured the coastline below. Gibusil banked to the left, head roving about as he followed the scent of Lòfroy's griffin. Shifting in the saddle, Eyoés glanced over his shoulder to where they had come from. He regretted his decision to forge on ahead of Gwyndel and Kerensa as they had insisted. Yet what most troubled him was the revelation of Fedrik's true identity. Eyoés struggled to sort out his conflicting disgust and compassion, but he could not shake the weighty dread that settled upon him. In his uncertainty, one thing was clear.

I know why Lòfroy pursues us with such irrational determination.

As he studied the land ahead, Eyoés felt a sudden tightness in his gut, and gripped the reins with white knuckles. Gibusil growled, his crown of feathers raised. The unmistakable grey shape of a griffin drew their eyes downward. Grazing for vermin across a small peninsula, the creature stopped and lifted its head to sniff the air. At the sight of Gibusil gliding above, the creature crouched, wings outstretched in a display of savagery.

Tucking in his wings, Gibusil shot downward. Before Eyoés could realize the speed at which he had fallen, Gibusil alighted before the other griffin and crept forward, his talons digging into the sod. The other creature roared in defiance.

"Silence, Taesyra," a familiar voice commanded. The sound put Eyoés' teeth on edge. As his eyes fell upon Throst's malicious grin, he fought the flare of rage boiling under his calm demeanor. He bit his tongue as the pain of Throst's betrayal pierced him again. Now, even deception was beneath him.

Erling struggled against his captor's hold, and Fedrik cried out. Unsheathing his dagger, Throst pressed it against the boy's throat. Erling's wild eyes widened and Fedrik curled his arms over his head, looking desperately to Eyoés. Eyoés clenched his fist till his fingernails bit into his palm.

The raven smirked. "It is an honor, Eyoés, that we should meet again," he said, his voice smooth. "Perhaps it makes you regret your decision to spare my life." Eyoés unbuckled and slid from the saddle in a single motion, helping Fedrik to the ground.

Drawing his sword, Eyoés fought to deny Throst the satisfaction of seeing how unsettled he truly was.

In my mercy, I spared my blade, and in return, Throst exploits my compassion.

Eyoés ventured forward, and Throst pressed his dagger harder against Erling's throat. Extending a wary hand, Eyoés stopped. "Release the boy, Throst," he said, fighting to hide his spite and panic. "Erling has no quarrel with you."

Throst's smile grew, and a mocking laugh slipped past his lips, laced with a venom that Eyoés could nearly taste. "Look at you. Straining to conceal your anger. Perhaps you now understand my pain as *you* lose hope. It was once said that 'a man's shoes rarely fit another'. What a pity that you cannot see my point of view this time, Eyoés," he said with a harsh squint. "You and your precious griffin are not the champions of Edeveros—despite whatever Neifon Vassaros may say. Even Roseen and Raulin Estworth will not escape the fire of Galeras' temper. And when this game is at its end, I shall snatch the throne of Edeveros for myself. I wish I could see the horror on Caywen's face."

As his wild eyes alighted on Fedrik, Throst unintentionally squeezed Erling tighter. He ground his teeth. "Hello, *Father*," he hissed with a feral hatred. Like a prisoner condemned, Fedrik ventured forward, chin trembling. Throst sneered. "You attempted to escape your punishment, Father, like the churl that you are. And by your act of self-preservation, have brought my wrath down upon my half-brother." He pressed the tip of the dagger harder against Erling's throat. At the sight of dripping blood, Fedrik sobbed. Throst chuckled. "The boy's life for yours, Fedrik. Or do you wish to add his death to the number of those you have slain?" he asked.

Fedrik dashed forward before Eyoés could restrain him. Throst shoved his captive aside, and Eyoés rushed to snatch Erling away. He whistled and Gibusil sprang for Fedrik, but Taesyra leapt in front of him.

The griffins circled each other, and Fedrik turned to face Throst. As their gazes locked in a tense silence, the years of conflict came to rest in the very air they breathed. Fedrik sighed, giving himself the freedom to weep. "I have done evil things, son. I will not hide it. I've butchered men. I've beaten you and your mother. And I have harbored so many evils in my heart that I dare not count them. I deserve your hatred in all its wrath. But for *your* sake, I ask you to consider forgiveness," he said.

Blinking away tears, Erling gave a trembling smile. "*I* forgive you, Father!" he shouted. Throst froze, and Fedrik turned with tears of hope toward Eyoés and Erling.

Nodding, Eyoés squeezed Erling's shoulder. "I hold nothing against you," he said, his voice cracking.

Mouth agape in disbelief, Throst blinked back tears, and the scorn in his eyes faded to sorrow and hurt. He suppressed a sob and his glare transfixed Fedrik like an arrow. "You put me through *hell*!" he roared, beating his chest. "Mother could not forgive you, and neither can I. Even if these two fools do."

Weeping, Fedrik took a bold step toward his son. "I have let the King's royal mercies atone for my wrongs. What will it take to prove my repentance to you?" he muttered through his sobs.

Throst looked steadily into his father's eyes. Squeezing his dagger for a final time, he threw it to the ground. His eyes watered. With a sneer, he drew his sword, his hand shaking. Eying the blade, Fedrik swallowed. His face softened with a loving smile, and he resigned himself.

Unnerved by his father's calm, Throst gritted his teeth. His eyes gleamed with misery. "Your blood is proof enough," he said, voice broken. With an anguished roar, he plunged his blade into his father's body. Eyoés and Erling gaped in horror. Fedrik fell, and his eyes drifted to the sky in a final plea for the Guide's mercy.

Erling's face contorted in sorrow. Tearing himself from Eyoés' arms, he rushed at Throst, blinded by his grief. "YOU *BLACKHEART!*" he shouted in accusation. Eyoés raced forward to pull him back.

Taesyra leapt—and the ground shuddered as Gibusil tackled her to the ground. The grey griffin slipped free, swiping for his chest but missing her mark. Gibusil struck her with his tail, and Taesyra darted for her foe's blind spot. Latching onto Gibusil, Taesyra yanked the griffin off balance and wrestled him to the ground. Gibusil kicked her off his chest, and she shot upward. Gibusil was faster, colliding into the grey griffin to knock her out of the sky. Pinning Taesyra to the earth, Gibusil fought to control her as she struggled to free herself. With a snarl, Gibusil pushed her harder against the unyielding ground. The smaller griffin slumped in submission with a weak chirp of surrender. As Gibusil stood back, Taesyra hung her head in a display of defeat. Gibusil shrieked a warning to further solidify her place.

A blur of movement flashed at the edge of Eyoés' vision, and he spun around and ducked under Throst's

blade, feeling the steel hum past his ear. Shoving
Erling out of the way, Eyoés drew his sword and
blocked Throst's wild blows. Countering a feint with
finesse, he stepped to the side, seized his opponent's
shoulder, and wrenched backwards, throwing Throst to
the ground. Gibusil started forward, but Eyoés threw
out a hand to stay him.

Throst sprang to his feet and swatted Eyoés' blade
to the side. Blocking an overhead blow, Eyoés forced
his adversary to retreat. Throst fell backward over a
knob of ground with a curse, and his sword fell from
his grip. Eyoés halted, his sword poised to kill his foe
where he lay.

As Throst eyed the sparkling blade leveled at him,
a smile overtook his face. With a mocking laugh, he
rose to his feet, throwing his arms wide to expose
empty hands. "You have bested me again, Eyoés
Kingson, and now my story ends," he said, his
mocking eyes belittling the goodness of his foe. "Kill
me in your reckless vengeance, so I may die knowing
that my death will bring you guilt." He gave a spiteful
chuckle as he saw the conflict in Eyoés' eyes.

The Hero of Asdale hesitated, grinding his teeth.
He remembered vividly Vikar's look of horror as
Throst's mob demanded his life. Caywen's words rang
through his memory, as she related the story of her
childhood friend's betrayal. Even in the years after
Rehillon's civil unrest, whenever he had met with
Caywen, he had seen the anguish on her face at even
the slightest mention of Throst. In his quest for power,

the man had afflicted hundreds with Everwheat addiction.

His blade quivered, eager to end the villain's legacy of torment, but Eyoés' heart sank at the thought.

Fedrik's evils were just as great as his son's. I forgave him, but can I not also forgive Throst?

Reveling in his enemy's indecision, Throst smirked. "It is my mind against yours, Eyoés, and it is now clear whose mind is the strongest," he said.

Eyoés swallowed the knot in his throat—and lowered his sword. "I offer you my forgiveness. I will not hold your past evils against you," he said. "Surrender to me, and I will take you to the authorities. Even as you pay the penalty for your wrongs, your heart may be restored. You can choose a different way."

Throst's triumph slipped through his fingers. His arms fell limp at his sides, and his brow furrowed as he struggled to understand. He wavered, taking a partial step forward. At the last moment, he shook his head and snatched his sword from where it lay. He curled his lip in contempt. "Forgiveness is for the weak," he snapped. With a roar, he dashed forward, sword poised to run Eyoés through.

A shriek and a blur of gold startled Eyoés. With a beat of his wings, Gibusil tackled Throst and plucked him up in his talons, gliding over the cliff's edge and dropping him into the void. The roaring waves drowned out the raven's screams.

The thump of his griffin's wings rang hollow in Eyoés' ears. With a sad smile, he stared out to sea, his heart aching over Throst's rejection of redemption. Silenced by the tragedies he had witnessed, Eyoés embraced Erling.

Throst's misery had finally ended.

Rain deepened the mourning of Fedrik's death, giving life to the ground that would accept him. In the distance, wolves howled in unison with the keening of Kerensa and Erling. Mother and son held each other tightly, and the rainstorm washed away their tears as it trickled down their cheeks. Gwyndel watched Eyoés pile stones upon Fedrik's shallow grave. As she envisioned Fedrik's lifeless face beneath the soggy earth, a hollow emptiness sank in her chest. Her eyes flashed blue, and the intense sorrow of Kerensa and Erling nearly knocked her to her knees.

The vision came true. I thank the Guide for the opportunity to share truth with Fedrik in life.

Eyoés set the final stone with a clack, his fingers slipping across its cold, moist surface as he retracted his hand. He shot a glance of pity toward Kerensa and Erling. Beside Fedrik's grave lay a commemorative burial mound. Eyoés shut out the image of Throst's broken body washed out to the sea's endless depths, never to be recovered.

The sound of their weeping sickened Eyoés, and he leaned against the monument of rock. Fighting off despair, he shook his head and brought the face of the

Guide to the forefront of his thoughts. Squeezing his eyes shut, Eyoés recalled the vividness of his eyes, and the pure white hood that surrounded his royal face like an aura. Words like the warm winds of Gald-Behn drifted into his reflections.

Fedrik died a free man. I spoke to him when you could not, and I freed him.

Stricken mute, Eyoés stepped back, his boots squelching in the soggy ground. A gentle rainfall cleansed the mucky stones. He regarded the two graves dwelling in each other's unexpected company, and his solemn manner deepened. It was a tragedy that they could not bring themselves to reconciliation. Death alone had brought their discord to an end.

His memory stung as he remembered Throst's life in Rehillon. Eyoés knelt, his weary legs collapsing under the weight of his journey. Shivering as the rain's touch chilled his skin, he laid a hand on the stones. Throst and Fedrik had both fallen victim to wicked men—and in turn, become wicked themselves.

I did what I could to help them find peace.

He sighed. Behind him, Eyoés could hear Gibusil and Taesyra stir uneasily behind him as they sensed his melancholy. Though the two griffins remained distrustful of one another, Taesyra's recognition of Gibusil as her alpha had stabilized their hostility. Eyoés felt his downcast heart stir with delight at the rare opportunity to witness the genesis of a griffin pack.

Gibusil and Taesyra had achieved what Fedrik and Throst could not—they had come to an understanding.

41

2ⁿᵈ of Rynéth, 2209 SE

2nd of Rynéth, 2209 SE

Sunlight cleared the clouds over Mithlon, but failed to lighten Haeryn and Marc's hearts. As they strolled in the castle courtyard, Mithlon's grand keep loomed over them like the memory of Neifon's passing. Marc stared, and Haeryn saw love for the Hero in his eyes. Haeryn winced as his companion's longing for his second father sparked his own heartache anew. He fought to drown his grief with strength of will. Haeryn willed himself to live as Neifon had.

Fearless and exemplary.

Hope sparked within him as his mind turned to Falrey O'Dyre. With calm certainty, Haeryn laid an assuring hand on Marc's shoulder. "Neifon will be avenged by the law. As he would have wanted," he said.

Marc nodded, his eyes brightening. "He once told me—'A strong leader does not tolerate lawlessness, either in the public square or in the privacy of his heart'. Now, more than ever before, I agree with him. We cannot bring Neifon back, but we can take the mantle he has given us," he replied. Haeryn felt the remnant of his wrongheaded fervor be crushed under the weight of the sentiment. Through their shared trials, he had come to trust his friend, and his convictions reminded him of Neifon.

"Rider approaching with airborne escort!" one of the sentries cried from Mithlon's gate.

Haeryn and Marc hastened up the stairs to the ramparts, pushing past a soldier who attempted to stay them. "Make way for the last Wynrence!" Marc shouted. At the authority in his voice, the guards atop the ramparts turned, standing at attention as Haeryn crested the stairs. The Wynrence colors on his outer coat inspired respect in the men around him. With a look of gratitude to Marc, Haeryn leaned against the merlons and gazed out. His face beamed.

A gust of wind surged over the ramparts as Gibusil soared above them. In his wake, a second griffin followed, its grey feathers tipped with crimson. Haeryn ducked as the creature swooped low, nearly knocking him and several other soldiers from the walls. He rose and helped Marc to his feet, remembering Neifon's conversation prior to his father's departure.

Lòfroy's griffin?

Staring after the creature, Haeryn ran down the stairs with Marc following close behind. Taesyra dove into the courtyard and spread her wings to land. Scrambling down the ramparts, soldiers surrounded the griffin, and with the click of loading crossbows, aimed at the beast. The line faltered as the creature screeched, slashing the stones with its claws. It thrashed its tail, knocking two men onto their backs. The guardsmen shouted curses at the beast and hastened to aid their dazed fellows. Haeryn's heart sped at the peril of their position. One false move could easily spark a disaster.

Gibusil alighted in the courtyard, charging through the dashing soldiers with feathers flared. The grey griffin lowered its head under its alpha's imposing presence. From the saddle, Eyoés held out a hand. "Stay your men!" he demanded. At a hasty command from their superior, the sentries lowered their crossbows. The castle gates swung open with a clang.

The clop of hooves rang out as Gwyndel and Kerensa rode into the courtyard, drawing up beside Haeryn and Marc. Dismounting, Gwyndel embraced Haeryn with a bright smile, oblivious to the peril that had been avoided.

"It's good to see you Aunt Gwyndel," Haeryn said, the warmth of her embrace comforting him.

Gwyndel released him with a beaming smile and helped Kerensa down from the horse's saddle. "I've worried ever since Eyoés told me he left you in Mithlon. From what I've heard, this place is home to many crimes," she said. At the sight of Haeryn's companion, she hesitated, stepping forward with an incredulous stare. "Marc?" she wondered.

Marc smiled, sweeping his arm to the side with an extravagant bow. "The very same, miss," he said with a laugh of delight.

Gwyndel embraced Marc with an astonished laugh. "I never thought I would see you again!" she exclaimed, holding him at arm's length. "You've joined the Knights of the Lance, your childhood heroes?"

Marc nodded, beaming. "I am a squire of the order. It was time I considered it more than just a childhood fancy," he answered.

Eyoés dismounted from Gibusil's saddle and helped Erling to the ground. The boy hid in the man's shadow with an uneasy glance to where the grey griffin lingered, growling. As he ushered Erling to his mother's side, Eyoés summoned two guards. "Give them food and shelter. They have endured too much suffering for one journey," he said. With a nod, the men tenderly grasped Kerensa and Erling's shoulders, escorting them to the keep.

Kerensa turned to Eyoés, pressing a hand over her heart. "Thank you," she said, eyes glistening with tears of gratitude. "We owe you our *lives*." Erling nodded, biting his lip to keep it from trembling.

Eyoés sighed with a compassionate twinkle in his eye. "The Guide is the one who ultimately guards life. Not me," he said, his own inadequacy evident in his humble manner. "Your lives can begin anew without fear or peril." He watched Kerensa and Erling follow their escort up the steps to the keep. They had been through so much together, that seeing them leave to claim a new life for themselves brought a wistful smile to Eyoés' face.

Turning to Haeryn, Eyoés embraced him, closing his eyes with a relieved smile. "I hope all is well?" he asked. Haeryn did not immediately reply.

A growl turned Haeryn's attention elsewhere. Aware of the grey griffin's scrutiny riveted on him, he faced the creature and fought to hide his unease. Eyoés laid a hand on his son's back and nudged him toward the beast. The soldiers surrounding the griffin eyed him with an incredulous stare. Haeryn locked eyes with the griffin as he came to stand before it. Behind the wild glint in the creature's eyes, he glimpsed the same steadfastness he saw in Gibusil. Clenching his jaw, Haeryn moved to touch the griffin—and his hand shrank back as the creature rumbled in wariness. Eyoés patted Haeryn's shoulder. "In time, Taesyra will become accustomed to us," he said.

Haeryn frowned, looking up at his father. "What do you mean?" he asked.

Eyoés grinned. "She is Lòfroy's griffin no more. She recognizes Gibusil's dominance, and will be coming to Asdale with us," he answered. "Taesyra is yours, Haeryn." Haeryn's eyes widened, and he stared at Taesyra, transfixed. The sight of his son's excitement warmed Eyoés more than Asdale's sun ever could. He motioned to the guards standing warily nearby, clutching their weapons. "Take Taesyra to a secure stable—and let Gibusil keep her in check," he said. The soldiers awkwardly led her away, with Gibusil flanking her. She growled as Gibusil nudged her along with his left shoulder.

As he turned to Haeryn, Eyoés glanced to the keep of Mithlon. "Where's Neifon?" he inquired.

Haeryn fought to keep his composure. "He was poisoned. We buried him in the Noble Mausoleum," he said. Face blanched, Eyoés clenched his jaw and looked away.

Haeryn set a hand on his father's arm. "There is much to tell you. I will bring you and Gwyndel to Roseen Estworth," he said.

42

3ʳᵈ of Rynéth, 2209 SE

Night secured its hold upon Castle Mithlon and its surrounding hamlets. An ever deepening ebony blanket spread across the crimson Aggas forest, reaching for the moorlands beyond. A chill wind swept through the air. Illuminating the darkness, the orange glow of lanterns lined the ramparts of the castle. Standing in rapt attention at their posts, soldiers peered into the night with eyes squinted and ears attuned to all sight and sound.

Haeryn and Eyoés watched as well, concealed in the shadows of an unmanned parapet. Crouching, Haeryn placed a hand against the cold stone wall to steady himself. Beside him, Eyoés surveilled the courtyard below. Glancing along the ramparts to his left, Haeryn caught sight of an armored guard not far away. He understood their risk. Should he and his father be discovered, they risked the chance of falling into the hands of Galeras' men. He trembled at the thought. Creeping closer to the ramparts, Haeryn looked down to the Aggas forest below. The glow of lanterns lined the forest road, glistening through gaps in the crimson canopy. The guiding light was a welcome sight for late night travelers, mostly servants and soldiery.

Within the forest of crimson leaves, Marc surveyed the road in total concealment. The knowledge of having partners in his errand eased Haeryn's strain, knowing Marc would aid him should his vigilance fail.

Haeryn pressed his lips together, searching for any sign of Falrey O'Dyre's coming. In his letter to Neifon, Falrey had indicated his date of arrival for that evening. Not even Neifon's death would stop Falrey's hammer from falling on Galeras.

Haeryn shook his head with a triumphant smirk, envisioning Galeras' shock at Falrey's unexpected visit. From his concealed position upon the ramparts, Eyoés tore apart the shadows with his gaze. He could not indulge in the luxury of lenience. The clopping of approaching hooves on the castle road drew them to the ramparts. Wetting his dry lips, Haeryn warily eyed the nearby sentries as he and his father leaned over the battlements.

Emerging from the forest, a large force of horsemen came into view. They rode in a diamond formation, and firelight sparkled off their sleek Fenaboran armor. Several riders lingering at the edges held lanterns aloft. In the midst of the diamond formation, a tall figure held himself upright in the saddle. Though distance obscured his face, his confident and dominating presence was discernible. Haeryn glimpsed bronze buckles neatly fastening his dark leathern overcoat. Riding at the head of the group, a flag bearer hoisted an azure pennant, embattled with purple and bearing the head of a bull as its charge. Though he did not recognize it from memory, Haeryn knew whose presence it heralded. As he inspected the approaching riders, Haeryn saw Marc lingering at the forest's edge. His courage swelled.

Haeryn turned around as Eyoés tapped his shoulder, pointing. Three shadows crossed the courtyard to Mithlon's keep under cover of darkness, before disappearing behind a hidden door. The sight assured Haeryn, knowing Neifon's former spies would bring Roseen word of Falrey's arrival.

Eyoés made for the nearby stairs, and Haeryn's heart pounded as he heard a loud voice. "Open the gates for Baron Falrey O'Dyre of Fenabor! Make way!" the flag-bearer shouted.

For a moment, the soldiers upon the ramparts hesitated, boots scuffing on the stone as they leaned out over the battlements. Then, with a shouted command from the garrison, the loud grinding of the gates and portcullis drowned out Haeryn and Eyoés' soft footsteps. Keeping to the shadows, Eyoés pulled his son beside him as they approached the gate.

The gate swung wide to admit the approaching party, and the portcullis clanged as it retreated into the gatehouse above. The clopping of hooves rang out as Baron Falrey's entourage paraded into the courtyard. Eager for the stable, the horses snorted and whinnied. Haeryn pressed himself against the wall as the commanding figure of Falrey passed by mere feet from Eyoés. Followed by a small cohort, the Captain of the garrison descended the ramparts and blocked their path, raising a hand to stay them. Falrey's standard bearer motioned for the company to halt. Haeryn nearly intervened, but Eyoés held him back.

Baron Falrey O'Dyre rode through the parting ranks of his entourage, heedless of the command. Coaxing his horse to stop beside the Captain, he studied the man with an unwavering composure. "What is this?" he inquired. Hidden in shadow, Haeryn was caught unawares by the confidence in the man's rich baritone voice.

Removing his plumed helmet, the Captain gruffly gestured to the keep. "His Baronship cannot receive your Grace until morning. As you are a foreign guest, protocol must be obeyed," he said, unwilling to lower his hard face in respect.

Haeryn clenched his jaw. Though such a diversion did not promise complete deliverance for Galeras, he knew they could easily leverage the excuse to frustrate the foreign baron into leaving.

Falrey examined the man with skepticism. Inhaling an invigorating breath of night air, he looked toward Mithlon's grand doors. A gentle smirk grew on his features, and he laughed quietly. "I am not bound by your *protocol*," he said cooly. "My business will not be brushed aside, as your baron is in the habit of doing." Before the Captain could object, Falrey dismounted and advanced toward Mithlon's doors. The small cohort of guards stumbled aside with curses as the entourage of mounted cavalry rode through them.

Haeryn smiled to himself.

Falrey is less needy than we suspected.

Galeras' debts had come due.

43

Roseen Estworth cradled a goblet of wine in her hand, observing the festival's inaugural banquet from under lowered brows. Amid the affairs of petty conversation, none ventured to speak with her. Her forbidding manner assured it. The idle conversation of the courtiers turned her stomach and pricked her indignation to life. Music rang out in celebration of the coming festival, stirring the hearts of the guests to excitement for jousting, buying, selling, and other pleasures. The news of the mercenary's capture had instilled in the people a fierce craving for merrymaking. Roseen recoiled at the frivolity. As she saw the carefree foolishness glowing on their faces, she wrinkled her nose.

Galeras conditioned them to be simple-minded. Perhaps they will abandon their idiocy when their baron finds himself at the mercy of another.

Swirling the wine in her goblet, she glanced toward the chamber door and idly fussed with her caul and veil. Chancellor Leofas helped himself to a scone, eying the door to the banquet hall with cool expectancy. Gwyndel picked at the sleeves of her dress, the constriction making her fidget. Roseen downed a draught of wine to steady her nerves.

Roseen caught a glimpse of her haughty brother-in-law among the crowd. With grand gestures, Galeras flaunted a story of some false escapade to the responding whispers of admiration from his audience. Roseen curled her lip in disgust and fell into a disdainful silence. Galeras gained many friends due to his theatrical personality and high position.

A position gained through treachery.

The chamber doors opened with a clang. Soldiers entered, their sleek armor bearing a crest Roseen did not recognize. The idle conversation ceased as all eyes turned, aghast at the intrusion. Chancellor Leofas adjusted the collar of his robe with a smirk. Gwyndel spun to face the door, and Roseen glimpsed a flicker of blue in her eyes. At the sight of Galeras' reddening face, Roseen smiled. Clasping his hands behind his back, the baron struggled to contain his wrath as he asked, "What is the meaning of this?"

Striding through the doorway, a standard bearer held a small banner aloft, displaying a foreign coat of arms. "Make way for Baron Falrey O'Dyre of Fenabor!" he proclaimed, heralding the guest's arrival according to customary Edeveran tradition. With this, he and the other soldiers stepped aside. Whispers rose from the crowd of guests as an imposing figure strode into their midst.

The man's leathern overcoat was unbuttoned halfway in Fenaboran fashion, revealing a lavish red tunic underneath. Crisp trousers added to his height, and polished shoes reflected the surroundings like a mirror. His imposing presence silenced the crowd.

Sharp angles outlined his face, as if hewn from the weathered mountains of Iostan. Raven-black hair crowned him, trimmed short to compliment his chiseled features. His deep, cold amber eyes held the attention of all, transfixing them with a demand of respect. The crowd of guests genuflected in honor, with only Galeras and Gwyndel standing dumbstruck in their midst.

As Falrey stood before Galeras, a modest smile spread across his face. "Ah, Estworth," he said, his deep voice filling the silent banquet hall. "It has been too long." Falrey motioned for the crowd to stand.

Galeras swallowed. Smiling weakly, he placed a welcoming hand on his guest's shoulder. Through his beaming expression, Roseen glimpsed his unease. "Welcome, my friend, to the ancient land of Edeveros! Please, allow me to celebrate with you," he said, wrapping an arm around Falrey and swiftly ushering him through the crowd. As they approached the table of wine, the crowd returned to their conversation with renewed gossip, and the minstrels again took up their song. Roseen and Chancellor Leofas bowed to their guest.

Catching sight of them, Falrey stopped and inclined his head in courtesy. A knowing smile freshened his sharp features, and he tilted his head. "And who might these excellent people be?" he inquired, raising an eyebrow.

Galeras froze. Roseen and the Chancellor seemed unsurprised by Falrey's unexpected arrival. His fists gripped the hem of his outer coat as he frowned, regarding the two of them. With a sudden understanding, his eyes widened, and he shot a livid glance at Roseen. Struggling to still his trembling, he gestured toward her, "This is Roseen, Lady of Gahidros. My sister-in-law." He spoke through clenched teeth. "This is Chancellor Leofas," he said. "And Gwyndel of Asdale."

Gwyndel locked eyes with Falrey, and her face paled. Clenching the hem of her sleeve, she swallowed, yet stood resolute. For a moment, Falrey paused, caught off guard by her reaction. As he eyed Gwyndel, he flashed a smirk.

Seeing Gwyndel's pallid face, Roseen laid a hand on her friend's arm. "Gwyndel, are you alright?" she asked, inspecting her with a critical eye.

Gwyndel nodded. "I'm fine. Just tired, that's all," she rushed to add.

Brushing aside the odd introduction, Falrey turned to Galeras. Seeing the man's suppressed rage, he shook his head. "My pleasure, friends," he declared. He turned to study the crowd. "Where is Neifon Vassaros?" he inquired.

Roseen's face fell, and she stared down into her wine goblet. Clenching his jaw, the Chancellor closed his eyes to blot out the tragic memory. "He was poisoned and buried in the Noble Mausoleum," he replied.

Falrey's eyes narrowed. "I see," he said.

Galeras' pasted smile faded as he shot a wary glance at his creditor. "What is the purpose for your visit to Mithlon?" he asked, his voice squeaking. He shirked back, dreading to press the matter.

Falrey paid no heed to the baron's feeble inquiry. Turning his back to Galeras, he calmly took an empty goblet from the table. At the gentle sound of pouring wine, Galeras squirmed under the oppressive silence, idly wringing his hands.

Blind to the warning in Gwyndel's haunted glance, Roseen clasped her hands. The beauty of Galeras' discomfort was not lost on her.

Galeras' schemes are falling in on him. What poetic justice.

Returning the pitcher of wine to the table, Falrey took up his goblet and turned to face the nervous Baron. "It appears I arrived at an opportune time, Galeras. I was informed by your retainers as to the reason for the festivities. With the capture of Lòfroy, *other* issues can now be addressed," he answered. Galeras blanched.

Falrey regarded him with a probing stare. Drawing himself to his full height, he took several steps forward. "They call you the fox, Galeras. A fox is swift, and not so easily caught," he said, swirling the wine in his goblet and taking a sip. "But we shall see."

Falrey intruded upon Galeras' chamber with authority. Galeras, Roseen, and Chancellor Leofas trailed behind him. Ushering Gwyndel in despite her reluctant footsteps, Haeryn, Marc, and Eyoés entered only when assured no one was following them. Candelabras surrounded them like a jury at attention, and the fractured light of the full moon coursed through the tall windows to illuminate Galeras in his vulnerability. Haeryn rubbed his stiff jaw as the door to the chamber shut with a click of the lock, sealing Galeras' fate. The foppish Baron of Edeveros had abused his subjects long enough.

Clenching his fists, Haeryn turned toward the chamber door. His eyes flickered to where Roseen and Chancellor Leofas stood restless, struggling to hold their anticipation in check. Eyoés pulled up a spare chair and sat, pressing a fist to his lips as he eyed Galeras and Falrey. As Haeryn studied Marc, his smirk faded. The squire paced. His brow furrowed in wrathful anticipation, then transformed into a look of worry. The struggle that showed itself upon his features burdened them all.

Haeryn's stomach turned in guilt, and he checked his desire for vengeance. Out of respect for the baron's status, Neifon had concealed his disdain for Galeras.

My gloating dishonors his memory.

Galeras turned to Falrey, stricken—his face robbed of its frivolity and childish temper. In his wide-set eyes there was no longer any hubris. Only distress.

Falrey remained silent, his presence exercising an utter dominance over those around him. Clearing his throat, he leaned against a small table. Galeras squirmed where he stood. As the two seated themselves, Haeryn and Marc drew near, along with Roseen and Chancellor Leofas.

Gwyndel lingered a distance from the others, stricken dumb as she stared at Falrey, rubbing her folded arms. Sensing her agitation, Eyoés touched her hand. "What is the matter?" he whispered. The brightness in her unsteady eyes unnerved him.

Tugging at her braid, Gwyndel bit her lip. "I do not know," she replied. "But Falrey is not what he seems to be." Her uncertainty cast her conclusion into doubt. Eyoés regarded Falrey with indecision.

As Haeryn met Falrey's gaze, a slight chill crept up his neck. Though glad of the challenge to Galeras, he felt a hint of apprehension in Falrey's presence. The words he spoke sounded foreign to his tongue—as if they were not truly his own. Haeryn placated his misgivings as he reveled in Galeras' discomfort.

Falrey folded his hands upon the table and faced his debtor. "I wish to end our troubles in a civil manner —as men of the nobility," he said. He turned to Galeras in an unspoken demand for agreement.

Galeras swallowed, pulling at the collar of his shirt. "Hard times have befallen Edeveros, Falrey. My treasury is inadequate, and I cannot tax the people further," he replied.

Falrey frowned, leaning against the back of his chair. His brow furrowed. "By the extravagance of the festivities, I doubt your honesty. I consented to your trade proposition with full confidence in your capabilities. Now, I am compelled to enforce greater taxes upon my own people to offset your irresponsibility!" he said, his words biting like arrows despite his calm manner. "And you excuse your childish behavior by blaming your bleeding treasury?" He leaned forward, his keen brow furrowed with a severity that unsettled Haeryn. "No longer will I disregard your corruption, Galeras. Your debt will be paid in full—or I will be compelled to report your misconduct to King Fohidras," he declared.

Galeras gasped, seizing the sides of the table with whitened knuckles. "No—please! Give me more time!" he insisted.

"How great is the debt?" Chancellor Leofas inquired, shaken by the baron's extreme response.

Falrey raised an eyebrow and stroked his chin. "Thirty measures of gold coin," he replied. His words fell like bricks.

Roseen's eyes bulged. Chancellor Leofas' look of silent triumph crumbled under the weight of the sum. "It is impossible to pay such a sum from the treasury," Roseen stuttered.

With a sigh, Falrey looked to Roseen and Leofas with regret. "Selling land seems to be your only recourse. I wish it wasn't so," he said, pinning Galeras with his wintry glare. "Otherwise, Fenabor must resort to war in order to resolve the matter."

"We will offer you Toldan and the surrounding lands south of the Airys river," Chancellor Leofas declared, wiping the sweat from his brow. "The matter will be settled with the Lords when a new Chief of Court is appointed." He gave a knowing, but urgent look to Roseen.

Stunned, Eyoés gawked at the Chancellor. "But the people of Toldan will be forced to relocate. They will lose their homes and livelihoods," he said, hoping for a better alternative.

Roseen put her head in her hands to hide her tears. "If Edeveros falls, they will lose even more," she said.

Gwyndel ran her hands through her hair. "There are matters at stake that surpass the needs of Edeveros," she said quietly to Roseen, glancing sidelong at Falrey. Clenching his jaw, Falrey pretended to not have heard.

"There is no other way," Roseen answered.

Galeras seized his chair and dashed it against the floor. He picked up two of the broken chair legs and threw one at Roseen. "Usurper! You seek to force my hand!" he shouted. Haeryn and Marc drew their weapons and dashed forward. Brandishing the other leg, Galeras turned to face them with eyes wild and teeth bared. "Edeveros is mine! I surrender it to no one!" he screamed. The rage and fear caged within him tore free as he clumsily swung his makeshift club.

Falrey seized the baron by his hair and yanked him out of reach of Haeryn and Marc's blades. He slammed Galeras onto the table to restrain the man's fury. "DULLARD!" Falrey roared. "You are but a child caged in a man's body. Control yourself!" He gritted his teeth to calm himself.

The fury in Galeras' eyes transformed to dread as he saw the depth of Falrey's displeasure. Breaking free, he scrubbed his face with his hands and cowered.

"Forgive me! I lost my decorum," he pleaded, his weak voice barely discernible.

Falrey lowered his head, tracing his jawline with his hand. Gwyndel and the Chancellor helped Roseen to her feet. Shaking, Roseen pushed a stray lock of hair back under her caul. Eyoés hastened to Gwyndel's side and embraced her, dismayed.

Falrey sighed and stepped away from Galeras. As the prominent shadow left him, Galeras rose to his feet. Falrey wheeled on him. "I will be in Mithlon for the remainder of the celebration. Do not blacken your name by ignoring me again," he said. "I only wish to keep Fenabor stable. You no longer have my trust, Galeras. Once this festival is over, I will call for your abdication." Bowing to Roseen, he departed in silence. Eager to escape, Galeras leapt up and followed, shooting Roseen a parting glare.

Neither the Chancellor nor Roseen spoke a word, instead taking their leave of the baron's personal quarters. Marc sheathed his sword and followed suit. With a weary glance at his son, Eyoés accompanied Gwyndel out of the chamber. Haeryn lingered with nothing but shadows and the light of the candelabras to keep him company.

Haeryn's gaze roamed about, studying the white walls and elaborate embellishments with apathy. As he contemplated Galeras' lavishness, a bitter taste came to his tongue, and he shook his head.

Galeras endangered all of Edeveros simply to coddle himself? Revolting.

Taking one last glance at the broken chair lying against the wall, he started for the door—and a slight movement caught his eye. He stopped. Lingering at the edge of his vision, a shape came to a standstill, sensing the youth's attention.

Haeryn spun on his heels and drew his sword in a swift motion. The shadow faced him in turn. Lifting the tip of his blade, Haeryn cautiously approached. The hooded shape was cloaked in shadow and mystery— tranquil, yet appearing to speak a threat with its silence. "You are a Phantom Leaguer," he guessed aloud. "I have heard much of your bloody ilk."

The tall figure stepped forward, and threw back its hood. His chiseled features mimicked a stag's proud face. A scraggly beard blanketed his tapering jaw, and disheveled hair covered his wide forehead. An intent stare met Haeryn's iron look, unafraid. "I am no longer one of their kind," he said, raising his empty hands to assure Haeryn he was unarmed.

Haeryn's eyes narrowed, and his blade lowered. The man's unexpected reply confounded him. "Then what is your business in Castle Mithlon?" he asked.

Glancing at the chamber door, the man lowered his hands. "I am the Crimson Mark," he answered. "My affairs are my own, but I say this—beware, lest your heart be deceived." Pulling his hood over his head, the Crimson Mark edged toward the open doors. From under his hood, the Crimson Mark regarded Haeryn with a nod of respect. "There are those in Mithlon who feign friendship, but plot betrayal," he said.

Haeryn blinked—and the man was gone.

44

Galeras Estworth's festival surpassed Raulin's grand parade in Gahidros. Music and laughter hung like a shining cloud over the township of Mithlon, spreading its merriment across the nearby hamlets and farms. Bright colored banners graced with ornate motifs hid nearly every wall from view. Garlands were spread from rooftop to rooftop, tracing across the streets above the people's heads. Stalls and tents were scattered about in a mad rush to claim the choicest locations.

Placed among the merchant's tents and places of entertainment, a long section of exposed ground was chosen to host the much anticipated jousting tournament. A dividing fence sectioned off the jousting lanes. Tiered rows of benches were placed on either side of the arena under wide canvas roofs. Spectators gathered—men of high standing conversing with one another in polite tones, and women watching the knights with flirting looks. As they all examined the list of contenders, bets were made. Several of the men wiped sweat from their brow as they fretted over losing their coin. The Jousting Master spoke with the knights and squires in turn, assuring the lists were accurate and the equipment was in satisfactory condition.

At the end of the field, Galeras overlooked them all from his seat of state. By his side, the Treasurer and Court Magistrate sat in silence, complicit in their baron's corruption. Chancellor Leofas, seated at the far end of the dais, wore a long-suffering frown at the misfortune of being seated among his enemies.

Reclining upon his high seat, Galeras pressed his knuckles to his lips. He stared at the jousting arena, feigning disinterest as he adopted a relaxed posture. His courtiers were oblivious to his strange demeanor. He shifted his gaze to where Falrey O'Dyre stood beside the nearest tier of benches, lingering in patient silence at the crowd's edge. Gripping his armrest, Galeras was conquered by a flare of wrath. He sneered at Falrey while he wasn't looking.

He sees me as a fool. I will reveal my true mastery and gloat over him as he is carted away like a criminal!

Galeras turned his eyes to the chairs placed in front of the dais. Raulin and Roseen sat before him, their backs turned as if in a subtle display of defiance. In a show of spectacle, Raulin had arrived at the festival accompanied by the Knights of the Lance, stirring the approval of the people. Once, such a blatant assault on his pride would have incensed Galeras. But with his plans in play, he did not mind. Pressing his lips together, he turned his attention back to the jousting preparations. His foes posed no threat to him now.

Standing at attention beside Raulin and Roseen, Haeryn and Marc searched the jousting grounds with piercing looks that made several nearby spectators cower in discomfort. As they sat on the edge of the dais, Eyoés and Gwyndel sipped water from leather skins. Rather than adopt the formal attire of their hosts, they had insisted upon wearing simple, clean garments that blended in with the peasantry. Adjusting the collar of his fine tunic, Haeryn scrutinized the knights and squires for any sign of treachery. He remembered the desperation in Galeras' eyes, and shivered because of it. Desperation made fools quicker than opulence.

An unsettled mind not only harms itself, but those it influences.

Roseen waved a hand to summon him and Marc to her side. As they leaned down to hear her, she motioned toward the merchant tents. "Go ahead and enjoy yourselves," she said with a genuine smile. "The contest will not be ready for some time yet."

Pushing away from the dais, Eyoés nodded his agreement and patted his son on the shoulder. "Don't worry about us. There's yet time, and we're watching out for each other," he said.

Haeryn glanced up to the baron's seat. "Galeras is in a desperate position. What if he tries something?" he whispered.

Raulin waved the youth's worries aside and clasped Roseen's hand with a disarming smile. "Galeras may have fine raiment, but his audacity is not nearly as bold as his clothing. He cannot risk estranging himself from the public, and he is not so brazen enough to face me with violence," he said with firm assurance. "Go. I did not emerge from hiding to be guarded at every turn. Enjoy yourselves—but don't enjoy the mince pies *too* much! I hear they're some of Galeras' favorites!" Raulin slapped his knee, and his hearty laugh boomed across the jousting field.

Glancing at each other with uneasy looks, Haeryn and Marc departed.

As Haeryn and Marc ambled out of sight, Galeras' face grew dark. Leaning forward in his seat, he clenched a fist and pressed it to his lips in a struggle to keep his composure. He transfixed Roseen and Raulin through their chairs with his intense stare, though they remained ignorant of it. A smirk soiled his handsome features. They seemed so fearless, so confident—but at the day's end, they would feel otherwise.

Through the blood rushing in his ears, Galeras heard the gentle tap of soft footsteps behind him. Over his shoulder, he glimpsed Gawter steal up and over the edge of the dais, slipping into the shadowed area behind the baron's seat. The sight of him unnerved Galeras. The elf's fair face was perpetually marred by his twisted mind. His narrow eyes were bright and cold with malice, perhaps thrilled by ideas of new methods of torture. Acknowledging his secret aide with a slight nod, Galeras turned his attention back to the joust.

Gawter leaned close to his ear, speaking through a twisted smile. "All is prepared, and my men will assure that all continues as intended," he whispered, shooting a bloodthirsty glance to Roseen and Raulin. "The thought of those prissy nobles being—"

Galeras elbowed him in fervent anger. "See to it then," he snapped quietly. Gawter pulled away with a snarl, slipping off the back of the dais and out of sight.

Marc and Haeryn walked together in silence, ignoring shows of indecency by several drunken patrons. Haeryn repeatedly loosened his sword in its scabbard and shoved it back into its sheath. He looked back to where the jousting field lay, and his brow furrowed in worry.

Will Galeras allow his authority to be stripped from him?

Marc caught his friend's uneasy look. Stopping, he grasped Haeryn by the shoulders and looked him in the eye. "I understand what troubles you. I know what desperation can do—I've seen it in Beydan and Galeras' eyes. But we are surrounded by our allies, Haeryn. Any violent schemes will be uncovered—" Marc's words halted, and he regarded Haeryn with a bewildered squint. As he followed Haeryn's stare into the narrow corridor behind them, a knot coiled in his stomach. Several suspicious men lingered within the shadows of the lofty, colorful tents. Haeryn and Marc ducked behind cover to observe.

Haeryn stifled a gasp as a small man bearing a knightly crest appeared among the group, pushing his way through the narrow spaces between the tents. The man cast wary glances about, and Haeryn and Marc ducked to avoid his sweeping gaze. Tentatively, they peered out from behind the edges of the tents.

As the squire spoke, Haeryn strained to hear over the sounds of the festival to no avail. Folding his arms, one of the men whispered in the ear of another. The other man retrieved a bundle of cloth from a hiding spot in the shrubbery. He lifted it with a grunt and unfurled the cloth to reveal what lay beneath. Haeryn's heart sunk as he recognized the block shape and stub of rope from his father's retellings of the Siege of Ellokon.

A Duraval bomb!

Haeryn caught Marc's eye, and mouthed the word "bomb". Marc started in alarm. As Haeryn turned back, he saw the small man disappear among the tents. With a shared glance of dread, they sprinted down the streets to the jousting arena. In his blind rush, Haeryn knocked aside a drunkard that wandered into his path. He stopped to apologize and make sure the man was alright before he resumed his chase. His father Eyoés had spoken of revenge, and how it rendered all reason helpless in its grip.

As he worked his way through the crowd, Haeryn prayed that he would arrive in time to prevent it.

"And Sir Thersos of the Lance against Rowan of Caylas," the Jousting Master concluded, rolling up the scroll once all the competitors had been introduced. "Let the jousts begin!" As the man spread his arms wide, the spectators gave a roar of excitement, leaning forward on the edges of their seats. The Jousting Master turned to Galeras with a bow and scampered off the field. As the applause died down, whispers of speculation took its place.

Roseen settled into her chair with a soft sigh. As the knights gathered at both ends of the lists, her heart warmed, and memories long left untouched surfaced with the tears prickling her eyes. A slight smile lightened her austere expression, and she laid a loving hand on Raulin's arm. She envisioned him riding among the knights upon his thick-muscled warhorse, sitting proudly with his helm nestled under his arm and his lance held aloft in the other. Her heart fluttered at the image, and she beamed at him. She longed to see him joust again, and rejoice at his victory.

No longer. Not after Galeras' sinister work.

Feeling his wife's eyes upon him, Raulin raised a playful eyebrow and kissed her. He noticed a wistfulness that betrayed her sadness. The jousting preparations had aroused painful memories. Her knight had fallen off his charger, never to take up the lance again.

Galeras felt no such sorrow. Upon the dais, his smoldering gaze clung to Roseen and Raulin like hot tar. Grimacing and trembling with expectation, he pressed himself against the back of his chair to restrain himself.

As they bleed, they will realize my true superiority!

Haeryn collided into a merchant as he bolted through the festival with Marc. The retorts of the passersby sounded dull in his ears as he struggled to keep up his pace. The cheers of the jousting audience chilled him. Gritting his teeth, Haeryn envisioned the ugly aftermath of Galeras' brazen vengeance. His heart skipped as he anticipated the blast shuddering through the air. They skidded round a bend in the path and found themselves behind the baron's dais.

Stooping with the bomb in hand, the small man stretched to place it underneath the dais platform. Beside him, a pole tipped with a candle provided a long-armed lighter. Haeryn and Marc seized the man by the ankles, yanking him out from under the platform. With a grunt, Marc enveloped his squirming captive in a bear hug while Haeryn retrieved the bomb from beneath the dais. At Marc's unyielding grip, the man snarled.

Haeryn gingerly lifted the bomb in his arms. "Galeras won't escape the consequences this time," he said.

Haeryn and Marc stepped onto the jousting field as the knights rode out to joust. Eyoés caught sight of them, and his eyes widened at the sight of the Duraval bomb. Gwyndel followed his gaze and stiffened. Gasps of horror erupted from the onlookers as they caught sight of the bomb. Before the crowd could flee, Galeras sprang from his chair, his smirk of triumph smothered by the facade of an astonished stare. As Roseen and Raulin leapt to their feet, realization dawned in their eyes.

Abandoning his plan of fleeing before the explosion, Galeras channeled his shock into a look of horror. His hand shot to his chest. "An attempt on my life was foiled!" he cried out, arresting the attention of the onlookers. Pointing an accusing finger to where Falrey stood, he fought to coax the people into a frenzy. "Baron Falrey O'Dyre is responsible! He tried to kill me to satisfy a petty gambling debt!" At Falrey's derisive laugh, the false pretense waned on Galeras face.

"Your fears are unfounded, Galeras!" a powerful voice shouted across the field. All eyes turned to the far end of the jousting grounds, and Haeryn and Marc hesitated at the unexpected turn of events.

Neifon Vassaros strode into their midst, his robe billowing behind him.

Haeryn and Marc embraced him with tears of joy. "You live!" Haeryn said, his voice breaking. Marc muttered his agreement under stifled sobs of joy. Eyoés rushed forward and clapped him on the back with a grin.

Neifon smiled. "In order to make Galeras over-confident, drastic measures were needed. The sap of the Weeping Brier is a little-known sedative that induces a death-like state. Both Roseen and Leofas assured the success of my plan," he whispered. "But enough about my death."

The triumph in his fellow Hero's expression hit Eyoés like a war hammer as he realized what kind of power struggle would have driven him to such extreme measures. The thought of Haeryn being caught up in such conflicts checked his joy.

As the revelation struck Haeryn speechless, Roseen cleared her throat and gave an apologetic nod to him and Marc. "Your grief at Neifon's false funeral brought me to to tears. I apologize that you both were kept in the dark regarding the matter," she said.

Clearing his throat, Neifon fixed Galeras with a penetrating stare and pointed at him. Lifting his voice, he addressed the crowd. "Your baron is unfit to rule, people of Edeveros! A body of evidence condemns him!" he said. Whispers of outcry spread as the people debated the validity of the statement. Raulin signaled to several of the Knights of the Lance, and they marched to the dais. Galeras raised his hands to ward them off, but the knights disregarded his wishes and restrained him.

Roseen and Raulin strode into the center of the jousting field. "The man who was imprisoned as Lòfroy is a scapegoat! Galeras deceived you so he could command the *real* Lòfroy to do his bidding! And he also ordered the murder of a witness that revealed his crimes!" Raulin shouted, motioning for Eyoés to stand beside him. "Do you believe the word of legendary Eyoés Kingson of Taekohar, slayer of Skreon the Murderer and also a member of the Five Heroes of Alithell? The son of Élorn, the fabled Protector of Taekohar?"

"Lòfroy is dead! But not according to the will of your Baron!" Eyoés announced, convincing the crowd with the strength of his voice and the certainty in his words.

"No! They speak lies to turn you against me!" Galeras insisted, beseeching the crowds in desperation.

Watching as the baron struggled against his captors' grip, Falrey moved to seal his doom. "Galeras indebted Edeveros to the territory of Fenabor to sustain his lavish living. His debt is worth thirty measures of gold coin!" he declared. The people lifted shouts of rage. Eyoés caught Falrey's glance, and to his surprise, saw a sly smirk upon the man's face.

As Galeras was torn from his place of honor, Neifon continued, hiding his shock at the proclamation of the debt. He nodded as several other Knights of the Lance ascended the dais and restrained the Treasurer and Chief Magistrate. "As Chief of Court, I hereby arrest and charge Treasurer Evraxis and Court Magistrate Tethenes with obstruction of justice. And I proclaim Galeras guilty of the High-Crimes of murder, treason against the people of Edeveros, and unlawfully indebting Edeveros to another territory. He has thereby forfeited the Baronship of Edeveros and earned himself a jail cell," he announced. "The Council of Lords will be summoned to determine your successor." Galeras paled at the verdict. The knights shoved him forward and escorted him off the jousting field to cheers of applause.

Neifon laid a hand on Haeryn's shoulder. "The new baron could use a Wynrence in his Court," he said with a questioning look.

Haeryn paused, then shook his head. "My heart lies in Asdale, not Edeveros. The Wynrences of old offer little to this land. Let Raulin and Roseen claim their rightful place."

Neifon smiled. "You are more akin to your father than you realize," he said.

45

5ᵗʰ of Bivyn, 2209 SE

The lines of tension that had once creased Eyoés' face faded under the light of Asdale's sun. Eyoés closed his eyes with a tranquil smile. The scent of his tea wafted up to greet him from the cup cradled in his hands as the steam curled and danced in the crisp autumn air. Leaning against the windowsill, Eyoés studied the streets of Asdale, covered in frost. Arching over the houses and roads, the barren trees weaved into a broken canopy of twisting branches.

Eyoés sipped his tea, feeling the warmth dispel the chill in him. Smoothing the front of his embroidered shirt, he ambled from the window, hearing the distant, entrancing song of a tin whistle upon the breeze. And as he wandered about his chamber, his mind wandered along with him.

Edeveros. Stopping at his bedpost, Eyoés sat on the edge of his bed with a sigh. In the capable hands of Raulin, Edeveros would regain stability and peace.

If he should need any aid, I will gladly give him my support.

He was pleased that the law hindering Raulin from regaining the Baronship had been repealed unanimously. Yet he shared Neifon's heartache over the loss of Toldan and the surrounding territory. Though he understood its necessity, he was sickened by it. The chances of Edeveros being struck again by a similar loss were slim, now that the Council of Lords had set precautions in place to assure they could not be exploited a second time.

Eyoés perked his head up at the flutter of wings outside his window. A raven alighted on his windowsill, eying him curiously. The breeze stirred the glistening black feathers, and he glimpsed the reflection of the sun in the bird's eye.

May the Guide bestow Erling and Kerensa with a peaceful life.

He stood, and the raven fluttered off its perch, croaking in surprise as it glided over the town below. Eyoés moved toward his desk, smiling at the laughter and bustle of the townsfolk.

One day, my people will understand, as Throst never could. When people focus on themselves, they miss the fulfillment found in virtue. Contentment will never be found in extravagance or self-centeredness.

A knock on the door caught him unawares. Placing his teacup on the windowsill, Eyoés turned. "Enter," he said, slipping the thumb of his free hand into his belt.

The door opened at his summons, and Gwyndel appeared. At the sight of her elaborate emerald dress, Eyoés pursed his lips and shot a confused glance at his sister. Gwyndel disregarded his unspoken question. Taking up his tea, Eyoés moved to press the matter.

The broad-shouldered figure of Vakros followed Gwyndel into the chamber, his dominating presence drawing Eyoés' attention. With a smile of welcome,

Eyoés embraced him, feeling the man's rough woolen scarf scratch his face. "It's been too long, Vakros," he said with a beaming smile.

Cordially releasing his brother-in-law, Vakros smiled and clasped Eyoés' forearm in a warrior's greeting. Seeing the questioning look in Eyoés' eyes as he looked at Gwyndel's dress, Vakros laughed. "I bought it for Gwyndel against her wishes. A woman should have at least one nice dress to call her own," he explained. He turned aside with a beaming glance behind him. "Rhoslyn is eager to see you," he said.

Eyoés' heart skipped as his eyes alighted on the small figure standing in the open doorway. Deep emerald eyes gazed back at him, and he lost himself in their beauty. Curly red hair hung free to her shoulders, parting over her pointed ears. Her round cheeks were dotted with tiny freckles, and a small, upturned nose gave her a mischievous appearance. Her resemblance to Gwyndel was striking. Fiddling with her hands, she wandered a step toward him and flashed a grin.

Kneeling before his niece, Eyoés opened his arms to embrace her. He smiled till his cheeks hurt. With a giggle, she sprang into his arms and clung to his neck. Eyoés lifted and spun her about, his chest drumming as he felt her heartbeat against his shoulder. He held her aloft with a laugh. "You've grown so much!" he exclaimed. Rhoslyn's thin, delicate body seemed weightless in his grasp.

Gwyndel leaned her head against Vakros' shoulder. "Rather tall for four years," she remarked, a gleam of pride in her eye. Glowing with a contented smile, she kissed Vakros on the cheek. He laughed to himself and squeezed her shoulder.

Eyoés lifted Rhoslyn onto his shoulders, holding her ankles fast. As he turned back to Gwyndel and Vakros, his grin faded. Despite the beaming joy in their eyes, a wistfulness dulled their happiness. There was more to be told—something they held back.

He glanced between the two of them. "Out with it," he said.

Gwyndel met her brother's look, then broke away, staring at the mountains in the distance. "I have decided to set aside active duty and become a Forester Liaison, though I could be summoned for short-term assignments. We will live in Castle Asdale and represent the Foresters to the people," she revealed, glancing sidelong at her brother. "I am the Keeper of the Sword Imperishable, Eyoés. Our people are becoming self-absorbed, disregarding others and turning to entertainment rather than to the King himself. You and Sharaf need my aid. In time, perhaps we can guide the people back to what matters."

Eyoés sighed. "I could never ask for better allies," he said, bouncing Rhoslyn on his shoulders as he adjusted his grip on her ankles. His smile dwindled as he caught a glint of tears in Gwyndel's eyes, which she hastily wiped away. He wished to hearten her, his eyes drifting as he sought for an adequate encouragement. "When I was a boy, I assumed Baron Dányth's duties were dull and of little consequence. Aványn would often jest that perhaps, if I was diligent in my work, I would ascend to the Baronship. Of course, I rejected the thought gladly. Now look where I am," he thought aloud. "The Guide leads us where he wills. You made your decision for the right reasons."

Sunlight filtered through the pine boughs craning above Haeryn's head, casting splotches of daylight upon the ground. The brisk wind chilled his face as it swept through Asdale's farradoth. Clasping a book in his hand, Haeryn smiled to himself, and his piercing eyes shimmered. From where he sat, he could look upon Asdale's keep with only a slight glance up from his book.

As Haeryn watched, a flock of songbirds clustered about the tower, swooping up to perch on the crenels and merlons that crowned it. The book slumped in his grip. As he stared up at Asdale's keep, he envisioned Mithlon's marble towers in its place, envisioning Neifon, Roseen, Raulin, and Marc watching him from its top. Haeryn recalled the poignant words Eyoés had spoken to him upon their departure from Mithlon.

I have seen rule by fear, trickery, perfection, and love, but the rule by indulgence is one of the most dangerous. Fear can be transcended, trickery can be uncovered, and love helps others become their best selves—but indulgence! An indulgent people are complicit in their own deception. Their eyes are always turned inward. Without restraint, degradation has little chance of being stopped. Our calling to serve Alithell's people is an opportunity for our redemption as well as for the redemption of our people.

Haeryn returned to his book, intent on honoring his father's exhortation.

A shadow passed over him. "Welcome back, mongrel," taunted a familiar voice.

Haeryn's face reddened with frustration, and he lifted his eyes to rest upon Tarrew's unwelcome figure. Glancing over his oppressor's shoulder, he noticed Gaery standing in complete silence behind him. The boy stared wide-eyed at Haeryn, wringing his hands and sidling into Tarrew's shadow. Raising an eyebrow, Haeryn let out a controlled sigh of irritation. "I'm touched, fellow mongrel," he said with a brief smirk of amusement.

Tarrew muttered a curse and folded his arms with a sneer. "Why not take a shot at me?" he said, stepping back and presenting his jaw for a clear strike. Haeryn returned to his book. The taunting look on Tarrew's face faded. "It appears Haeryn the Irongaze has lost his edge," he remarked with a loud snort. "So much for his beloved justice."

"Your punishment is not my duty," Haeryn said dismissively. He shot a fleeting glance behind Tarrew —and straightened with a smirk of triumph. "But it is *his*."

Two brawny hands seized Tarrew and Gaery by their shirt collars and hoisted them off their feet. A look of terror eclipsed Tarrew's malice as he stared into the livid eyes of Sir Thrynnis. The elder knight shook the two troublemakers like rags. "GUARDS!" he roared, making Haeryn's ears ring. Across the drilling field, two sentries jumped at the sound and hastened to answer his summons. As they drew up beside him, Sir Thrynnis shoved the two squires into their arms. "These two are unworthy of the glory of knighthood. Send the little swine home," he snapped. With salutes of wholehearted agreement, the soldiers escorted the troublemakers away, cuffing Tarrew on the ear as he lifted up a cry of protest.

"I owe you an apology, Haeryn. I should not have been so merciful to them in the past," Sir Thrynnis said, looking down to his squire. "You did not even retaliate this time. What made you follow the Farradoth's mandates instead of your own judgement?" he inquired.

Haeryn smiled. "It is a knight's duty," he replied, returning to the pages of his book.

EPILOGUE

13ᵗʰ of Rynéth, 2209 SE

Night did not catch Falrey O'Dyre unaware. It never could. Like a thief, it always came, seeking to find him in the weakness of sleep—only to find itself laid bare like a servant under the gaze of his master.

For Falrey O'Dyre never slept.

He stood at the edge of a marble veranda, watching the crimson leaves of the Aggas trees glow under the moon like a bloodstained canvas. The sordid sight inspired his aspirations, and as he contemplated the town of Mithlon from a distance, Falrey shook his head.

It's a shame Throst Ravenstrong met his end. As the Sage, I deceived him easily. His fragile ego made him gullible, and he became one of the most valuable pawns at my disposal.

But the loss did not worry him. Alithell's people were so consumed with their little lives that they were easy prey. Like fish in a net. Even those who fought for virtue were instruments in his hands. He laughed as the thought pleased him in its treachery. Falrey smiled, remembering Galeras' cowardice, and the hope in the eyes of those who fought for the baron's downfall. They had come to him with open arms, little knowing whom they were receiving with such gladness. The irony struck him.

Such children.

At the sound of footsteps behind him, Falrey turned. Gawter knelt before him, the glint of fear in his eyes, amusing. "Master, you summoned me?" Gawter asked.

Falrey nodded to himself and turned away, retreating into his scheming mind. "I have no further use for Galeras," he said, glancing over his shoulder. "Kill him in his cell. We depart tomorrow morning." With a bow of obedience, Gawter disappeared into thin air.

Closing his eyes, Falrey exhaled a long, slow breath. Like wax, half of his face melted in tendrils of black mist. Lidless, milky white eyes stared into the darkness.

"My crown is coming," he hissed.

To access exciting Sword and Scion freebies, please visit the Exclusive Content page on my website:

www.jacksonegraham.wix.com/jackson-e-graham

Password: AndiamasRademSS